Prior BAD ACTS

A CAIN/HARPER THRILLER (#1)

D. P. LYLE

SUSPENSE PUBLISHING

PRIOR BAD ACTS
A CAIN/HARPER THRILLER
by
D. P. Lyle

PAPERBACK EDITION
* * * * *
PUBLISHED BY:
Suspense Publishing

D. P. Lyle
COPYRIGHT
2020 D. P. Lyle

PUBLISHING HISTORY:
Suspense Publishing, Paperback and Digital Copy, October 2020

Cover Design: Shannon Raab
Cover Photographer: Shutterstock.com/ Mike Pellinni
Cover Photographer: Shutterstock.com/ Nerthuz
Cover Photographer: Shutterstock.com/ Zonda

ISBN: 978-0-578-72479-9

BOOKS BY D. P. LYLE

Cain/Harper Thrillers
Skin in the Game (#1)

Jake Longly Thrillers
Deep Six (#1)
A-List (#2)
Sunshine State (#3)
Rigged (#4)

Dub Walker Thrillers
Stress Fracture (#1)
Hot Lights, Cold Steel (#2)
Run To Ground (#3)

Samantha Cody Thrillers
Devil's Playground (#1)
Double Blind (#2)
Original Sin (#3)

Royal Pains: Media Tie-in Novels
Royal Pains: First, Do No Harm (#1)
Royal Pains: Sick Rich (#2)

Anthologies
Nothing Good Happens After Midnight
For the Sake of the Game
It's All In The Story
Thriller3: Love Is Murder
Thrillers: 100 Must Reads

Non-Fiction
Murder and Mayhem: A Doctor Answers Medical and Forensic
Questions From Mystery Writers
Forensics For Dummies
Forensics For Dummies, 2nd Edition
Forensics and Fiction: Clever, Intriguing, and Downright Odd
Questions From Crime Writers
Howdunnit: Forensics: A Guide For Writers
More Forensics and Fiction: Crime Writers Morbidly Curious
Questions Expertly Answered
ABA Fundamentals: Understanding Forensic Science

ACKNOWLEDGMENTS

To my wonderful agent Kimberley Cameron of Kimberley Cameron & Associates for her guidance, advice, dedication, and friendship. KC, you're the best.

To John and Shannon Raab and all the dedicated crew at Suspense Publishing. Thanks for your hard word and creativity and for making this book the best it can be.

To my always first reader and editor Nancy Whitley.

To Nan for everything.

PRAISE FOR D. P. LYLE

SKIN IN THE GAME
(*Cain/Harper Thriller* Book #1)

"D. P. Lyle writes wonderfully and with real insight. He's a born storyteller."
—Peter James, UK #1 Bestselling Author of the *Detective Superintendent Roy Grace* Series

"D. P. Lyle's novels are chillingly authentic. An expert technician just keeps getting better. Packed with edge of the seat tension, **Skin in the Game** takes hunting to an astonishing, and frightening, new level."
—Robert Dugoni, *New York Times* Bestselling Author of the *Tracy Crosswhite* Series

"**Skin in the Game** is *The Most Dangerous Game* on steroids. Fast, relentless, and cunning."
—David Morrell, *New York Times* Bestselling Author of *Murder as a Fine Art*

"Terrific—truly sinister, scary and suspenseful. Lyle never lets you down."
—Lee Child, *#1 New York Times* Bestselling Author

STRESS FRACTURE
(*Dub Walker Thriller* Book #1)

"D. P. Lyle's **Stress Fracture** is just what I love in a book: lightning paced, brutally executed, dynamic characters, and a story that grips you by the throat. If Michael Crichton had written an episode of *Law & Order*, here might be the result. Simply brilliant!"
—James Rollins, *New York Times* Bestselling Author

"Cutting-edge forensics and a whip-cracking pace make **Stress Fracture** a one-sitting read. If you love *CSI*, this is the book for you."
—Tess Gerritsen, *New York Times* Bestselling Author

"D.P. Lyle's **Stress Fracture** is an intense, nail-biting adventure. The author's knowledgeable voice adds a fear factor that can't easily be found. A wonderful, thrilling read, an excellent work of fiction—and more!"
—Heather Graham, *New York Times* Best-selling Author

HOT LIGHTS, COLD STEEL
(*Dub Walker Thriller* Book #2)

"A gritty and grisly tale of serial murder, told in the edgy style of classic noir but powered with a 21st century plot. Dr. Doug Lyle delivers a scalpel-sharp thriller."
—PJ Parrish, *New York Times* Bestselling Author

"A taut, hard-to-put-down, emotionally-satisfying thriller. Fans of James Lee Burke and Lee Child will be pleased with Lyle's Dub Walker. Really, a damn good read!"
—Andrew Gross, *New York Times* Bestselling Author

PRIOR BAD ACTS

A CAIN/HARPER THRILLER (#2)

D. P. LYLE

CHAPTER 1

PRESENT

Bobby Cain stood at the wall of windows in the St. Germain Place penthouse condo he shared with his sister Harper McCoy. Near two a.m. He enveloped a firm rubber ball in each fist, squeezing them in a to-and-fro rhythm. Right-left-right-left. The action made little inroad into the tension that gripped his shoulders, his entire body, but at least it was adding to his hand strength. The key, according to Uncle Mo. Whether climbing a tree, pulling off a second-story B&E, or attempting to survive a mano a mano fight to the death, grip strength offered the make-or-break advantage.

Rain streaked the glass and muted his view over the SoBro area and the lights from Broadway, a block away. Lower Broadway, the Bourbon Street of Nashville, rich with food, drink, and country music, was winding down. Lights winking off, drunks staggering home, musicians packing up, another gig finished. The city stumbled toward slumber.

Not so for Cain. The fourth night in a row fitful sleep had dragged him from bed to stand in this very spot. Not an uncommon occurrence. His dreams came off and on in no predictable pattern. Lately more on. Even during restful nights, they appeared as not-so-gentle nips along the edge of his dreamscape, coiled to flare up full-blown. When they did, sleep became impossible.

"Bad night?" Harper moved to stand next to him.

"Yeah."

"Which one?"

She meant which dream. Cain possessed a catalog to choose from. Not that the choice was his. Never his. Sometimes it was the traitorous Iraqi commander whose throat he had sliced just so. Dark room, third floor, dead of night. Never saw his face, but felt the warmth of his departing life ooze over his hands. Other times it was the Al-Qaeda bomb maker who earned Cain's blade up through his diaphragm and into his heart for dispatching three Marines with his roadside devices. Or one of the other two dozen sanctioned missions he had completed.

Sometimes an unsanctioned mission reared up. Like the three Mexicans, the ones who had killed his parents in Tyler and fled, thinking the border and the cartel they worked for would protect them. He and Harper tracked the trio to Juarez, dead of night, in and out, no shadow of their visit left behind. Only the three corpses.

Tonight? The Taliban scumbag who stood sentry while a pair of his compadres raped a young woman, her screams and cries still jangling in his head. Cain and the other assigned operatives—Seals, Marines, and Harper as the CIA controller—had completed their mission, the silent elimination of an enemy asset, and were hunkered down in a basement, waiting to hump it to the desert extraction site. But, the sounds of the girl's misery and fear had frayed his nerves to the point that sitting by was no longer an option. Harper had been there—the night of their reunion after a fifteen-year separation—and had helped. Without hesitation.

Their actions were unsanctioned, no permission granted, or sought. Risky move. Could have crashed both their careers. Turned out that was a moot concern.

Harper caught the sentry's attention. Cain over-powered and bled him through a deft puncture of his femoral artery, clutching him tightly, hand over his mouth, feeling his struggles wane as his vital energy faded. He and Harper then introduced the two rapists to their virgins. The girl scurried to freedom. If there was such a thing in that desert hellhole.

"You were there," Cain said. No other words needed.

Harper nodded.

"Want some tea?" she asked.

"Couldn't hurt."

They sat at the kitchen table. Cain placed the stress balls on the surface, settling them against the metal napkin holder. He cradled the warm cup, took a sip. The chamomile infused his nerves, softening the invading images.

"We need a job," Harper said.

He looked at her over his cup.

"Idleness makes you fret," Harper continued. "Drags up your demons."

That was true. They had had a month to unwind from their last job. Cain could do a week, even two, but a month? Too much downtime allowed the past to dig in its claws. Pull him from bed to the window where he watched the sleeping city, and fought internal battles.

It wasn't guilt. He never allowed that to enter the equation. Each of his sanctioned missions had been righteous. On point. A problem that he could best resolve. Even if they were off the books. Way off. No written orders, no records. It's the way it had to be.

And the others? The ones since he and Harper left military service behind? The three who had killed his parents? Never guilt over that one.

No, it wasn't guilt. It was simply images. A series of pictograms, movies no one should have to store in their memory banks. His were filled with such.

"You're right," Cain said. He stood. "Want some more?"

"I'm good."

He refilled his cup. His cell chimed. From the living room coffee table where he had left it. Caller ID read "Milner."

Well, they wanted a job.

CHAPTER 2

8 HOURS EARLIER

The gun appeared from nowhere, materializing at the end of an unsteady arm, the black hole of its muzzle searching for a target. Then the flash-bang of sudden, remorseless violence. The shock momentarily locking the scene like a still-life.

Who keeps a gun stuffed between sofa cushions?

For Dalton Southwell the answer was simple. A punk-ass little shit is who. A punk-ass like Tommy Finley, jacked up on his own stash. Wired to the point of implosion, leaving him no way to make a smart move. A desperate one, sure. It didn't save him and didn't save his family. Not that anything could have. Their shared fate had been sealed the moment Dalton arrived in town.

Everything had been so smooth. Exactly as Dalton had set it up. He had choreographed every move that his brother Dennie and Jessie Parker, a member of his crew, would make. His sources indicated that there would be four people inside: Tommy the punk, along with his father, mother, and sister. Dalton had hammered into their heads that they were to flank him so that they would have clean lines of fire if needed, and that they were to remain silent, leaving the talking to him. That's how it went down. He had been in total control, right up until he wasn't.

His knock on the door had been answered by the father. John, if Dalton remembered correctly. If not, so what? He didn't really give two shits.

The curious look on the father's face as he swung open the front door and asked what Dalton wanted was quickly replaced by shock when Dalton's Glock pressed against his chest.

Gathering the family in the den, Tommy, his sister, and his mother on the sofa, the father in a wing-backed chair at one end of the coffee table. Some stupid sitcom played on the big screen along the far wall. Dalton ended it with a single round spit from his silenced weapon.

That got their undivided attention, Tommy flinching, his mother covering her open mouth with one hand, only partially smothering her gasp. His father's face paled, his breathing quick and raspy, head swiveling, obviously seeking a way out, a way to defend his family. The father asked again what the three men who leveled guns in his direction wanted.

"You want to tell him who I am?" Dalton asked Tommy.

Tommy's gaze danced quickly to his father and then back to Dalton but he said nothing. As if his throat was clogged. Probably was. Dalton offered a half-smile.

"Then allow me to enlighten your family," Dalton said. "Bring them up to date on your recent activities."

The mother and sister stared with big eyes as he dumped the bad news on them. That he and his crew were there to settle a score, and to deliver a message. That dear old Tommy had tried to flex his own muscles, go out on his own. That was something that couldn't be allowed. Not from Tommy, not from anyone.

"I don't understand," the father said.

Dalton scratched his chin with his free hand. "You see, Tommy made a bad move. He tried to cut us out of his sales. He tried to hook up with another supplier and build his own crew." Dalton pointed the weapon at Tommy. "He'd been warned. He chose not to listen."

"Are you talking about drugs?" the father asked. He glanced at his son. "Tommy isn't into that anymore. He went to rehab and put it all behind him." He now slid forward on his seat and stared at his son. "Tell him. Tell him you're clean."

Dalton laughed. Clean? Not Tommy. His large, black pupils

were only partly due to fear, the rest from the meth that swept through his bloodstream. Dalton's meth.

"Tell him, Tommy," Dalton said. "Tell him what a good boy you've been."

"Listen, Dalton," Tommy said, "I didn't screw you or anyone else. I was simply trying to expand my operation and make us all more money."

The father now appeared to be in full panic mode. As if his worst nightmare had materialized. No longer relegated to the darkness of restless sleep but rather standing right in front of him. Dalton loved this. That brief slice of time when a victim realized that their personal apocalypse had arrived, that Dalton was the personification of their every fear. Heady stuff.

"Tommy, what're you talking about?" the father asked, his voice wavering.

"It's not what it seems, Dad."

Dalton laughed. "Actually, it's exactly as it seems."

Tommy's fingers fidgeted with the edge of the sofa cushion, then he wiped his hands on his jeans as he shook his head. "Dalton, I didn't go around you. I swear."

"What about the guy over in Knoxville? The one who's cooking for you?"

Tommy's left knee began to bounce, and his voice ticked to a higher pitch, the words coming quickly as if saying a lot was saying the right thing. "I don't know what you're talking about. What guy? I don't know anyone over there."

Dalton took a deep breath and puffed out his cheeks as he exhaled. "Tommy, Tommy, Tommy. Don't you know me? Don't you know you can't bullshit me? Don't you know we work inside a very small community? That every time a new cooker pops up, we know the who, the where, the what, and, most importantly, the how much before he even cranks out his first batch?"

"Listen to me..." Tommy began.

Dalton cut him off. "Shut the fuck up. This isn't a negotiation." He now waved his weapon toward the two women. They recoiled, wide-eyed. "And now you've dragged your family into this."

"What is it you want?" the father asked.

"I told you. To deliver a message."

The father nodded. "We're listening."

Dalton smiled. "The message isn't for you. It's for anyone else who might be tempted to follow in old Tommy's footsteps."

That's when the gun appeared. Tommy had shoved a hand between the cushions and came up with the .357. He managed to snap off a single round before Dalton punched a hollow point into his forehead. Then two into the father's chest, the man attempting to rise, his butt never clearing the chair's cushion before death arrived. The women released a chorus of screams, voices stretched to the snapping point, hands raised for protection. A pair of shots from Jessie's gun silenced them. The mother took it through her left eye, death following immediately; the daughter to the chest, now moaning and clutching at the red blossom blooming near her left breast. Dalton stepped toward her and ended her struggles with a single shot to the forehead.

He walked to where Tommy lay, crumpled on the sofa. The entry wound in his forehead was surprisingly clean. Very little blood surrounding the black hole. Of course, the back of his head and his brain were splattered over the sofa and the lamp that stood behind. Dalton searched Tommy's pockets. He found a wad of money, which he took, and two phones. An iPhone and a burner. The former he left, but the burner he slid into his own pocket.

Then Dalton saw his brother Dennie. He was on his knees, clutching his belly, left side, blood flowing between his fingers.

Goddamn it. This entire operation had just morphed from quick, easy, and smooth to screwed, blued, and tattooed.

The truly infuriating part was that Dalton knew it was his fault. He should have forgone the speech and taken out Tommy straight up. But for him, the preamble was the payoff. His victim's rising fear with its coppery taste, the look in their eyes, the begging and bargaining. God, he loved that. Like waves of electric current enveloping his entire body. The killing was simply the exclamation point.

CHAPTER 3

PRESENT

Cain's phone lay on the coffee table. He sat on the sofa and punched it to speaker. Harper settled next to him, leaning forward, brow creased, head cocked slightly.

Marcus Milner. Attorney at law. Senior partner at one of Nashville's most high-dollar firms, he was also Cain's and Harper's go-between for cases. He fielded the calls, set up the accounts, and made the deals. Then, turned them loose to do the fixing. That's what they did. Fixed things. Made things right. Or at least even.

For Milner to call at this hour, the job had to be time critical. Something that couldn't wait for sunrise.

"It's a kidnapping," Milner said. "Tanner's Crossroads. Over near Knoxville."

"Who?"

"The son of the client. A Dr. Frank Buckner. Runs a clinic near Charlotte, North Carolina."

Milner continued, filling in some details. Truth was, he didn't know much.

"When did this happen?" Harper asked.

"Around six or seven p.m. Say, seven or eight hours ago."

"Was he harmed?" Cain asked. "The son? When he was taken?"

"I don't think so."

"What else you got?"

"That's it, really. Are you on board?"

"We are," Cain said.

"Good. I'll tell the father. He'll be waiting for your call. He can fill you in. I'll text you his number."

"We're heading out in fifteen minutes tops," Cain said. "We'll get loaded up and call him from the road." He disconnected the call. "We'll take The Rig," he said.

The Rig was their black Chevy Suburban, modified for their needs. A cranked-up engine, extra fuel tanks, bulletproof glass and tires, and a satellite communication system. Because you never knew when a simple situation could shape-shift into something more dangerous.

"I'll gather the duffles," Harper said.

The duffles, eight in total, varied in their contents. Cain and Harper kept them ready to go at all times. For situations such as this. Where every minute created a colder trail, and a greater chance for a bad outcome. Some of the bags were packed for surveillance, some for full-on warfare, most somewhere in between.

A kidnapping could go in many directions. From a simple rescue to a hostage situation to a hellfire shootout.

Ten minutes later, they lugged four duffles to the elevators and descended to the basement parking area.

CHAPTER 4

Dalton wasn't panicked. Panic was not in his nature. But he was furious, and such fury had always been embedded in his DNA. Even as a kid, his switch could flip on a moment's notice, and with little provocation. That constantly simmering anger was probably the reason he did poorly in school and why he now did what he did. Dirty work for Frankie. Things like sending messages and settling scores. His fury never left room for panic. He always did what was necessary and completed the job. No matter what. That's what Frankie paid him for. He had no doubt that he would have to earn his keep before this night was over.

Dalton twisted and turned the black Lincoln Navigator through several of the quiet neighborhood streets. Jessie rode shotgun. Dennie lay in the cargo area, moaning. They had folded the rear seats forward so Dennie had room to stretch out.

"How bad is it?" Dalton asked.

"It's bad," Dennie said. "Hurts like a bitch."

"What're we going to do?" Jessie asked.

Dalton considered the question as he turned west onto Main Street. What could they do? This was supposed to be a clean hit. As simple as one, two, three. Take out the family, walk away, message sent. But now? Dennie's blood left at the scene, a huge stain on the light gray carpet. Tommy's un-silenced gun going off with explosive intensity.

Did the neighbors hear anything? Had they called the police already? The houses in the neighborhood were spaced a couple of hundred feet apart so they might've gotten lucky, but Dalton knew anything was possible and counting on luck was never an acceptable strategy. Sure, luck could smile on you, like drawing to an inside straight when the pot was piled high, but in Dalton's experience, it more often offered an unfriendly face. Like a gun appearing from nowhere. Fucking Tommy.

If they were in Memphis, he'd know where to go. The boss had a doc on retainer for just such emergencies. He could fix things off the radar, no record and no one the wiser.

But here? In Fucktown, USA?

"I don't know," Dalton said.

He rolled past the hospital on his right, and to the left, the town's park, quiet this time of night. Main Street became Highway 57, a narrow two-lane blacktop that wound into rural darkness. Dalton glanced back at Dennie. His bloody hands clutched his side and he winced with each bump in the road.

"Think you can make it to Memphis?" Dalton asked.

"No. I need a hospital now."

"That ain't going to happen."

"Come on, brother. Memphis'll take hours. It's on the other side of the fucking state."

Dalton's knuckles whitened on the steering wheel. "A hospital's out of the question. We might as well drive to the local PD and let them cuff us."

"You gotta do something," Jessie said. He spun in his seat to look back at Dennie. "He's losing a lot of blood."

The highway led them through what was mostly farmland punctuated with wads of trees. There was no real traffic. In fact, they passed only two cars, each headed in the opposite direction. A few miles out of town, Dalton saw a church. On the left, set back from the road a ways, it was a white frame structure with a wide gravel parking area. Empty at this hour. He wheeled into the lot and circled to the back, the chapel blocking them from the road.

"What are we going to do?" Jessie asked. "Pray?"

Dalton gave him a look, then pushed open the driver's door. The interior lights popped on.

"Somebody'll see us," Jessie said.

"Not here." Dalton climbed out and tugged open the rear door. "Let me see."

Dennie rolled out of his fetal position, and onto his back. He lifted his blood-soaked shirt.

It was bad. No way to sugarcoat this. The bullet had entered the left side of Dennie's abdomen. It had to have damaged some important shit inside. Dalton rolled Dennie to his right side, drawing a deep moan. He searched for an exit wound but found none.

"Hand me that towel," Dalton said to Jessie. He passed it to Dennie. "Hold pressure on the wound. The bleeding is slowing and that'll stop it."

"We've got to do something," Jessie said.

Dalton stood and looked up at the night sky. "Give me a second. I'll figure it out."

CHAPTER 5

7 1/2 HOURS EARLIER

"What happened to you, partner?" Dr. Bradley "Buck" Buckner asked.

The young boy was stretched out on the ER bed, lips trembling, eyes big, gaze directed down toward his loosely tied Nikes, as if afraid to look at Buck, as if all this would simply go away if he didn't. He sniffed and then gathered himself. Somewhat. "My brother hit me," the boy said, his voice small, frightened.

"Not an uncommon thing in our household." The woman sat in a chair across the stretcher from Buck.

"I take it you're Mrs. Newland?" Buck asked.

She nodded. "Joyce. Matthew and his brother are pretty rambunctious."

Buck smiled at her. "Let's take a look."

The two-inch laceration angled across his forehead just above his right eyebrow. Dried blood surrounded it.

"How'd this happen?" Buck asked.

"It was an accident." Matthew looked up. Tears glistened in his eyes.

"They were sword fighting," Joyce said. "That's what they call it anyway. It's an excuse to whack each other with sticks."

"Boys are fun, aren't they?"

Joyce rolled her eyes. "You have no idea."

"I was raised with two brothers. And a sister. They were all older. I got the short end of the stick—no pun intended—more often than not."

"Is it bad?" Matthew asked.

"I've seen worse." Buck tugged on a pair of surgical gloves. He gently touched the tissues around the wound. Matthew flinched.

"Don't touch it," Matthew said.

"That might make it hard to stitch it up, don't you think?"

The tears now welled in his eyes. "Can't you just put those little tape things on it? My friend Willie got those when he cut his arm."

"Not sure that's the right answer here. Don't want a big old scar on your face, do you?"

"Maybe. I'd look bad then."

"In a Frankenstein kind of way." That got a half-smile from Matthew. "Might scare the girls away."

Matthew sniffed. "I don't like girls anyway. They're too bossy."

Buck smiled. "Well, you sure figured that out at a young age." He winked at Joyce. "But girls are pretty nice, too."

"No, they're not."

"You're what? Eight?"

"Eight and a half."

"Just wait a couple of years and you'll feel differently."

"No, I won't."

"Want to bet?" Buck asked.

"Yeah. Like a gazillion dollars."

"I'm afraid I don't have that much. Maybe a pizza?"

"Or a cheeseburger? With fries?"

"You're on."

Joanie Campbell, one of the RNs appeared with a plastic wrapped suture tray and began setting it up on the bedside stand.

Now a tear rolled down Matthew's cheek. "Mom, I don't want stitches."

Joyce took her son's hand. "Matthew, what did I tell you? We have to do what the doctor says."

"But I want those tape things. Stitches hurt." He looked up at Buck. "It'll hurt, won't it?"

"A little. But only at first. After I put it all to sleep you won't feel a thing."

Matthew's face screwed down as he tried his best not to let the dam break.

"Look, I'll tell you everything I'm doing. I'll tell you when it'll pinch. No surprises. Okay?"

"I don't want to."

"I know," Buck said. "But you don't want to go to school tomorrow and tell everyone you cried, do you? Wouldn't you rather say that you weren't afraid? That you were a tough guy?"

He glanced at his mom, who nodded, and then he said, "I suppose."

Matthew was a real trooper. He panted and moaned a little but held still and in less than a minute the local anesthetic had been delivered. Buck then sutured the wound, leaving only a very fine line where the laceration had been.

"That's it. All done."

"Really?" Matthew asked.

"Really."

"That wasn't so bad." Matthew laughed, now almost giddy. Tension release will do that. He rambled on about how he couldn't wait to tell everyone how brave he was.

"Told you," Buck said. "The better news is that there are no stitches to remove. They're all inside and will disappear."

"That's so cool," Matthew said.

"I think so." Buck ruffled the boy's hair. "And you were very brave."

While Joanie applied a loose bandage over the wound, Buck and Joyce walked to the nurse's station.

"Keep it clean and dry," Buck said. "The bandage can come off tomorrow morning and you can leave it uncovered after that. Bring him back in three or four days and I'll make sure it's healing well."

She nodded. "You were very good with him."

Joanie walked up. "Dr. Buck is great with children."

"You just have to treat them like adults," Buck said. "Tamp down the fear and they do fine."

"Do you have a practice?" Joyce asked. "I'd like to bring my whole family to you."

"No. I only work here at the ER. And only for a few months. Then I'll be off somewhere else."

"That doesn't make sense," Joyce said.

"I'm doing what we call *locum tenens*. That's a fancy phrase for temporary hired help. Dr. Sally Wilkins is out on maternity leave so I'm here filling in until she returns."

"That's too bad," Joyce said. "We need doctors like you around here."

"I appreciate that. But that's not in the cards."

"You're an excellent surgeon," Joyce said, "I could barely see the cut after you finished."

"That's the path I was on. I did two years of surgical residency but decided ER work was more to my taste, so I switched. Then I decided I'd do this gypsy thing for a while."

Joyce smiled. "Well, when you finish your rambling maybe you'll come back to us."

"I guess anything's possible."

After Matthew and Joyce left, Joanie said, "We have one of our frequent fliers in. She's in cubicle 3. Looks like an infected injection site."

"Drug user, I take?" Buck said.

"Marla Jackson. A local girl. She was a beauty in high school. Cheerleader, homecoming queen, destined to be a model, or a movie star, something like that." Joanie sighed. "Then drugs strangled her into submission. Been on the streets for a while."

Buck had heard that story often enough. Good kids sliding down a drug-paved slope.

That Marla Jackson, in her earlier iteration, had been beautiful was evident. Large, round, blues eyes, great cheek bones, and blonde hair. That drugs had done their damage was also apparent. Thin, painfully so, sallow skin, her shoulder-length hair resembling dirty straw. Not to mention the lesions on her face and her teeth beginning to go south, each a gift from crystal meth.

"Hello. I'm Dr. Buckner. But folks call me Buck."

"Marla," she said. She held up her arm. "I think I have an infection."

She indeed had a nasty injection site infection. It was red, angry, swollen, and pus-filled.

"How long has it been like this?" Buck asked.

"A week. I could squeeze the pus out at first but now it's too painful."

"I bet that's true." He tugged on a pair of gloves and examined the area. "I'll have to open it up, drain it, clean it out, and then you're going to have to keep it covered and clean. Very clean. This could become a serious problem if you don't."

She nodded, rubbed her nose with the heel of her other hand.

"Let me guess," Buck said. "Meth and heroin?"

She nodded.

"Anything else?"

"Coke when I can afford it."

"A bad combination."

"Don't I know."

"When did you use last?"

All the signs of early withdrawal were present. A slight patina of sweat, quick head and eye movements, lip licking, nose rubbing, and a fine tremor in her fingers. Marla was beginning the spiral that would lead her to her next fix. The monkey had its claws in her back and was nipping on her neck. Soon he'd clamp down hard and she'd do anything to sooth the need. An addict's life.

Her gaze dropped, as if trying to avoid the question.

Buck didn't let up. "Maybe four or five hours ago?"

She looked at him. "How'd you know it was…" She stopped mid-sentence and gave a thin smile. "Of course you know. You're a doctor."

"And I've seen this roller coaster quite a few times." Buck now offered his own smile. "Why not get in a program and dump all this crap?"

"Done that. Three times. Doesn't seem to stick." She shrugged and licked at her dry, cracked lips. "So here I am."

"You know this stuff will eventually kill you. Right?"

"There're worse things."

"Well, let's not let it get to that."

After Buck opened, drained, cleaned, and dressed the abscess, Joanie gave Marla an antibiotic injection in her left hip.

"I'll give you an oral antibiotic," Buck said. "Take it regularly and don't skip any doses. Okay?"

"I will."

"Do you have a family doc?"

She shook her head. "Not anymore. I think they all gave up on me."

"Well, we won't. Come back here tomorrow so I can take a look at this. Okay?"

"I'll try."

"No. Don't try. Do. It's important."

"I promise."

"Where do you live?"

She shrugged. "Here and there. Sometimes over at Reverend John's."

"John Packard," Joanie said. "He was a real reverend at one time. But, he had his own drug and alcohol problems so he got tossed from his church. Now he's clean and has a boarding house down near the other end of town. He takes in addicts and runaways and does what he can. Good guy. Folks still call him Reverend John."

"He's saved me from sleeping in the rain more than a few times," Marla said. "And fed me when I couldn't buy a stick of chewing gum."

"Do you have any money?" Buck asked Marla.

"Some," Marla said. "About four bucks."

Buck took out his wallet and extracted a twenty. He extended it toward her. "Get something to eat. Okay?"

She hesitated a beat and then took the bill.

"That's for a good meal, not drugs," Buck said.

Marla nodded a thanks and then swung her frayed backpack over her shoulder and walked through the automatic doors into the night, her jeans hanging loosely from her boney hips.

"You know she'll use that money for drugs."

"Probably. That's up to her. But she does need a little help."

"She needs a lot of help. Just not sure she'll take it."

"She'll be back tomorrow," Buck said. "I'll work on her a bit more. Step at a time."

"The eternal optimist."

Buck smiled. "That's me."

Joanie raised an eyebrow. "You still coming over for dinner

tonight?"

"Sure am."

"Harvey's making his famous venison stew and I think he has a bottle of bourbon with your name on it."

"Tell him not to drink it all before I get there."

She laughed. "He just might. But he has a backup or two."

Buck glanced at his watch. "Pedro should be here any minute and then I'll head home, clean up, and be over in say...half an hour."

Dr. Pedro Padilla, another of the ER docs, had the night duty. The ER was quiet now so the handover should be quick.

"Perfect," Joanie said. "I'm out of here, too. See you soon."

CHAPTER 6

7 HOURS EARLIER

Marla Jackson walked down the ER entry ramp, her packet of antibiotics tucked into one back pocket, her $24 fortune in the other. Her arm ached, but that took a backseat to the withdrawal that twisted her gut, nipped at her nerve endings, and drove the cool night air into her chest. October nights could be chilly here in the hills, particularly on evenings like this when ribbons of ground fog settled into the low-lying areas.

She stopped on the shoulder of Main Street, slipped off her backpack, and knelt. Inside she found her stained and worn navy blue sweatshirt and tugged it on, pulling the sleeves down until only her fingers were exposed. Four months ago it had fit, now it seemed two sizes too large.

She needed to score. Get well. Kill the demons that warred inside her.

A tan sedan rolled by. Family of four, the woman in the passenger seat eyeing her with what she knew was disdain. She was used to it. Throughout high school, people had looked at her with a degree of awe that now had turned into righteous disgust.

She crossed into the park. Tommy Finley, her connection, would likely be hanging near his usual spot. She followed the gravel walking path that wound beneath the trees until she reached the large oak that sheltered one of the park's three small ponds. Where Tommy hung out and conducted his business. Nothing. Where the hell was he? She completed the loop through the park until she returned to where she had begun. Now what was she going to do?

"Looking for Tommy?"

The voice came from behind her. She turned. It was Jason Epps, Tommy's partner or whatever he was. In the few dealings she had had with him he came off as mostly a prick.

"Yeah," Marla said. "Have you seen him?"

"Nope. Looking for him myself."

She rubbed one arm through the sweatshirt. "I need some stuff. Can you call him?"

"I've tried. He ain't answering."

"Damn it." She looked around. A car cruised down Main. "Any idea where he might be?"

"Supposed to be here. He ain't, so your guess is as good as mine."

She heeled her nose, trying to kill the itch.

"You're coming down," Jason said.

She nodded.

"I can help you out."

"I thought Tommy handled your stash."

"Not all of it. So, want some of mine?"

Marla hated Jason. He was a real jerk. Treated her like vermin most of the time. When he wasn't hitting on her. But right now did she have a choice? Tommy, where the hell are you?

"What've you got?" Marla asked.

Jason patted his jean pockets. "Meth. Mexican Black Tar. What do you want?"

"A little of both."

He stepped close to her. Jason was small and thin, maybe five-eight and 140. She was a good two inches taller. His smile was more a sneer than a sign of friendliness. His closeness made her stomach clench.

"How much money you got?" Jason asked.

She stuffed her hand into her pocket and fingered the folded bills. "Twenty-four."

Jason shrugged. "That won't get you much."

"Look, it's all I got." She looked beyond him into the darkness of the park, hoping Tommy would miraculously appear. But her life didn't have any miracles attached to it. It hadn't for a long time. Maybe it never had. Not even when things had been good. "You sure you don't know where Tommy is?"

"I told you, he was supposed to be here. An hour ago. But he's been a bit flakey lately."

"Shit."

"I can give you a quarter of meth for twenty but a quarter of tar will be another twenty."

She wanted the meth but she needed the heroin. Both would be real good.

"Can I owe you for the smack?"

He rolled his eyes. "You know this is a cash and carry business."

"But you know me. You know I'm good for it."

"Do I? Exactly how much is your salary now?"

She wanted to scratch the smirk right off his face. "Why are you being this way? Can't you help me out here?"

"How would you pay me back?"

"I'm pretty good at panhandling. I'll have the twenty well before noon tomorrow."

He scratched one ear. "Maybe. But you'll need more product tomorrow. What then?"

She wrapped her arms around herself. "Come on. I need something now."

"And I told you what it'd cost. Unless."

"Unless what?"

Another sneer-smile. "We can work something else out."

CHAPTER 7

7 HOURS EARLIER

Dalton didn't think much of Tanner's Crossroads. Way too small and backwoods for his tastes. Memphis had everything he needed. Big, busy, and filled with bad guys. Some bad cops too, for that matter. Which was good for business and for staying out of a cage. Besides, if Memphis had been good enough for Elvis, it was good enough for him.

Here in this little speck on the map he had no resources, no backup. He knew no one and barely knew the town's layout. Just enough for a quick in and out. That possibility was gone now. Unless they cut and ran for Memphis that is. Could Dennie make it that far? It sure didn't look that way. But Memphis had the doc he needed, and the remainder of his crew. About now they were probably at some bar, maybe Turk's Lounge, Frankie's place. Should he call them in? If he did, Frankie would know he had fucked up. Better to let that news drop after he had resolved everything. Frankie liked his guys to be self-sufficient, think on their feet, and adapt to the situation.

But, what could he do here and now to smooth over his mistake and save Dennie?

It was at the church that the idea came to him. Who said the Lord couldn't supply inspiration? As ideas go, it was a good one.

Risky, sure, but it just might work. He had been standing near the open rear cargo area of the SUV, studying the back of the church while keeping an eye on the county road beyond, Jessie leaning over to apply pressure to Dennie's abdomen with the wadded towel. The bleeding seemed to have slowed, maybe even stopped. For now anyway.

Dalton had been racking his brain for some way out of this mess. He flashed on a girl he had long ago dated. He couldn't recall her name but remembered she'd been smart. A college girl who had majored in English Lit or some such. Even went to church and did all the other right stuff. She was dating some clean-cut athlete but Dalton had been her bad boy on the side. Worked for him, and apparently for her too.

It'd been a rainy night so they retreated to his apartment. She had been studying Shakespeare, lying in bed next to him, while he watched a baseball game on TV. She rambled on about some play she was reading. Something about the forest coming to some castle. He had thought that was odd since forests couldn't move but he let it ride. He didn't want to stir up some discussion. Not when he was finishing his cigarette and getting ready for round two of sex.

The memory of that moment flashed forward and the idea popped in his head. Who would have thought English Lit might save his brother's life?

Now, Dalton rolled down the county highway, back toward town. The two-lane blacktop crossed over Tanner Creek, the road now Main Street. Dalton kept his speed under the 35 miles-an-hour posted limit.

"Where are we going?" Jessie asked.

"I got an idea," Dalton said.

"What is it?"

"Hold on. You'll see." He glanced at Jessie. "If it works, that is."

They entered the downtown area. There was little traffic. Speed limit now 25. Dalton eased to a stop at a red light. To his right was the city park. Trees, park benches, a couple of walking paths he could see—it was dark and mostly empty now. He saw only two people. A couple standing beneath a broad oak, probably lovers looking for some alone time. Just ahead, on the left, was the emergency entrance to the hospital. When the light cycled, he slow rolled past. A paved ramp led up a gentle slope to the two-story structure. A backlit white sign with red lettering that said "Emergency Department" stretched above double glass doors. Two nurses walked out, chatting and laughing, heading toward their cars, the day's work done. It was seven o'clock.

"There's the hospital," Dennie said. "Are you taking me to the ER?"

"No," Dalton said. "Told you, that's not an option."

"Man, I'm in trouble. I've lost a lot of blood."

"Hold on, little brother."

Dennie moaned. "I'm trying but I don't think I'm going to make it." A louder groan. "Just drop me at that ER. I'll say I accidentally shot myself or that someone tried to mug me."

"And when they connect your blood to the stain you left on the carpet at Tommy Findley's place? Along with four bodies? What then?"

"Jesus. I'm going to die."

Dalton continued past the ER entrance. A block later he swung through a bank parking lot and climbed back on Main Street, heading back east.

"What are we going to do?" Jessie asked.

"If we can't take Dennie to the hospital, maybe we can bring the hospital to him."

"What the hell does that mean?" Dennie asked.

Dalton explained his plan.

"You think that'll work?" Jessie asked.

Dalton shrugged. "Fifty-fifty. It either will or it won't. Keep your fingers crossed. We're going to need a little luck here." The luck he didn't believe in.

Dalton swung into the ER parking area just as a nurse walked through the double automatic doors and angled toward a gray Toyota.

"Her?" Jessie asked.

"She'll have to do," Dalton said.

He tapped the accelerator and the vehicle moved forward. The plan was to slide behind her vehicle until Jessie could jump out, introduce her to his Glock, and let her know what was what. The nurse, now unlocking her car door, looked over her shoulder in their direction. Dalton slowed. But before he could pull in behind her car, a better option appeared. A much better one. A doctor. Had to be. Scrubs, stethoscope draped around his neck, white coat over one arm, briefcase in his other hand. Dalton hit the brakes.

The taillights, then the backup lights of the nurse's car snapped on and she backed out.

"She's getting away," Jessie said.

"Sit tight," Dalton said.

The nurse drove by, cell phone to her ear, not paying attention to them.

"Now what?" Jessie asked.

Dalton pointed ahead. "Him."

The doctor walked to a white Toyota Land Cruiser with North Carolina plates and unlocked the door. He placed his keys on the roof, then tugged open the back door and tossed his coat and briefcase inside. Dalton turned into the slot next to him and jumped out of the Navigator.

"Are you a doctor?" Dalton asked.

The young man looked up. "Yes."

Jackpot. Maybe some luck was coming their way after all.

"Can you help us?" Dalton asked. "It's my brother. He's been injured."

Concern settled over the doctor's face as he walked toward him. "What is it?"

Dalton lifted the rear gate of the SUV exposing Dennie, still on his side, still clutching bloody hands to his belly. The doctor seemed to study the situation for a beat and then looked at Dalton.

"I'll get a stretcher and get him inside."

"I don't think so." Dalton raised his Glock. "Do everything I say, no questions, and this will work out for you."

The doctor recoiled, taking a step back.

Dalton clutched his arm. "Get in."

The doctor hesitated. "What is this?"

"My brother needs help and you got elected."

The doctor looked back toward Dennie. "What happened?"

"Hunting accident." Dalton pressed the muzzle against the doctor's ribs. "No more talk. Get the fuck inside and help my brother."

CHAPTER 8

PRESENT

"Thanks so much for calling, Mr. Cain." Dr. Frank Buckner's voice fell somewhere between panic and exhaustion.

"Please, call me Bobby."

"Okay. Thanks for taking this on."

"Hopefully we can help."

"From what I hear, that's a given."

"I'm curious," Cain said. "How did you find us?"

"Colonel Walter Fromeyer. He was a college classmate. An old friend. I didn't know what to do. This being far away and in a small town. Probably with limited resources. I knew Wally would know how to proceed."

Cain knew Colonel Fromeyer. From his military days. He had run a couple of Cain's missions. Back in the day.

Buckner continued, "He told me about you. What you do. I called Mr. Milner." He sighed. "And here we are."

"You're on speaker. Me and my partner, Harper McCoy. We're leaving Nashville. Should take a couple of hours to reach Tanner's Crossroads."

Cain was driving. Harper held her phone, speaker mode.

"What do you know so far?" Harper asked.

"Buck—his name's Bradley, but everyone calls him Buck—is

doing temporary work in the ER over there. A *locum tenens* situation. Are you familiar with that?"

"We are."

"Only been there a few days. He apparently was leaving work and was abducted at gunpoint. Taken away in an SUV or something."

"Witnesses?"

"Only one that I know of. I got a call from the chief of police. Her name's Cassie Crowe. She and her officers are looking for him now."

"I take it they have no suspects?" Harper asked.

"Not when I last talked to her. An hour ago now. And they still have no clue where to look."

"When did she first call you?" Harper asked.

"Maybe three, four hours ago."

"The abduction was just a few hours before that? Correct?"

"That's right. Around seven p.m. Local time."

Cain mulled that. Witness to the kidnapping, calls cops, who call father, who tracks down Cain and Harper. All in a few hours. "That's good," Cain said. "Means we're entering the fray early on. Not the next day, or the next week."

"Was Buck injured or harmed in any way?" Harper asked.

"I don't know. The witness couldn't be sure."

"Do you know if he had any issues with anyone there?"

"None. Like I said, he's only been there a brief time. I don't see how he could."

"Tell us about him," Harper said.

"Buck is a bright young man. Always near the top of his class. High school, college, med school. He attended Duke for undergrad and med school. Did a couple years of surgical residency, then left the program."

"Why?" Cain asked.

"I wish I could answer that. Believe me, I've tried to fathom it. You see, I head a medical group over here near Charlotte. Multi-specialty. We have twenty-two docs now. Buck's two older brothers and sister are all MDs and work here. I'm over seventy and not all that well, so I'll be turning it over to them before too long. Anyway, Buck was going to become a general surgeon and join us. Take over our surgical programs. But he decided that ER work was for him. Then, he got the travel bug and signed on with a *locum tenens* group." An audible sigh. "Been doing it a couple of years."

"I take it you weren't pleased with his decision?" Harper asked.

"I wasn't. Neither were his siblings. But, Buck is headstrong. Always has been. Danced to his own tune." He cleared his throat. "We butted heads over his stubbornness more than a few times."

Headstrong stubbornness just might serve Buck Buckner well about now. If it didn't get him killed. And if he was still alive.

"What else can you tell us?" Harper asked.

"Is all this important?"

"Very. The better we know him the better we can predict his decisions. His choices and actions. How he might react to his captors."

"I suppose. I can tell you he's smart. Thinks well on his feet. That's why he was top of his residency class. He's tough-minded. Maybe his best skill is that he's good with people. He's a good looking young man with a sense of humor. People like him."

Cain hoped that included his captors.

"Was he an athlete?" Cain asked.

"Yeah. We hiked and hunted and fished when he was younger. When I was younger. In high school he ran cross-country on the track team."

"Do you have a photo of him?" Harper asked.

"Sure. I have as many as you need."

"Send me a couple." She gave him her email address.

"What now?" Buckner asked.

"You sit tight. Let us get boots on the ground and see what the story is. Then, we'll be in touch."

"I wish I could come there. But travel isn't in the cards. I have Parkinson's. It's very limiting. And since timing can always be unpredictable, and at times maddening, his brothers are away. One in Europe on an anniversary trip, the other in Australia at a medical conference. His sister is eight-months pregnant. She has two. The youngest is ten. This one was the later in life surprise."

"Don't worry," Cain said. "We'll do our best for Buck."

CHAPTER 9

6 1/2 HOURS EARLIER

"No way," Marla said. "I'm not going to fuck you for a fix."

"Not what I hear," Jason said. "You fuck Tommy all the time. Rumor is you'll lay down for anyone with a dose of meth. Or money. Or whatever. Maybe you just like to get down and dirty."

She wanted to punch him in the face, rip his eyes out, kick his balls up into his throat. None of that was really an option. He held the keys and right now she needed him to open the medicine jar.

He gave her another sneer-smile. "What makes you think I would fuck a skank like you anyway?"

His words, like a knife, physically hurt. God, she hated him. God? There's a joke for you. If He were real, He'd deliver Tommy and wipe Jason from the Earth. She hadn't seen God, or Jesus, or the freaking Holy Ghost since Sunday school. Another lifetime ago.

"Oh," Marla said. "I thought that's what you meant."

"I was thinking more along the lines of a blow job."

"Not a chance."

"Okay. Have a nice evening." He turned and started to walk away.

"Wait."

Jason spun toward her and waited, saying nothing, just looking

43

at her with that same smirk.

A chill worked its way into her bones. Nausea rose in her stomach. Withdrawal or revulsion? Probably both. Her mind raced, seeking some other option, but finding none. She was short on cash and had nothing to barter with, except herself. But blow him? Right here in the park? Did she have a choice? As bad as she felt right now it was only going to get worse. A lot worse. Should she tell him to fuck off and hope Tommy showed? And if he didn't, what then?

Finally, she sighed. "Okay."

"All right. Twenty and a blow job will get you a couple of quarters of each."

"I'm not going to do that and also give you twenty bucks."

"That's the deal. Take it or leave it." He glanced at his watch. "I've got somewhere to be so make up your mind."

Five minutes later he stood with his back against a large oak tree, Marla on her knees before him. It seemed to take forever. She was sure he was delaying his release on purpose just to fuck with her. But finally he did, grabbing her hair and pulling her to him. She choked and gagged and pulled away, coughing and spitting.

"You fucking asshole."

"Part of the deal, bitch."

She stood and slugged his arm.

He laughed. "You're pretty good. Maybe I could sell you on the street. Bundle you with a gram of coke. I could call it a blow and blow package."

"Fuck you."

He removed two small glycine folds from his pocket and handed them to her. She gave him the twenty.

"Meet me here tomorrow night and we'll do it again," Jason said. He laughed and faded into the night.

She spit a few more times as she made her way to one of the park benches, where she sat, her backpack on the ground between her feet. Maybe a little taste of the meth first, she thought. Her fingers trembled as she unfolded the glycine wrapper. Using the single long nail she had, left little finger, she lifted a dose of crystals. She snorted it, felt the raw burn in her nose, and sat back, waiting for the rush. Didn't take but a few seconds and it was a good one.

Hard and heavy. Her heart pounded and her anxiety began to melt away. God, she loved that feeling.

She looked across Main, toward the hospital. She felt bad about using the money that doctor—what was his name?—she couldn't remember—gave her for drugs, but she needed meth more than she needed food. Besides, Reverend John always had something she could eat.

The hammering of the meth began to smooth out. She dug inside her backpack until she found her spoon, lighter, syringe, and rubber tubing. Using the same nail, she scooped up a bit of the heroin and dumped it into the spoon. She flicked the lighter to life and in a few seconds the white powder became a dark bubbling liquid. She drew it into the syringe. She propped one foot on the bench, pushed down her sock, and near her ankle found a vein that was still in reasonable working order. The needle entered smoothly and she depressed the plunger. The warm rush hit her immediately. She leaned back on the bench, enjoying the ride. Nothing felt like this. Nothing she had ever experienced anyway.

Her vision blurred but across Main Street she saw the wavering image of the doctor walk through the ER doors, his white coat draped over one arm, some kind of satchel or briefcase in his other hand. Dr. Buckner. That was his name. He had said people called him Buck. She liked that name. He opened the back door of a white SUV and tossed the coat and case inside. A large black SUV pulled into the lot, hesitated a beat, and then swung into the empty space next to the doctor's vehicle. Two men got out and approached. One, the taller one, waved a gun and herded Buck into the rear of the vehicle. The two men climbed in and the SUV spun onto Main, heading into downtown.

She watched the entire ordeal unfold through a haze. Not the ground mist, the fog in her brain. She needed to do something. Tell someone.

The drug curtain settled over her. She slouched on the bench and rode the wave.

Move, Marla. Get up. Walk into the ER.

Her eyes closed and she melted into a world of black tar.

CHAPTER 10

6 1/2 HOURS EARLIER

Buck knelt in the rear cargo area of the SUV as the driver rolled down Main Street into town. His mind raced as he tried to sort out what was happening. Other than the obvious. He had been abducted at gunpoint. The driver, the taller of the men, had a hard face. Buck knew the type. They often ended up in the ER with a gunshot wound, a product of the world they inhabited. The guy in the shotgun seat sat twisted his way, a gun in his right hand, aimed at Buck's chest.

"What's your name?" the driver shot over his shoulder.

"Buck."

"Okay, Dr. Buck, let's have your cell phone."

"Why?"

"Gee, let me guess? Give me the fucking phone."

Even in the dark, the rearview mirror reflected the threat in the man's eyes. He was lean, yet muscular, his dark hair slicked back into a ponytail.

Buck removed his cell from his scrub shirt pocket and passed it to the driver. He handed it to the guy riding shotgun. Buck heard it thud to the floorboard and then the crunching of glass and the twisting of metal. The guy picked up the mangled phone, mumbled something that sounded like, "That ought to take care of that." He lowered the window and tossed it out.

"What's this about?" Buck asked.

"My brother needs help," the driver said. "Now do some of that doctor shit."

Buck turned toward the injured man. "Let me take a look."

"I got shot, Doc." The young man grunted as he rolled to his back and lifted his shirt. In the darkness, the blood that covered his abdomen looked more black than red.

"Hard to see much in the dark," Buck said. "Can we have some light back here?"

"Hold on a sec."

They continued through town and a couple of minutes later Main Street became Highway 57, a winding two-lane road that led west. After a half mile, the driver slowed, whipped onto a dark gravel road. The SUV gyrated over the uneven surface. The man laying beside Buck groaned with each bump. The vehicle crunched to a stop and the interior light popped on.

Now Buck could see the entry wound. A small hole in the mid-left side of his abdomen. Buck reached around the man's back but felt no exit wound.

"The bullet's still inside," Buck said.

"Tell me something I don't know," the driver said. "How bad is it?"

Buck did a mental inventory of the possibilities. Spleen? Probably a little low for that. Obviously not the aorta or the vena cave. The wound was too lateral for that—not to mention, if that were the case, the man would be long dead by now. Most likely bowel, maybe kidney. But it could be anything. Bullets do odd things inside a human body. They can bounce and ricochet and tumble around in almost any direction. Especially if they strike bones. Buck had seen gunshots to the chest where the bullet ended up near the bladder. Or some that entered the abdomen and found their way into the chest. Anything and everything was possible.

He began his examination, pressing on the man's abdomen. He winced and withdrew.

"I know it hurts," Buck said, "but I need to see what's going on."

The man nodded and gritted his teeth.

"What's your name?" Buck asked.

"Dennie."

"Shut your fucking mouth," the driver snarled.

"You ain't the one shot."

Buck ignored the brotherly feud. "Hold on, Dennie. This will be a little uncomfortable."

His abdomen was soft and not swollen badly, which was a good sign. At least it wasn't filled with blood. Not yet, anyway. Buck knew that the fact the man was alive, actually awake and not in shock, was a good sign. Meant the bleeding was slow at worst and might even have ceased.

"How long ago did this happen?" Buck asked.

"Maybe an hour," the driver said.

Buck sighed. "Odds are there's damage to one or more of the internal organs. Maybe the kidney, probably the bowel." He looked at the driver. "He needs surgery. He needs a hospital."

"I told you, Dalton," Dennie said. "You got to take me to the ER."

Okay. Dennie and Dalton. Two names down.

"Listen to him," Buck said. "He's right."

"Dennie ain't exactly thinking clearly right now."

"He makes sense to me," Buck said. "Why don't you drop us off at the ER and then you two can take off?"

"That can't happen," Dalton said. "What I need to know is if you can fix him?"

"With what? My fingernails?"

"Listen, smart ass, if you can't help, you're worthless to me."

The guy riding shotgun waggled the muzzle of the weapon he pointed toward Buck.

"And if I can't help?" Buck asked. "What then? You going to shoot me?"

"Yes," Dalton said.

He hadn't hesitated or wavered or even offered a maybe. A simple and absolute yes meant that Dalton wasn't the sort you could bargain with. At least, not right now. He was amped up, probably scared, and Buck got the feeling he'd shot people for less. Still, the facts were the facts. Buck couldn't simply wave a hand and make Dennie better.

"Look, this isn't like the movies," Buck said. "He needs major surgery. Not a couple of stitches and a Band-Aid."

"Like I said, if you can't fix him, you're of no value. So I suggest you figure it out."

Jesus. How did he end up in this mess? They didn't teach him this in med school. Sure he could do the surgery. They did teach him that. But in an OR. Not here in the backseat of an SUV. Did he have a choice? Neither of the two guys with the guns looked like the types that would listen to reason. Not to mention, he believed that Dalton, whose black eyes now stabbed at him from the rearview mirror, would indeed kill him. Why wouldn't he? Buck didn't yet know what had happened but this certainly didn't smell like an accident. Certainly not a hunting accident as Dalton had said. And if it wasn't, it presented a lot of ugly scenarios.

Think, Buck, think.

"I'll need some equipment," Buck said.

"What kind?"

"Little things, like surgical instruments, IV fluids, antiseptic solutions, anesthetic meds. That's just for starters."

Dalton scratched his chin with the muzzle of his gun. Buck now noticed that the weapon had a thick silencer on it. These guys weren't just drug-addicted punks. Guys that got into some O.K. Corral shootout with some other punks. They were pros. Who else would have a silenced gun? No way that helped his cause.

"I saw a pharmacy back in town," Dalton said. "Would that work?"

Buck shook his head. "No. They won't have half of what I need. But there's another one. A larger one that also stocks hospital supplies."

"Then that's our next stop." Dalton slipped the SUV into gear and spun a U-turn toward the highway. "Where is it?"

"Over on Elm Street."

"Where's that?"

"Head back into town; turn right on Fourth. It's a block down on the corner of Fourth and Elm."

It only took a few minutes to reach Shaffer's Pharmacy and Hospital Supplies. The cinder block building, white with black trim, was dark except for a weak light filtering from the rear of the interior.

Dalton drove around the building and parked near the metal rear door. He killed the engine. Through the drizzle-misted windshield, Buck saw a smear of light spilling through the pharmacy's rear window. A shadow moved by.

"Someone's inside," Dalton said. "I suspect with most of the lights off it's the manager closing up." He opened the SUV's door. "We might've just got lucky." He stepped out. "Sit tight." He nodded toward his partner. "Listen up, Jessie. If he tries anything stupid, shoot him."

Okay...Dalton, Dennie, and Jessie. He had their names. Not that that would likely help him much.

Dalton disappeared inside. For less than a minute. He returned holding a middle-aged man's arm. He led him to the vehicle.

"This here's the owner. Tell him what you need and we'll get it."

"I need too much," Buck said. "It'll be better if I go in with you."

Dalton hesitated a beat, as if considering options, but finally said, "Let's go then."

Buck climbed out. Jessie did, too.

"Hang in there, Dennie," Jessie said. "We'll be out of here in a hot minute."

Inside, Buck said to the man, "I'm Dr. Buckner. You the owner?"

"Wilbert Shaffer."

"Sorry about this," Buck said.

"Cut the fucking chatter," Dalton said. "Get all your shit and let's get out of here."

Shaffer hesitated.

"It's okay," Buck said. "Just give me what I need and we'll leave."

Shaffer grabbed a wad of plastic garbage bags and he and Buck walked the aisles, filling them with everything Buck saw that he might need. Surgical drapes, packages of gauze, tape, surgical gowns, gloves, masks, two large plastic bottles of Betadine Scrub, a handful of scalpel handles and blades, hemostats, scissors, an automatic blood pressure device, several boxes of sutures, oral airways, IV lines and bags of fluids. While they worked the shelves, Dalton moved with them, standing at the end of each aisle, keeping them in sight.

Buck whispered, "His name is Dalton, his brother Dennie is

the injured one. The other guy is Jessie."

Shaffer gave a quick nod.

"Didn't I say no talking?" Dalton said. "Shut the fuck up and get what you need. We have to roll."

"Any anesthetic agents?" Buck asked Shaffer.

Shaffer led them into the back area of the pharmacy. The part off-limits to customers where the drugs and other controlled items were stored. A long counter with three arched pass-through windows and a single door separated the area from the rows of shelves available to customers. Buck did a quick survey. Rows of medication bottles and in one corner a wire cage, the controlled drug area. Shaffer unlocked it and they entered.

He and Shaffer worked together gathering Versed, morphine, Valium, Vicodin, Xanax, and Narcan. An array of bottles of Noctec caught Buck's eye and he grabbed a couple.

"Look at what we got here," Dalton said. He stood in the doorway, his gun hanging at his side. "The good stuff." He waved the weapon. "Take it all."

Of course, Buck thought. Take the drugs. Profit is where profit is found.

He swiped several rows of bottles and vials into one of the bags.

Buck looked around. Did he have everything he needed? Hard to be sure. He hadn't had time to think or even formulate a reasonable list. Rather he had grabbed everything he saw that might prove useful.

"That about it, Doc?" Dalton asked.

"I think so."

"Be sure. This is a one shot deal."

"Want me to sit down and make a list?" Dalton glared at him. "I'm doing the best I can under the circumstances."

Dalton's jaw tightened. He then turned to his partner. "Jessie, get all this shit outside while the doc thinks."

He gathered up the four trash bags they had filled, two in each hand, and carried them toward the rear door.

"I think that's it," Buck said.

Jessie returned. "Dennie ain't looking so good. We need to get out of here."

"One more thing," Dalton said. He walked to the cash register and tried the drawer, finding it locked.

"Open it," he said to Shaffer.

He did.

Dalton fisted all the bills inside and stuffed them into his pocket.

"Not bad. Now it'll look like a good old-fashioned robbery." He looked at Jessie. "Take the doc back to the car. I'll finish up in here."

Jessie waved a hand toward the door, headed that way. Buck followed. As he passed one of the cash registers, he made sure Dalton wasn't looking, and quickly removed his wallet from the back pocket of his scrubs. He snugged it against the edge of the register and trailed Jessie outside.

CHAPTER 11

6 HOURS EARLIER

Marla floated on a heroin wave. Her arms, legs, entire body was heavy with that welcome tingly feeling. To her, the ride always felt as if she were enveloped in a warm, comforting blanket, curled before a fire. One of the few memories she still held from her childhood. The remainder had long ago been fractured and scattered. Her past now only appeared in snapshots and brief distorted images. Laughing with friends in the school cafeteria, movies with buttery popcorn, leading cheers on the sidelines, even siting at the dinner table with her parents. But these flashbacks were increasingly fragile and unreliable, as if they might not have really happened.

The heroin fog, and the ground fog, thinned. Above her, she saw the outline of tree limbs against the dark sky, but no stars or moon. She had slouched down on the park bench, head back, her neck now stiff. A single drop of rain struck her forehead. She heard others tap against the leaves.

She sat up, twisting to relieve the tightness in her back. She wiped drool from her chin with one sleeve.

How long had she been here? Seemed an eternity but she knew heroin voyages only lasted twenty minutes, max. God, she wished they were longer. Like forever. That would be perfect. Hang weightless in that mist, never come out, never have to deal with this shitty world again.

She sat up. Her foot banged against her backpack. Next to her, the bag of heroin sat on the bench, along with her needle and spoon. She collected them.

Maybe one more ride. More raindrops.

Shelter. That's what she needed now. The temperature was dropping and if she got soaked it would fall farther. Time to head over to Reverend John's. Hopefully, he had a bed for her. If not, she would have to crash on the floor. Right now either would be welcome.

She stood. Unsteady.

Across the street, the lights of the hospital's ER caught her eye. "Emergency Department" in red block letters on an illuminated white sign.

What was it? Something niggled at her brain. Something she needed to remember. But, what? It had slipped away as the heroin enveloped her.

She grabbed her backpack and walked that way, stopping at the edge of the road. Nothing. She couldn't recall what had earlier seemed important. But was it? Did anything important ever happen in her life? Other than the next fix?

The raindrops now became a drizzle. She turned along the road's shoulder toward town, toward Reverend John's.

She suddenly stopped. Remembered. Jason. What he made her do. Took almost all of her money. The twenty the nice doctor had given her. She spun toward the ER. The doctor. Someone had forced him into a big black vehicle. Hadn't they? Or was it a dream? She had those all the time and couldn't always remember what was real; what had really happened and what had simply rolled through her brain.

She shifted the backpack to the other shoulder and crossed the street. The ER parking area was mostly empty, only four cars. An ambulance sat to the left of the sliding-glass entry doors, lights off, engine quiet.

There it was. The doctor's SUV. A Land Cruiser. The left rear door stood open. She approached, looked around, saw no one. Inside, a briefcase and a white coat lay on the rear seat. On the rooftop, keys.

The entire scene replayed in her head. She hadn't imagined it. It hadn't been a drug dream, it really happened.

The ER doors whooshed open and she entered. It was quieter than it had been before. The waiting room empty, two nurses standing near one of the curtained cubicles chatting, only the sound of a floor polisher whirring away somewhere down a hallway. The woman behind the reception desk—Marla knew her name but couldn't recall it—greeted her with a quick smile, her fingers still working her computer. Her keyboard tapping fell silent.

"Marla? What brings you back? Is everything okay?"

"I don't know. I think I saw something."

"Like what?"

Marla glanced toward the entrance. Did she really see what she thought she did? Yes, yes. The car keys, the door open, the stuff inside. But what had she actually seen? The image of the tall man materialized. The gun. She looked back toward the woman.

"I think I just saw that doctor get kidnapped."

The two nurses standing nearby now approached. Marla recognized Mona Faulk, the older of the two.

"What do you mean?" Mona asked.

"I was in the park. A black SUV pulled up as the doctor—what was his name?"

"Buckner. Dr. Buckner."

Marla nodded. "He was nice. I liked him."

"What happened?" Mona pressed her.

"He was getting into his car when they pulled up. Two guys held a gun on him and forced him inside the back of the SUV."

Mona didn't seem convinced. "Are you using?"

It wasn't like Marla hadn't heard that before. No one ever believed her. "What difference does that make?"

"Maybe you imagined this? Dr. Buckner went home earlier."

"I'm telling you he didn't make it out of the parking lot by himself." She massaged her nose with the heel of one hand. "I know what I saw."

Mona shrugged.

"You don't have to believe me." Marla turned toward the

entrance. "Come see for yourself."

CHAPTER 12

Chief Cassandra Crowe didn't know what to make of the call. A doctor kidnapped? From the ER parking lot? That made no sense. Had Tanner's Crossroads ever had an abduction? Well, one that she could remember. Back when she was a young officer and her father was the chief, an estranged father took his five-year-old daughter. Not very far. Just to a local diner for breakfast. The mother had been hysterical but all was resolved after the child finished her pancakes and licked the syrup from her fingers.

The other thing that struck Cassie as odd about the call was that Mona Faulk had said the witness was Marla Jackson. Not exactly the most reliable human she knew. Not anymore.

Seeing, even thinking of Marla, always disturbed her. Churned up feelings of failure. Not just Marla's but also her own. She and Marla had been classmates, and friends. Back in the day. Where Cassie had been the best female athlete in school, Marla had been the prettiest. By far.

Unlike some of the others in their class, Cassie never envied Marla's looks, believing, even at a young age, that such beauty carried heavy burdens. Always on display, the focus of ardent male attention at any gathering, and having to deflect unwanted advances on a daily basis. That Marla had a knack for rejecting such come-ons, while making the dejected souls feel okay about it, had always amazed Cassie. Marla had a gift beyond her beauty.

Cassie never felt Marla envied her own athletic prowess. Some did, but never Marla. In fact, she had been one of Cassie's biggest supporters. Never missing one of Cassie's softball or basketball games, the latter being Cassie's best sport.

During their senior year, when Marla began experimenting with drugs, Cassie tried to dissuade her. For a while, she believed she had. After graduation, as Marla slid ever more deeply into the drug culture, Cassie again stepped up. As a young cop, she had arranged rehab for her. Twice. Neither took and Marla continued on her own private road to hell. Anyone who saw her today would know she had arrived but, unless they knew the old Marla, they could never imagine just how far her fall had been.

That was the source of Cassie's feelings of failure. Why hadn't she been able to help? Why couldn't she find just the right words, the right buttons to push, to get Marla back on track? She had always prided herself on her abilities to persuade others to do the right thing and stay on the right path. But everything she tried fell flat and Marla was lost.

Cassie swung into the ER parking lot, slid into a space near the entrance, and walked to where Mona and Marla stood. Near a white Toyota Land Cruiser. A mist of rain filled the air.

"Chief," Mona said. She held an umbrella. "Maybe you can figure this out."

"What's the story?" Cassie asked.

Mona nodded toward Marla, who wore a hoodie, cinched around her face, hands stuffed in its pockets, a blue backpack over one shoulder. Marla told her what she had seen. She spoke rapidly, stumbled out the story. She kept her eyes down, rarely glancing up at Cassie, like a kid trying to convince a parent they were innocent.

"You sure?" Cassie asked.

Marla sighed. "Yes, I was using. Yes, I wasn't sure at first. But I walked over here and found the car door open and his stuff inside."

Cassie saw a white coat and briefcase on the backseat.

"And then I saw those," Marla pointed to the vehicle's roof.

Cassie saw a wad of keys on a gold metal ring with a matching tab that read "Buck." The ring also held the fob and the key to the

Land Cruiser. Cassie picked them up.

"I know what I saw," Marla said.

Cassie circled the vehicle. The other doors were closed. No evident damage, nothing laying on the concrete nearby. When she returned to where Marla stood, she said, "I believe you."

Marla visibly relaxed.

"What did they look like?"

"I was over in the park." She pointed that way. "Sitting on the bench, so I couldn't see them all that well."

"Do your best."

"One was tall. Over six feet for sure. He had dark hair in a ponytail. The other guy was smaller and wore a cap or something. Both wore black clothes."

"Their vehicle?"

"An SUV. A big one. All black and the windows looked tinted."

"Did you get the make or license plate?"

Marla shook her head. "I don't know cars all that well."

"Anything unusual about it? Odd lights, decals, anything?"

"Not that I saw." She rubbed her nose. "Sorry."

"You're doing great." Cassie smiled. "Which way did they go?"

Marla pointed. "Toward downtown."

Cassie turned to Mona. "Did you call him?"

"Yeah. His cell went to voicemail. I left a message for him to call us back." She pulled a scrap of paper from her jacket pocket. "I wrote the number down for you. I figured you'd want it."

"Thanks."

"I started to call his father but thought I'd better wait to see what you thought."

"Who's his father?"

"He's the emergency contact Buck gave us."

"Buck?"

Mona smiled. "Dr. Buckner. His name's Bradley, but everyone calls him Buck. He insisted we did, too."

"Is he new?" Cassie asked. "I haven't met him."

"Yeah. Been here less than a week. Filling in for Dr. Wilkens."

Cassie nodded. "When's she due?"

"Three weeks, I think."

"You have the father's number?"

"Yeah. Inside. He's a doctor back in North Carolina where Buck is from. Apparently runs a fairly large clinic." Mona's eyes widened. "Do you think this could be a ransom thing?"

"Don't know. Doctor's son. I guess it's possible. But if he's over in the Carolinas, it seems a bit far away to abduct someone and then collect the payout."

"That makes sense."

"Then again," Cassie said, "criminals aren't known for their smarts."

Mona smiled.

"I'll get a couple of my folks rolling and we'll see if we can find this SUV. I'll give the father a call while on the road." Cassie turned to Marla. "Good job."

Marla shrugged. "It just seemed so odd."

"I'm glad it did. And that you followed up on it."

Marla scratched an arm through her shirt sleeve, stared at her shoes.

"Where're you staying tonight?" Cassie asked.

"Probably head over to Reverend John's."

"Good idea. This rain's supposed to get worse."

Marla looked up. "You think he'll be okay?"

Cassie sighed. "Depends on who's got him and what their agenda is."

Marla looked down, kicked one foot at the asphalt, sending a small pebble skittering. "He was nice."

"Come on," Cassie said. "After I get the phone number, I'll take you over to Reverend John's."

"I can walk."

"It's raining."

Marla shrugged.

"Humor me," Cassie said.

CHAPTER 13

5 HOURS EARLIER

Buck did his best to divide his attention between caring for Dennie and memorizing where they were going. No easy task. For sure, they had turned north at The Crossroads, but after that Dalton seemed to meander in no particular pattern. Up, down, right, left, paved roads, gravel roads, and a couple of U-turns. He tried to locate distinctive landmarks in case he found some way out of this and had to run for civilization. He pictured doing that with bullets flying. But, the farther they traveled the less likely that seemed a possibility. In truth, he now had no idea where they were or what direction they were going.

"Do you know where you are?" Buck finally asked.

"I'll figure it out."

"We're running out of time here. Your brother can't last much longer."

"He'd better."

"Then land somewhere," Buck said. "It's the only chance he has."

"I'm trying. Now shut the fuck up so I can think."

"Thinking won't help him much."

Jessie twisted in his seat. "Dennie don't look so good, Dalton."

"We got to find the right spot."

"How you going to do that driving around in circles?" Jessie said.

Dalton glared at him. "That pharmacy dude said there were lots of cabins up here."

"I know," Jessie said. "We've passed a bunch of them."

"Not isolated enough. We need a place where no one can find us."

"How come he told you that?" Jessie asked. "About the cabins?"

"I convinced him it'd be good for his health if he helped a little bit."

Dalton slowed. He pointed to a pair of dirt and gravel tracks that led up into the trees. No house was visible.

"This might work," Dalton said.

"I don't see anything," Jessie said.

"There's a mailbox. Right there beside the road. There must be a house of some sorts."

He turned up the slope, the SUV gyrating over its rutted surface, the overgrowth of weeds scraping the undercarriage. Dennie moaned with each lurch but said nothing. Dalton switched off the headlamps. The darkness was instant and deep. Almost disorienting. A hundred yards ahead on the left, a house appeared. Dark except for a single window that emitted light through a curtain.

Dalton eased to a stop a couple of hundred feet short. He leaned forward, examining it over the steering wheel. He switched the engine off.

"Wait here," Dalton said. "I'll check it out."

The interior lights seemed harsh when he opened the door. Dalton eased it closed and walked up the road. Buck watched as Dalton veered to his left and disappeared into the stand of trees that flanked the home.

"How are you doing, Dennie?" Buck asked.

"Not so good. I'm cold and thirsty. And my belly hurts like a bitch. It's throbbing like a smashed thumbnail."

Buck felt his wrist, finding the pulse. Weak but steady and not too fast.

"You going to be able to help me?" Dennie asked.

"I'm not sure."

"You're a fucking doctor. I thought you guys could fix anything."

Buck looked at him. "If we were down at the hospital, in the operating room, I'd say your chances would be very good. Out here in the middle of nowhere, it's not that certain."

Dennie groaned and clutched his belly. "Jesus. We should've taken the nurse."

"Nurse?" Buck asked.

"A nurse came out of the ER right before you did," Jessie said. "Dalton was going to grab her, and then like a miracle, you appeared."

"Lucky me," Buck said.

"You ain't the one that needs luck," Dennie said. "I do. Maybe the nurse would've been better seeing as you don't know what to do."

"I know what to do, I'm just not sure it'll work under these conditions."

"Great. Just fucking great."

"Listen, Dennie," Buck said. "I was a surgeon for a couple of years before I moved over to ER medicine. I've done this more than a few times." He looked out the window, "Just not in a place like this."

"Where the hell is Dalton?" Jessie asked. "You think he ran into some trouble?"

"Dalton can handle himself," Dennie said.

CHAPTER 14

4 1/2 HOURS EARLIER

Fifteen minutes later, Dalton reappeared, walking down the drive as if he didn't have a worry in the world. He climbed in and cranked the engine.

"Looks good. We're all set."

"Who lives here?" Buck asked.

"No one," Dalton said. "Probably a vacation home."

Why would they leave a light on? Buck thought. His impulse was to ask, but he said nothing. Not the time to stir the pot.

The rutted tracks ended at a garage door. Dalton angled to the right and behind the house, parking the SUV in the backyard beneath a tree, well hidden from the drive and the road.

The home was wooden, single-story, and had a plank rear gallery that extended its width. The back door, flanked by two windows, stood open and light, from what Buck saw was a kitchen, spilled through, casting a trio of lit rectangles across the deck.

While Jessie carried the bags of stolen medical supplies up the four steps and inside, Buck and Dalton helped Dennie from the truck. He groaned with every movement and when he finally stood, he wavered, leaning his weight on Buck's shoulder.

"Stand still," Buck said. "Get your legs under you."

Dennie gritted his teeth. He looked toward the house. "Looks a million miles away."

"Come on. You can make it."

With Buck's help, Dennie shuffled up the steps, through the kitchen and dining area, and into the living room, where he stretched out on a plaid sofa.

"Where you want to do this?" Dalton asked. "One of the bedrooms?"

"Let me check things out," Buck said.

"Just so you know," Dalton said, "I cut the phone line."

"I assumed you would," Buck said.

"What's that supposed to mean?"

"That you don't impress me as the sort to leave much to chance."

Dalton nodded. "Probably something you should keep in mind."

The house was cozy. Dining room, living room, and kitchen a single large space. Two bedrooms. The largest just off the living area had an attached bath. The other down a short hallway, a second bath across the way. Buck returned to the kitchen to find Jessie rummaging in the refrigerator.

"Look at this," Jessie said. "They got some cold cuts, cheese, milk, and half a chocolate cake in here."

He flipped open the overhead cabinets. Dishes, glasses, bread, crackers, cereal, a bag of cookies, cans of tuna, and two jars of peanut butter. The final cabinet held bottles of whiskey, gin, vodka, and scotch.

"Jackpot," Jessie said. "We got food and alcohol."

"Good," Dalton said. "I'm starving."

"Hey," Dennie yelled from the living room. "What about me?"

"Chill, Dennie. Dr. Buck's figuring out where he's going to cut on you."

"Jesus," Dennie moaned. "You sons-of-bitches are going to fool around and let me die."

Dalton looked at Buck. "What's the decision?"

"Dining room table. It's stable and the right height to work."

"All right. Let's get to it."

"Who's going to assist me?" Buck asked.

"Assist you? Can't you do this on your own?"

Buck shook his head. "I'm going to need you both. One to work with me and help with the instruments."

"You mean like blood and stuff?" Dalton said.

"Yeah, blood and stuff."

"Jessie'll do that," Dalton said.

"Why me?" Jessie asked.

Dalton glared at him. "Because I said so, that's why. Besides, you're the big hunter. You've skinned and gutted more deer than I've ever seen."

"I'm not a goddamn deer," Dennie shouted.

"Let's get to work," Buck said.

He dragged the chairs away from the table, lining them up against one wall, out of the way. He turned on the overhead light and moved a floor lamp from the living room, stationing it near one end of the table. Not exactly surgical lights but it was the best he could do.

Buck spread a blue surgical drape over the table. He had seen two TV tray tables in the living room and brought them in, placing them on one side of the table. He draped them also. He then grabbed the trash can from beneath the kitchen sink and settled it on the floor nearby.

"Let's get your clothes off, Dennie," Buck said.

"Why you got to do that?"

"Because they're dirty and bloody and right now you don't need them. Or an infection."

It took a few minutes and a lot of moaning and complaining from Dennie, but finally his clothes were removed and he was stretched out on the table.

"This ain't very comfortable," Dennie said.

"Once you go to sleep, you won't feel a thing," Buck said.

"Asleep? You ain't going to knock me out. No way."

"If you'd prefer, we can get you a stick to bite on while we dig around in your belly." Buck shrugged. "That's how they did it in the Civil War." He looked down at Dennie. "Of course most of them died in the process."

"Goddamn it."

"Relax. It'll be okay."

"So now you're all confident and everything?" Dennie said.

"Put a cork in it, Dennie," Dalton said. "Let the man do his job."

"You ain't the one he's going to cut on."

"Yeah, but you are. So shut up and do what he tells you."

"You two want to knock it off?" Buck said. "So we can get to work?"

That ended the brotherly squabble. For now, anyway. Siblings did that. He knew; after all, he and his brothers had had their spats. But this wasn't the time or place. Buck needed Dalton's focus. Later? Maybe he could use a good spat to his advantage.

If Dennie survived. If Dalton didn't shoot him as soon as he finished. Both were distinct possibilities.

Buck started an IV, hanging the fluid bag on a standing hat rack Dalton had dragged in from the entryway. He opened up the flow rate and over the next few minutes got half a liter of fluids into Dennie. He gave him four milligrams of morphine, two of Versed, and a gram of the antibiotic Cefazolin. Dennie eased into sleep. Buck wrapped the blood pressure cuff around one arm and checked his BP. Ninety. Low but survivable. Maybe. He scrubbed his chest and abdomen with Betadine.

After slipping on surgical gloves and showing Jessie how to do the same, Buck went through a few sterile procedure techniques, mainly telling Jessie not to touch anything unless he said so, and making sure Dalton understood that when he opened instruments and other materials he must avoid touching anything inside. They seemed to understand but Buck knew that was probably wishful thinking.

Following Buck's directions, Dalton opened several instrument packages, dumping scalpels, scissors, hemostats, sutures, and two high stacks of gauze on one of the draped TV trays. Buck took a quick inventory, deciding he had most of what he needed.

"One more thing," Buck said. "Once I give him more drugs to take him way down into unconsciousness, you're going to have to breathe for him."

Dalton stared at him. "Mouth to mouth? Not a chance."

"No." Buck pointed to the Ambu bag and mask he had collected at the pharmacy. "With that."

"I don't know how to do any of that."

"I know you don't. That's why we should be doing this in a

hospital where they actually have people who do all this for a living."

Dalton glared at him.

Buck stared back. He saw this as an opportunity to take some of the power away from Dalton. This was his domain and Dalton was definitely uncomfortable. Buck even detected a hint of fear in his eyes. Probably not a common emotion for Dalton.

"You have the guns. You're in charge of all this." Buck waved an arm toward the living room. "But here," he nodded toward Dennie, "I'm in charge. You do what I say, when I say it, or he dies. That clear?"

Dalton smiled. "And if you let my brother die, I'll kill you in flash. Is that clear?"

"Crystal. You just do what I tell you and we'll muddle through."

Dalton hesitated a beat and then nodded.

Buck placed an oral airway into Dennie's mouth, sliding it over his tongue to keep it out of the way. Dennie gagged, weakly, the drugs having taken effect. He strapped the face mask around Dennie's head, seating the mask over his mouth and nose. He attached the Ambu bag to the mask. He showed Dalton how to slowly and rhythmically squeeze it, indicating that the rise and fall of Dennie's chest meant all was working. Dennie sputtered a pair of feeble coughs.

"What's wrong?" Dalton asked.

"Nothing. He's reacting normally to having air forced into his lungs. You ready?"

"I guess."

Buck injected another ten milligrams of morphine and three of Versed through the IV. Dennie went completely limp. He knew this wasn't truly general anesthesia, only that Dennie was in a deep coma, and might still react and try to withdraw, even fight him. He could only hope it would be enough.

Buck stripped off his now-contaminated gloves and tugged on a fresh pair.

The big test would be the initial incision. If Dennie reacted to the pain, Buck would have to use more anesthesia, and with Dennie's blood pressure already low, that could cause him to crash. Buck took a breath and drew the scalpel blade through the skin just left of the midline. No reaction. So far so good. He quickly extended and deepened the incision until he was in the abdomen. He tugged Dennie's flaccid abdominal wall open.

"Here," Buck said to Jessie. "Slide your fingers in here and pull his belly wall toward you."

"Put my hands inside him?" Jessie said.

"I need space to work," Buck said. "And I can't do both."

Jessie hesitated but did as he was told.

"Wider," Buck said. "You aren't going to hurt him."

Jessie did. Dennie's abdomen opened before them.

"Jesus," Jessie said. Sweat dotted his forehead.

"Take a couple of breaths," Buck said. "It'll be okay."

Inside, Buck found wads of clotted blood and scooped them away, lifting the dark mahogany clots out and dropping them in the wastebasket near his feet. Jessie paled. Sweat now covered his face.

"Hang in there," Buck said.

"I ain't never seen anything like this," Jessie said. "It's gross and then some."

"You're doing fine."

And Jessie was. He did everything Buck asked of him, which fortunately wasn't much more than holding Dennie's belly open with one hand and with the other handing him scissors, hemostats, sutures, and gauze whenever Buck asked. Buck found that Dennie's bowel was intact. Very good news. If the bowel had been breached and its contents released into the abdomen, Dennie's chance of avoiding a serious and potentially lethal infection would be nil. As it was, the only real damage was the completely trashed left kidney.

"Okay," Buck said. "This isn't as bad as it could be. But this kidney is history."

"What does that mean?" Dalton asked.

"It means it's coming out."

"What? You're going to take out his kidney?"

"He's got another one." He looked at Dalton. "Don't try to tell me what to do. Clear?"

Dalton's eyes narrowed, his jaw flexed, but he gave a nod.

Buck cross-clamped the renal artery and vein, freed and removed the kidney, and then tied off the vessels. He found the bullet embedded in the back of the abdominal wall in the cavity where the kidney had been. He extracted it with a hemostat and held it up.

"Here's the culprit."

After Buck made sure the bleeding was under control, he closed everything up.

As Buck stripped off his gloves, he said, "The hard part's done. Now he'll need a little luck." He looked at Jessie. "Good job."

"I ain't so hungry now," Jessie said.

"I'm starving," Buck said. "I'll hang another liter of IV fluids and run that in while we eat something."

"What am I supposed to do?" Dalton said. "Keep squeezing this bag?"

Dalton had done a good job, too. He had kept a steady rhythm to the Ambu bag the entire time, breathing for the unconscious Dennie. Buck considered leaving him there, ventilating Dennie, just to piss him off. But, did he really want Dalton pissed? Besides, Dalton would probably pass that task on to him.

"I'll give a little Narcan," Buck said. "It'll counteract the morphine and he should wake up enough to breathe on his own."

"Good. My hands are cramping."

"Least you didn't have to get no blood on you," Jessie said. "Or stick your hands inside Dennie."

CHAPTER 15

PRESENT

A steady drizzle had accompanied Cain and Harper as they traveled east on I-40. By the time they veered north off the interstate onto the two-lane blacktop that would carry them to Tanner's Crossroads, it became a steady rain. Cain slowed, following the wet curves that ascended into the Appalachian foothills.

Throughout the two-plus hour trip, Harper had worked her iPad, researching the town, and the surrounding area. She related to Cain what she had uncovered.

Tanner's Crossroads, ninety miles from anything one might reasonably call a city, got its name from Tanner's General Store, which was now down to the fourth generation of Tanner ownership. For eighty years it had staked out one corner of the intersection of two county highways; 43 running north and south, 57 east and west. The Crossroads, as locals called it. That more or less marked the western edge of town. Beyond lay deep forested hills and patches of farmland.

Two major streams tumbled out of the hills and joined a half mile west of The Crossroads. The townsfolk apparently referring to it as The Confluence. The river they formed continued tumbling toward Chattanooga.

Population was 8,400 according to the town's website. The

current chief of police was Cassandra "Cassie" Crowe. From her website picture she looked around 30, fit, with short, spiky blonde hair, blue eyes, and a stern face. At least for the photo. The entire force consisted of a dozen officers, including a couple of guys listed as "volunteers."

The town boasted an active tourism industry. Mostly hunters, fishermen, and folks who wanted a cabin to get away from the big city. Rentals were plentiful, suggesting most were second homes.

It had one hospital. Their destination.

Cain rolled to a stop at The Crossroads and turned right toward town. Highway 57, now Main Street, bisected the compact business district—ten blocks or eight traffic signals long, depending on how you wanted to count it, and two blocks wide. Residential neighborhoods wrapped the commercial area. At the east end they found Tanner Medical Center, across from a tree-studded park.

Cain slid The Rig into a parking slot outside the ER entrance and they entered through sliding glass doors. Quiet inside. Understandable at this hour, around five a.m. A nurse sat behind a counter and looked up as they walked toward her.

"What can I do for you?" she asked.

"I'm Bobby Cain. This is Harper McCoy."

"Mona Faulk. I'm the charge nurse tonight." She eyed them. "What's the problem?"

"None," Harper said. "Not a medical one anyway."

"We're here about Dr. Buckner."

Mona's head jerked up. Confusion erupted on her face. "Did you find him?"

"No. But that's why we're here."

Her confusion deepened. "I don't understand. Who are you?"

"We're private investigators," Harper said. "From Nashville. We were retained by his father. We understand he was kidnapped. Or something like that."

She stood. "Have you talked with Chief Crowe?"

"Not yet," Cain said. "We just drove in. This is our first stop."

"From Nashville?"

Cain explained the two a.m. call, them hitting the road, driving straight through.

Mona seemed to digest that. "Let me get this straight. His

father called you three hours ago, and now you're here?"

"Time is critical," Harper said.

"Tell us what happened," Cain said.

"I'm not exactly sure. We got the story from Marla Jackson. She's one of our local druggies. She was here earlier. Dr. Buck—that's what we call him—took care of her. I think it was an infected injection site. Anyway, she went over to the park and shot up. A lot of kids around here use the park for that. It also seems to be the spot for dealing. She apparently saw two guys with guns put Buck in their vehicle and drive away."

"Any idea who?" Harper asked.

Mona shook her head. "The chief and her guys have been looking for them."

"What kind of vehicle?"

"Marla said it was a big black SUV, but she didn't know the model." She massaged her neck. "Look, Marla's a headcase. Hell, it could've been a red sports car and I'm not sure she would've known the difference."

Cain nodded.

"I better call the chief," Mona said.

"Probably a good idea," Cain said.

CHAPTER 16

Mona grabbed a pair of coffees from the break room for Cain and Harper. Black, strong, bordering on bitter. Like most hospital coffee in Cain's experience. But it was hot and had caffeine so it did the trick.

Mona had called Chief Crowe and after she hung up had said, "She's on the way."

"Tell us about Dr. Buckner," Harper said.

"Buck? He's been here less than a week but he's good people. A good doc. The patients love him."

"So he fits in around here?" Harper asked.

"More than that." She gave a quick glance over her shoulder, then leaned forward slightly. "All the doctors we have here are good. We're lucky there. But Buck is something else again. Really good with trauma. Cuts and scrapes and contusions, broken bones, stuff like that. He did two years of a surgical residency before turning to ER work. Good with his hands."

"That's what we heard," Cain said. "From his father."

"Yeah, well, I don't think his father was pleased with him splitting from that program. I talked with Buck about it once. Just a couple of days ago. How he ended up here in our little slice of paradise." She smiled. "He said that the plan was for him to be a surgeon and return to the big medical group his dad had created. He decided he'd rather see the world and do the ER thing." A quick head nod. "We're sure glad he did."

"I take it he had the day shift and was heading home when this happened?" Harper asked.

"Yep."

"Where does he live?"

"The hospital got him an apartment. It's not far. Maybe three or four blocks."

The automatic entry doors slid open. Chief Cassie Crowe entered. She looked just like her photo. Now that Cain could see all of her, she was fairly tall, maybe five-ten, lean and fit, with long legs. She wore jeans and a Navy blue shirt and jacket, the PD logo on the left chest. Service weapon on her right hip. She walked toward them with confident strides.

"You the ones looking for Dr. Buckner?" she asked.

Cain and Harper introduced themselves. Handshakes followed, Chief Crowe saying they should call her Cassie since everyone else did. Cain explained they had been hired by Buck's father and that they had left Nashville around two and had just gotten into town.

"Three hours ago you were in Nashville?" Cassie asked.

"We were."

She raised an eyebrow.

"Like we told Mona," Harper said. "Time is critical in these cases."

"I see." Cassie examined each of them, sizing them up for sure. "I take it you know Dr. Buckner's father?"

"No. A friend of a friend."

She nodded. "When I spoke with him, he didn't mention calling in anyone else."

"He probably didn't know then," Harper said. "Needed to process things, I suspect."

"And after he did, he called you?"

"He did."

"What exactly do you do?" Cassie asked.

"Solve problems," Cain said.

"That's pretty vague."

Cain smiled. "So is our job description. Each job is different."

Cassie sighed. "Why do I get the impression that you might get in the way here?"

"We won't," Cain said.

"We're here to help," Harper said. "Find Buck Buckner. Find whoever grabbed him."

Cassie mulled that, said nothing.

"Like right now," Cain said. "I imagine you could use an extra pair of eyes to track down this mysterious SUV." He shrugged. "We're not too busy."

That almost drew a smile from Cassie. "Can't say I'd turn that down."

"Look," Harper said. "This is what we do. In many of our cases. Track someone down. We're pretty good at it."

"Based on?"

"Training," Cain said. "US military."

"That explains the way you're dressed?"

They were decked out in combat pants, shirts, and jackets. Black, snug, efficient.

"Sure does," Harper said.

"What? You guys were MPs or something."

"Not exactly."

"Exactly what then?"

"Harper was with the CIA. Me? Let's go with special ops."

"You mean like a Seal or something?" Cassie asked.

"More like a something."

"Care to elaborate?"

"Later," Cain said. "Right now we need to get on the trail."

"I hope I don't regret this but we're a small department and could use all the help we can get."

"That's why we're here," Cain said. "To help."

"What's your search plan?" Harper asked.

"You know anything about this area?" Cassie asked.

"Some," Harper said. "At least the general layout."

Cassie seemed to consider that. Probably still wondering exactly who they were. How they got a call and drove here on such short notice. How they had already done at least some research. Cain expected more questions but Cassie simply moved ahead.

"I have guys out roaming in every direction. But, to be honest, we only have a vague description of the vehicle. From a less than reliable source."

"Marla Jackson," Harper said.

Cassie couldn't hide her surprise. "How do you know that?"

Harper nodded toward Mona.

"I gave them the thumbnail of Marla's problems," Mona said.

Cassie gave a slight head shake. "Yeah. She's followed a rough path."

"How reliable do you think her description is?" Cain asked.

Cassie shrugged. "I don't know for sure, but I suspect even Marla would know a big black SUV when she saw one."

CHAPTER 17

On the way out to the parking area, Cassie told them that she had three other units working the area. Most of the town had been covered and covered again. Now they were spreading out, mostly north and west as those directions were less populated and might be good directions to go in if staying off the radar was the main concern.

"Any idea why they'd kidnap a doctor?" Harper asked.

"Maybe disgruntled patients," Cassie said. She smiled. "Actually, I have no idea." She looked across the road toward the park. "Maybe it's a ransom thing. He's a doc, so is his father. So I guess that's a good bet."

"We considered that too," Cain said. "So far the senior Dr. Buckner hasn't been contacted. No money demands. Anything like that."

"Might be too early," Cassie said. "Maybe they're hiding out somewhere. Waiting to make the call."

"Let the pressure rise," Harper said. "And the fear. That can translate into a larger payout."

"I suspect that's true."

"But kidnappings are risky," Cain said. "You have to keep the person alive. For a while anyway. Not to mention the money exchange. Big time exposure."

"And if it isn't a ransom deal?" Cassie asked.

"Then I'd say Dr. Buckner is in even worse trouble."

Cassie gave Cain her cell number and said in no uncertain terms that if they saw anything suspicious they should call, not confront.

Harper climbed in The Rig, behind the wheel. They watched Cassie's black Jeep Cherokee turn left on Main, back toward downtown. The rain had stopped, leaving a cool night in its wake.

"She seems matter of fact," Harper said.

"She does."

"Probably best not to step on her toes. Too much." Harper snapped her seatbelt into place. "Not sure she's overly thrilled with us being here."

"She welcomed our help though."

"Maybe she was just being polite."

Cain eyed her. "We could've given her references."

"Yeah. But they'd scare the hell out of her." Harper cranked the engine. "How do you want to proceed?"

"We don't know the area. Whatever we do will be random."

"Sometimes random stumbles on random."

That was true. Any soldier, any cop too, will tell you that they'd rather face a pro. More predictable, more likely to follow protocols and expectations. Understand the rules of engagement. Amateurs tend to be erratic and unpredictable. Often volatile and emotion driven. Can lead to some dicey situations. Of course, both Cain and Harper were trained for just such deviations. Virtually every operation Harper ran for the CIA and every mission Cain completed for the guys up the food chain were fluid. Constantly changing. Never an iron-clad plan. At least not one that couldn't be altered as things unfolded.

"All we have is a satellite map." Cain held up his iPhone. "But it's a valley."

"My thoughts exactly."

High ground. See if there were any overlooks along the roads that climbed and fell and twisted through the hills that cradled Tanner's Crossroads. Harper turned east and then north, looping back until she found a gravel turnout that faced south and looked down on the park, the hospital, and westward over the town. Harper parked. A two-foot high rock wall edged the area, the ground falling away beyond. Harper climbed on top. Cain opened the rear hatch, then one of the duffles. He joined Harper on the wall, passing her one of the two pairs of binoculars he held.

Cain switched to night vision and began scanning the terrain. The park was empty, the town quiet; few lights, no traffic.

"Got a vehicle," Harper said. "Two o'clock. Looks like a residential area just south of town."

Cain saw it. He zoomed in. Black Jeep Cherokee, white door panel, PD logo in gold, female driver, spiked blonde hair. "That would be the chief."

Over the next fifteen minutes they saw the two other patrol cars roam into and out of town, mostly to the west, toward The Crossroads and The Confluence. They also tracked a half dozen other vehicles. Three merely passing through, the others entering and parking downtown. Probably shop owners arriving early to set up for the day. But no black SUV.

It was just after six a.m.

A flash of headlights caught Cain's eye. Behind and to his right. He nudged Harper.

The lights bounced off the trees and then came toward them up the road that fell away in that direction. As the vehicle swung into the parking area, Cain saw that it was an old Olds 442, gold. It angled their way and stopped. Not too close, washing them with light. It sat, engine idling for a few seconds before the driver's door swung open. The interior lights revealed a heavy set man. Same jacket the chief had worn. He rolled out, stood behind the open door, both hands on the top frame. He was heavy, thick, with a full head of salt-and-pepper hair.

"How you folks doing?" he asked. His voice was deep, a little raspy.

"Just fine," Cain said.

The man didn't move. "Mind if I ask what you're doing?"

"Same thing you are. Looking for a black SUV. The one that snatched Dr. Buckner."

"You mean like the one you're driving?"

Cain jumped from the wall. The man's back stiffened, his right hand dropped to his side. Toward the weapon Cain knew he must have on his hip.

"You might want to stay where you are, partner."

"You must be one of Chief Crowe's deputies," Harper said.

"That's a fact."

"We just had a chat with Cassie. Down at the hospital."

"You on a first name basis with her?"

Harper stepped off the wall and walked to where Cain stood. She smiled. "She said that's what we should call her."

"I see."

"We were hired by Dr. Buckner's father to find him," Cain said. "I'm Bobby Cain. This is Harper McCoy."

"William Hackford. Folks call me Hack." He looked around, settled on Cain, then Harper. "You telling me his father called you? This quickly? We just found out about it a few hours ago."

"He called us maybe three, four hours ago," Harper said. "We came over from Nashville."

"Nashville? Who are you guys?"

"We do private work."

"That's pretty vague. What kind of work?"

"It varies," Cain said. "But kidnappings and missing persons are sometimes the job."

Hack hooked a thumb in his belt. "You guys look like you're dressed for combat."

"We are," Cain said. "With kidnappings you never know what might happen. Best to be prepared."

Hack gave a slight nod as if he understood. He waved a hand. "What brought you up here?"

"High ground," Harper said. She held up her binocs. "Getting the lay of the land. These night vision glasses help."

"Night vision? I've heard of those. Never seen them though."

Cain held out his pair. "Take a look."

Hack walked toward them and took the binocs. He scanned the city for a couple of minutes and then handed them back to Cain. "If that don't beat all." His cell buzzed. He answered. "Yeah." Listened. "Okay. See you there in five." Hack slipped the phone in his pocket. "Got to run. The chief wants a pow wow."

"Mind if we join you?"

"I 'spect that'd be up to her."

"We'll follow you," Harper said.

"Gracie's Tavern. It ain't far."

CHAPTER 18

Gracie's Tavern, a typical small-town café, was already bustling when Cain and Harper arrived. They followed Hack through the front door. A dozen tables were occupied by hunters, farmer types, and locals, loading up on eggs, bacon, and pancakes. The aromas reminded Cain that he and Harper had eaten little in the past twelve hours. He saw Cassie at a table toward the back with two young officers. Hack led them that way.

"Mind if we join you?" Cain asked.

"They followed me here," Hack said. "I guess we should keep them." He tossed Harper a wink.

Cassie smiled, then nodded toward a pair of empty chairs. "Don't see any reason why not. You were kind enough to help with the search. I take it since I didn't hear from you that nothing turned up."

"Nothing."

Cassie introduced the two younger officers: Rick Fowler and Scotty Duckworth.

A middle-aged waitress poured coffee. Welcome on a cold, drizzly morning. Orders were taken and conversation laced with a hint of sleep-deprived giddiness followed. Not completely lighthearted since a kidnapping was still in progress and they had no clue where to look, but relaxed and friendly. A small southern town staple regardless of the situation.

They learned that Cassie had been chief for two years, having taken over when Hack stepped down. Said he was too old and too tired for the job. Cassie jabbed him, saying he had more energy than Rick and Scotty put together. Hack, in turn, had inherited the job from Cassie's father who had been chief for nearly two decades. Killed in the line of duty. A shootout at a rural meth lab. Being the chief's daughter, Cassie had hung around the station from age ten and often did odd jobs and typing. She took a more or less official part-time position while in high school. After graduation, she joined the force. She had been there just over a year when her father was killed.

"What about you guys?" Cassie asked. "You were pretty vague about exactly what you do."

"Things like this," Cain said. "Find folks who are in trouble."

"You any good at it?" Hack asked.

Harper smiled. "We are. We were trained by the best."

"Oh?"

"Me, the US Navy. Bobby, the US Army."

Hack ran a finger around the lip of his coffee cup. "I know lots of ex-military folks. Some are pretty sharp; others couldn't find their way into or out of a paper bag."

Cain gave a thumbnail of their careers. Leaving out most of it.

"So you guys are partners in this...whatever it is you do?" Cassie asked. "I'm still not sure I grasp it all."

"We're actually brother and sister," Harper said.

Fowler stared at her. "Brother and sister?"

"Yeah, we get that reaction a lot," Harper said. "We were raised by the same family. Until around age twelve, anyway."

Cain added, "Our family wasn't the picket fence variety. More like gypsies."

"And this family adopted you both?" Cassie asked.

"Sort of," Cain said. "I was apparently abandoned in a bus station in Houston. Two months old. The family scooped me up from a waiting room bench." He nodded toward Harper. "The story is she was purchased from her mother for a few bucks and a couple of bottles of whiskey."

"You're kidding. Right?" Fowler said.

"My mom was apparently half Cherokee," Harper said. "Indian

blood and alcohol don't mix well. She was an alcoholic."

"What happened to her?" Cassie asked.

Harper shook her head. "Don't know. Didn't even know her name. I was only one at the time so, like Bobby, I only know what I was told later."

"When I was twelve," Cain said, "Harper thirteen, the family got taken down by the FBI."

"The FBI?" Hack asked.

"We were more or less a traveling show. Plus scams, thefts, all kinds of mischief."

"We were packed off to an orphanage and then adopted into separate families," Harper said. "Didn't see, or even know what happened to each other until fifteen years later."

Cain picked it up. "Our paths recrossed while on a mission. In Afghanistan."

"What kind of mission?" Hack asked.

Cain captured his gaze. "The kind that never existed."

"Black ops? CIA? That kind of thing?"

"Let's just say we were tracking down a bad guy."

"And then?"

Cain shrugged, opened his palms.

Hack gave a nod, said nothing. No one said anything for a full minute, then Cassie took charge, brought the conversation back to the present. Laid out a search plan. One that expanded out from the town. Everyone was assigned a different area to explore.

Cain paid the bill. Cassie protested. He insisted.

Cassie's cell chimed. After she answered, she mostly listened, then said, "Okay. We'll be over in a few."

"What is it?" Fowler asked.

"Something going on over at the Finley place."

"What?" Hack asked.

"Don't know. Neighbor said it didn't seem right."

"Probably Tommy doing something stupid," Hack said.

"I'll go check it out," Fowler said.

Hack stood. "I'll do it. I can handle Tommy." He smiled. "He's afraid of me." He headed toward the door with a wave.

"Tommy Finley," Cassie said. "One of our local drug dealers. Good parents. His sister is a star student and one of our best athletes. Tommy's an asshole. And a handful for his folks." She forked her fingers through her blonde spikes. "For me, too."

CHAPTER 19

Dennie had had a rough night. So had Buck. Even though he had dragged a fairly comfortable chair from the living room into the bedroom where Dennie was now ensconced, he got very little sleep. Only what he could grab between tending to Dennie and listening to his moaning and murmuring, which at times bordered on being coherent. He hoped that in Dennie's post-anesthesia haze he might reveal something useful, but, in the end, he could only decipher a word here and there, the rest simply noise.

Dennie's BP had bottomed out a couple of times, once around three a.m., falling to 60. Buck hung the third liter of IV fluids and ran it over the next hour. That helped. He was essentially flying by the seat of his pants. He had no cardiac or 02 Sat monitors, no lab results, no X-rays, none of the equipment he'd have access to in an ICU—where Dennie belonged.

Buck had no illusions that he would get out of this alive. Not a chance. He had seen them, knew their names. If whatever they had done, whatever got Dennie shot, precluded a trip to the hospital, it damn sure meant a witness wouldn't be cut loose. Unless he found some way out of here, his fate was in Dalton's very dangerous hands.

Calling for help wouldn't happen. Dalton had told him the phone lines had been cut and to make sure, Buck had tested one while no one was looking. Dead. He had seen three cell phones.

Jessie's, Dalton's, and a third that was probably Dennie's. But they kept them close at hand or in their pockets. Didn't matter anyway. During the night Jessie had let it slip that the cell service up here in the hills was nonexistent.

Since communication with the outside world was impossible, running seemed his only option. Not a good one, and not one he could likely pull off, but if things fell into place at least he had a plan. Sort of. Probably wouldn't work but what the hell. Right now, time was his ally. As long as he could make them believe that Dennie would die without him, he was safe. Truth was, now that the surgery had been done and Dennie was as stable as he'd ever be, they could easily load him in the SUV and make a run for it. Wouldn't be without risk, or without pain for Dennie, but it was doable. Buck would guard that little bit of information with his life. Literally.

Dalton and Jessie had taken turns on watch. Watching him. He had still managed to get a feel for the place. He had already explored the interior layout and, whenever the opportunity arose, he peeled back a curtain to briefly survey the surroundings. A small front and a larger rear yard, the narrow dirt road they had driven up, and a single car garage. Otherwise he saw only trees. Nothing to orient him. No feel for anything beyond a few dozen yards away.

Even if he managed to get out the door, where would he go? Which direction led to help? The final mile or so of the drive here last night seemed to pass through only wilderness. Trees mostly, a few patches of open land, but no signs of civilization. He had tried his best to keep north and south straight but the road twisted, turned, rose, and fell so much that it was a futile effort. Not that it would really help, anyway. Other than somewhere downhill, he had no feel for which direction would lead back toward town.

Another disturbing thing was last night's dinner. Left over fried chicken, cheese, crackers, and milk. All fresh. There was no way the owners were gone for any extended period of time. Everything looked and felt like they had gone to the movies or out for dinner and would be back at any minute. They never returned, however. Not all night. Where were they? What would happen if they did unexpectedly return?

He knew that whatever Dalton and his crew were into wasn't pretty. No doubt illegal and lethal. Who had shot Dennie? Under what circumstances? What happened to the shooter?

The door opened and Jessie walked in. "How's he doing?"

"Rocky but better."

Jessie nodded and took another bite from the drumstick he held. "Want something to eat?"

"Not right now."

Jessie walked to the window, pulled back the edge of the curtain, and peeked out. "Looks like the rain's picking up. Feels like a storm's brewing."

"Who's place is this?" Buck asked.

"Don't know."

"Lucky they weren't home last night."

Jessie shrugged. "I guess luck's part of everything."

"Until it's not."

"What's that supposed to mean?"

"What happens if the owners return?" Buck asked.

Jessie glanced toward the door, the window, and then back to Buck. He seemed uncomfortable with Buck's line of questioning. Good. Maybe he'd say something he shouldn't. Something Buck could use. No doubt he was the weak link. Dalton impressed him as the kind who made few mistakes. Seemed to always stay focused. But Jessie seemed more relaxed and not nearly as sharp.

Buck continued, "I imagine they wouldn't be very happy with their dining room becoming a surgery suite and this bedroom an ICU of sorts."

"That's a fact."

"But, like you said, luck's part of everything."

Jessie gnawed off another bite from the drumstick. "I suspect they're gone for a few days."

"I guess we'll see."

Jessie seemed to search for a response, finally coming up with, "This is pretty good chicken. You should have some."

"Maybe in a few minutes." Buck checked the IV flow rate, trying to appear casual, distracted. "What happened?"

"Happened?"

"How did Dennie get shot?"

"It was an accident."

Buck looked at him, holding his gaze until Jessie looked away. How far could he go? Right now they needed him, and as long as he could keep that need alive he would be safe. Gave him a sliver of power. After he became expendable the story would definitely change. Pushing Jessie might not be smart but neither was doing nothing. Divide and conquer seemed his only viable strategy.

"Come on, Jessie. I've seen too many gunshot wounds. This was no accident."

"Sure it was. He was cleaning his gun."

"Then why not take him to the hospital? Where he could get the right care?"

"Seems like you did pretty good. Old Dennie looks to me like he'll make it."

"That your medical opinion?"

That caused a pause. Jessie glanced toward the open door. "Let me give you some advice—don't go asking this kind of shit to Dalton. He ain't as pleasant as me and he don't like folks digging into his business."

"I'll keep that in mind."

"I would if I was you."

Time to change course. Maybe draw in Jessie a little.

"You did good last night," Buck said.

Jessie shook his head. "I ain't never seen nothing like that. That's for sure. I mean, the way you just ripped that kidney right out of him. Sewed him right up."

"He was lucky that's the worst of his injuries. Had the bullet hit his liver or his bowel or one of the big blood vessels in there, we would be having a different conversation."

"I guess luck does come in all sorts."

"Sure does. Especially with gut shots." Buck sat down in the chair. "But I meant what I said, you did a good job."

Jessie tossed the chicken bone in the trashcan. "I just did what you told me to do."

Buck smiled. "All without throwing up or fainting."

Now Jessie smiled. "I guess I did do pretty good."

"What's going on?" Dalton said. He stood in the doorway. He had loosened his ponytail and his hair splayed out in a tangle behind him. His dark and dangerous eyes focused on Buck, then Jessie, then back to Buck. "What were you guys talking about?"

Jessie shuffled his feet, head down toward the floor.

Buck jumped in. "I was complimenting Jessie on his work last night with Dennie." He smiled. "You did good, too."

"I'm thrilled with your approval." Dalton walked to the bedside and looked down at Dennie. "How's my brother doing?"

"He had a few problems during the night. Low blood pressure, things like that, but right now he's more or less stable."

Dalton nodded. "When can he travel?"

"If you mean down to the hospital, we can leave right now," Buck said.

Dalton glared at him. "You can give up on that idea. I mean to Memphis."

Memphis? So they were from Memphis. A long way from home. Why were they here? What was Dalton's agenda over here in this little spit of a town?

"Memphis is a long way from here," Buck said. "That where you're from?"

Dalton's glare did not waver. "You ask too many questions."

"You wanted to know when he could travel. I simply wanted to know where. How far."

"And now you know. So, when?"

Buck looked at Dalton across Dennie's bed. "Two or three days at best. And that's if all goes well and a post-op infection doesn't rear its head."

"Ain't that what all those drugs we stole were for?"

"Some of them. But they don't guarantee anything. Just lessen the likelihood." Buck waved a hand toward the living area. "The surgery wasn't done in exactly the most sterile environment. A wound infection is a distinct possibility."

Now Dalton looked uncomfortable. Laced with a hint of aggravation. Or was it fear?

"Not sure we can wait that long," Dalton said. "We need to get on up the road."

"I'd plan on a couple of days then."

Dalton started to say something, but hesitated. He turned and walked toward the door. "I'll make some coffee."

Twenty minutes later, Buck, Jessie, and Dalton sat at the kitchen table eating the eggs and toast Jessie had made and sipping the coffee Dalton had brewed.

Dalton examined his cell phone. He shook his head.

"What's the problem?" Buck asked.

"Not that it's any of your business, but there's no service up here." He placed the phone on the table. "And I need to make a couple of calls."

Buck glanced toward the kitchen area and the wall phone near the refrigerator. "Probably shouldn't have cut the line on that one." He nodded that way.

"You'd like that wouldn't you? Give you a chance to call for help."

"Or let you make your call."

Dalton's stare became cold, hard. "No real problem. I'll drive down the hill later. Go into town, make my calls, and pick up some supplies. See what the buzz is."

"Buzz about what?" Buck asked.

Dalton stood. "You worry about my brother. I'll worry about everything else."

CHAPTER 20

Cain drove. He followed Cassie's black Jeep Cherokee to the Finley home, four blocks and two turns from Gracie's Tavern. They parked in tandem behind a pair of patrol units. The rain had dissipated and the sun was out. It reflected off Hack's vintage 1968 Olds 442 that sat in the sloping driveway, Hack standing next to it. They walked his way.

Earlier, after Hack, Fowler, and Duckworth left Gracie's, Cain and Harper remained with Cassie. Another cup of coffee and more conversation. Then Cassie got the call from Hack.

"What've we got, Hack?" Cassie asked as they approached.

"It's bad. Real bad." He hiked his pants, a futile attempt to restrain the belly that lapped over his belt.

"All of them?"

Hack's head twisted toward the front door. "Yep. The entire family."

Cassie shielded the morning sun from her eyes and looked up at the house. "Show me."

Cain and Harper followed them inside, Cassie saying, "Don't touch anything."

"We know the drill," Harper said.

"Figured. Just making sure."

It was bad. Very bad. Reminded Cain of the inside of a mud hut he'd walked into once in some desert shithole. After a pair of Marines had taken care of business. Six bad guys, a couple still clutching their Kalashnikovs in a death grip. He guessed they shouldn't have placed the IED that took out a transport, killing four soldiers, or tried to ambush the Marines who came to investigate. Karma is as Karma does.

"Jesus," Cassie said.

"The Baby Jesus had nothing to do with this," Hack said. "This is some evil shit."

Cassie pointed. "On the sofa are Martha, son Tommy, and daughter Jennifer. Over there," she nodded toward the man slumped in a wingback chair, "is John."

Cain circled the sofa, carefully avoiding the blood spatter. All three had been shot. The most disturbing image was Martha. Her left eye had been blown out, along with the back of her head. He stopped next to the chair where John Finley's corpse lay draped over one arm, right hand dangling near the carpet above a pancake of congealed blood.

"John caught two in the chest," Hack said. "Jennifer, chest and forehead, and Martha in the face. Gruesome." He pointed toward Tommy. "Tommy basically got it between the eyes."

"So what?" Cassie asked. "The killer, or killers, lined them up and shot them?"

Hack forked his fingers through his hair. "A real turkey shoot, I'd say."

"I take it there wasn't any forced entry or anything like that?" Harper asked.

"Nope. But there's a twist to the story."

"I hate twists," Cassie said.

Hack shrugged. "Me and you both."

Hack walked over to a credenza that sported a big screen TV and picked up a plastic evidence bag. He held it up, revealing that it contained a handgun.

"The twist," Hack said.

"The murder weapon?"

"Doubt it. I found it on the floor near Tommy's feet. Only one round fired." He handed the bag to Cassie and then pointed behind her.

Cain turned toward the large circular blood stain in the

carpet. He had noticed it coming in but hadn't yet understood its significance. It was a good ten feet from the sofa, the coffee table between. "One of the killers took a round," Cain said

"That'd be my guess," Hack said.

"I have to ask," Cassie said, "but I'm sure I know the answer—you called the hospital?"

"Sure did. Nothing. I've got Poppy checking with every hospital within fifty miles. Haven't heard back yet."

Cassie explained that Poppy Phelps worked dispatch and did just about everything else at the station. Indispensable and then some.

"And there's more," Hack said.

"Great."

"Maybe a motive," Hack said as he led them down a hallway to one of the bedrooms. Tommy's no doubt. Metal band posters on the wall, a laptop computer on a messy desk. Clothes tossed in piles near an open closet. A pair of evidence bags lay on the unmade bed. Hack picked one up. Inside a smaller bag of white powder.

"Looks like meth," Cassie said.

"Probably." Hack dropped the bag back on the bed. "Could be coke or heroin. I found it in the drawer over there." He indicated a chest, the top drawer open. "Along with some cash." He picked up the second bag. "Two hundred and forty bucks."

Cain and Harper stood just inside the doorway. Cassie turned to them and continued with what she had told them about Tommy Finley earlier. He had been more than a little familiar to Cassie and everyone else in the department. A smart-ass punk. Always had been. A long drug history. Been to jail, been to rehab, and Cassie was sure he was still dealing. Never was able to hang that charge on him but she had no doubts. The meth and the money reinforced that belief.

"Sure smells like a drug hit," Cassie said. "No doubt Tommy was dealing. Probably pissed off the wrong people."

"As druggies are wont to do," Hack said. "Until someone settles the score with this kind of shit."

Cassie let out a deep sigh. "Why does this crap have to land in our backyard?"

"Why not? It seems to land everywhere else."

She gave a slow nod. "I hate it when you're right."

"Which I usually am." Hack smiled and gave her a wink.

"That you are." She looked around the room. "Who called this in?"

"I was just fixing to tell you," Hack said. "That's the other twist."

"I'm about twisted out here."

"Jason Epps."

"You're kidding?"

"Wish I was."

"Who is Jason Epps?" Harper asked.

Cassie explained. Jason was another punk. Long time buddy of Tommy's. Also a user and probably worked with Tommy to push product. Another case she could never make. She almost had Jason once. Nearly caught him red-handed. But when she grabbed him, over in the park where most deals seemed to go down, he was clean. Had about $800 in his pockets but no drugs. His good fortune and her bad luck.

"Where is he?"

Hack hooked a thumb toward the kitchen. "Out back. Waiting for you."

Jason was a punk. Cain could see it in his entire being. Stringy hair, slouched shoulders, and a flat attitude that suggested he couldn't be bothered with other people's problems. Like the massacre of his so-called friend's family. He could probably use a couple of years in the Marines to stomp that attitude into submission.

Jason sat at a redwood picnic table, rolling a Dr. Pepper can back and forth over its top as if playing some game of tin can hockey. He didn't appear overly concerned, or upset, or really anything. Looked more like he was bored. Cassie sat across from him. Cain and Harper stood behind her.

"Who are they?" Jason asked.

"Backup singers," Cassie said. "Now focus on me."

He shrugged, kept rolling the can.

Cassie reached out and stopped it. That got his attention.

"Tell me about it," Cassie said.

"Not much to tell. I came over to see Tommy. Rang the bell. No one answered so I looked through the front window and saw all of them. Pretty freaky. So I called you guys."

"Was Tommy expecting you?"

"Not really. We were supposed to hook up last night but he never showed. I came by to find out why."

"What time were you supposed to meet him?"

He shrugged. "Six, seven, eight. Something like that."

"Sounds pretty vague."

"We're busy guys. Schedules are sometimes hard to keep."

"Busy with what?" Cassie asked.

"Stuff."

The more Cain saw of Jason, the less he cared for him. His first visual impression had been right on but only to a point. Jason was worse. Not simply a smart-ass, he was cold, unconcerned. Seemingly disinterested in what had happened to Tommy and his family. If there was no love lost between Jason and Tommy, which seemed to be the case, did Jason see this as an opportunity? If they both dealt, were partners in the business, then could this be a partner liquidation? Was Jason involved in the killing? Did he do it himself? If not, did he know who did? These questions, and a handful of others, surged in Cain's head. He wanted to slap the answers right out of Jason's mouth, but he held all that in and let Cassie do her job.

Cassie leaned her elbows on the table edge. "Where were you guys going to meet?"

"The park."

"Why there?"

"We hang out there a lot."

Cassie smiled. "I know."

He shrugged but said nothing.

"You guys still dealing?"

"We never did that. That's just some shit you guys made up."

"I doubt that. Tommy have a habit of not showing up?"

"Not really." Jason raised one shoulder in a half-hearted shrug. "He usually appears sooner or later. But, like I said, we're busy guys."

He reached for the can but she backhanded it off the table.

"Listen to me, smart ass," Cassie said, "if I even suspect you had anything to do with this, I'll bury you. Are we clear on that?"

"You think I did this?"

"Did you?"

"No. Tommy was my friend."

"Where were you when this happened?"

He gave her a half-smile. "When did it happen?"

"Jason, do not fuck with me. Am I clear?"

He stared at her but said nothing.

She went on. "Walk me through last night. Step by step."

"I was in the park until maybe ten-thirty, eleven. Then I went over to Big Bill's. Had a few beers. Went home around one."

"That's it? Nowhere else?"

"It's what I said."

"Anybody who can confirm that?"

"I drank at the bar. With Bill Keener. Talk to him."

"I will."

Jason's chin came up. "You do that."

"Okay, let's say you didn't do this," Cassie said. "Any idea who might've come in here and killed an entire family in cold blood?"

He fidgeted with the collar of his tee shirt. "No."

"Why do I think you're lying?"

"That's what you guys do, isn't it? Think everyone's lying?"

Now Cassie smiled. "Only the ones who are."

"Well, I ain't lying. I don't know nothing about this."

Cain knew they were wasting their time with Jason. He wouldn't talk. At least not until they had some way to squeeze him. The thing about criminals, virtually all criminals, is that they're self-serving. Clamp down on their balls and they talk. Until then, they were team players. The question here was, who were Jason's and Tommy's teammates? Who had a hard on for Tommy? Enough to wipe out his entire family?

"So you guys didn't step on the wrong toes?" Cassie asked. "Anything like that?"

He looked at her. "Don't know what you're talking about."

She stood. "Have a nice day, Jason. We'll be in touch."

CHAPTER 21

"What do you think?" Cassie asked. She removed her Glock from its holster, laid it on her desk near the phone, and dropped into her old but comfortable swivel chair. It had been her father's, then Hack's, and now passed down to her. The chief's seat. A few repairs here and there, but still sturdy enough. She guessed if it held Hack during his tenure, it should have no problem with her for many years to come. Which was good since her budget wouldn't easily allow for a new one. Or a new anything else.

The Tanner's Crossroads' PD occupied a low brick downtown building that had once been a furniture store. The old PD, where she had spent much of her childhood, where she first became a cop under her father's wing, was down the street a couple of blocks in a white frame house that began its life as a private residence. It was now an antique store. The new digs, now three years old, were larger and more centrally located but Cassie missed the old one. So many memories. Seeing the front window piled with antiques somehow didn't seem right to her. But it was progress, she guessed. Not to mention that the sale of the house and the deal they got on the current location put a few bucks into the PD's bottom line.

Hack sat in one of the two chairs that faced her desk, the fingers of his right hand snugged beneath his belt as if to help hold his belly in. A posture he frequently adopted. He tugged at one ear as he spoke.

"You mean about those two investigators? Or whatever they are."

"I was thinking of the murders, but yeah, what's your take on them?" Cassie asked.

"Not rightly sure. They seem okay. They sure have an interesting history."

"You think? Gypsy family? Military? Now problem solvers? Whatever that means."

"Love to know more about what they did in the military."

"Me, too. But the question we have before us is can they be helpful in this?"

"I suspect they might. If they can track down people in Afghanistan maybe they can here."

Cassie considered that. The truth was, she had the same impression. But with a few reservations. "This isn't Afghanistan. I suspect over there whenever they found their target a shootout followed."

Hack gave a nod. "That's a concern. Then again, from what I saw over at the Finley place, these guys aren't afraid of a shootout themselves."

"Don't even think that."

"Just making conversation." He smiled.

"Unfortunately, now you've put it out in the cosmos."

"I suspect it was out there long before I bumped my gums about it."

"Back to the murders. Any initial thoughts?"

"Seeing as how nothing was stolen and there wasn't no break in, in the classic sense, I'd say someone in the family knew the killers. Invited them in, so to speak. And since John and Martha and Jennifer are stand up citizens and Tommy is a jerk-off, I'd say it'd be a smidge shortsighted not to think he was the one that knew them. Or at least they knew him. That means this ugliness reared up from his world. Don't you think?"

She loved Hack. He had a way of cutting through the fog and getting to the heart of any matter. Not to mention telling it in such colorful ways. He probably should've been a writer or a newspaper man or something like that, but the truth was he was a good cop. He had been a good chief, too.

Cassie nodded. "Tommy's world is drugs."

"Yep. Which means we got some bad actors in town."

"From what I've seen, this isn't their first rodeo."

"That'd be my take."

Cassie let out a frustrated sigh. "The question is, who?"

Hack lifted the front brim of his department-issue Stetson with an index finger and looked at her. "With hunting season on us, there're a ton of strangers in town about now."

Fall and winter in Tanner's Crossroads attracted game bird, deer, rabbit, turkey, and other hunters. Spring and summer brought in the fishermen. Both seasons pumped dollars into the local economy. Also pumped up the population of new faces in town.

"You mean like the bar fight over at Gracie's the other night?" Cassie asked.

Gracie's Tavern, where the crew had eaten breakfast that morning, had been a Tanner's Crossroads institution since before Cassie was born. Opened in the 1950's by the long dead Gracie Mueller, her grandson Wally now in charge, it was the focal point of drinking and dining for both locals and visitors. Last week, a couple of hunters had gotten sideways with one another, as Hack had put it, over who won the fifty bucks they had bet on bagging the day's largest turkey. The dispute evolved into a few punches, a bloody nose, and a couple of broken beer mugs. Then all was forgiven. Once the damages were paid.

But, such incidents, even with the influx that hunting season always dragged in, were rare. Made the massacre of the Finleys even more disturbing.

"That and just the general insanity of anyone who hunts." He smiled. "As you would know."

Hack was a big fisherman. He lived down on the lake and fished whenever he could. He had even taught Cassie how to snag bass and crappie when she was in grammar school. Cassie never cared for it. Too passive and boring. She gravitated toward hunting. Something her father had taught her. Mostly rabbit and squirrel, rarely duck and geese. She got her first .22 at eight and her first 16 gauge shotgun at twelve. Some of her favorite memories of her father involved hunting trips.

"How do you want to approach this?" Hack asked.

"Sniff around Tommy's world. Which means Jason Epp's world." She squared a stack of papers on her desk. "He knows more about this than he let on."

"Sure does."

"Maybe we can dig up some leverage on him," Cassie said.

"We been trying for the better part of a year and so far we got bupkis."

"Maybe this'll up the ante for him. I mean, he has to have at least a sliver of concern about what happened."

"He sure didn't seem overly troubled to me."

Cassie nodded, and then said, "It's still possible he did it."

"He passed the GSR test the boys did at the scene."

"Could've washed his hands."

"Jason ain't that smart." Hack angled his neck one way and then the other as if trying to work out a kink. "Besides, I don't think he has the stones for something like this. This was pro. Someone on up the food chain."

Cassie massaged one temple. "I hate this crap."

"Chief?"

Cassie looked up to see Poppy Phelps standing in her doorway. Hack twisted her way.

"There's been a shooting over at Shaffer's Pharmacy."

Cassie stood. "Just now?"

"Don't know. But it's Mr. Shaffer who got shot."

"What?" Cassie stood. She scooped her Glock off her desk.

"That's according to Penny," Poppy said.

"Did she call an ambulance?"

Poppy shook her head. "She said he was dead."

CHAPTER 22

Marla had slept poorly the night before. Even an extra dose of the heroin she'd gotten from Jason hadn't helped. Not that she was allowed to shoot up, or take any drugs for that matter in Reverend John's place. He had rules. Some were stricter than others but the use of drugs was a big-time taboo. Even having them on hand was forbidden and she'd seen more than one person tossed on the street for using in the house. But it still happened. What was he going to do? Strip search everyone who flopped there?

She now sat on the edge of the bed, legs drawn up, chin resting on her knees, attempting to beat back the throbbing in her head. Sunlight slanted through the knobby curtain in thin shafts, painting ovals of light on the hardwood floor. She counted them. Thirty-two if you included the fuzzy ones near the chest of drawers along the far wall. She counted again and got the same number.

She still tried to grasp what she had witnessed last night. Why would anyone kidnap a doctor? A nice one like Dr. Buckner had been?

About now, that seemed long ago. She often got her days and nights confused, and rarely if ever knew the exact day of the week, but she was sure it was just last night that this had happened. She touched her bandaged arm, pressed it, feeling the aching pain of her infected tissue. Yeah, no doubt it all happened last night.

Sleep-deprived nights were no stranger to her. Unless she

managed to make a connection, score some heroin, turn her brain off for a while. Even that didn't always work. The problem was that all the what-ifs and why nots of her life too often had a party in her head. She hated her life and had done so for years now. It seemed that every night she replayed some event or another from her previous life. The good one. Back when she was pretty and popular, and had a future. When dating and social circles meant something and she hung with the most sought-after clique in school.

All that was gone. Now former friends avoided her. They never stopped to chat when she passed them on the street. They acknowledged her existence with a quick smile and a darting gaze that quickly moved away from her. As if she were contagious. As if the monkey on her back might leap off and glom on to them.

She knew exactly the night her life took its irrecoverable turn. It was during her senior year when she took that trip over to Knoxville. The weekend she had spent over at UT with…what was her name? She was a year ahead of Marla in high school and now a freshman at UT. Why couldn't she remember her name? Jesus, sometimes her brain refused to work.

The party had been on a houseboat tethered near the bank of the Tennessee River, Neyland Stadium towering over them. It was where most fans gathered on fall weekends to cheer on the Volunteers. Many folks preferred to hang out on their boats rather than brave the crowds and actually enter the stadium to see the game. They called it the Vol Navy, or some such shit. She had spent the afternoon there, the racket from the raucous crowd spilling over stadium walls, almost, but not quite, drowning out the music from the massive sound system the boat's owner had installed. Alcohol and weed had been plentiful. Made college seem like one big party. Marla already had her acceptance in hand and couldn't wait to leave Tanner's Crossroads behind and take on the world of Knoxville.

But later, after the game, after almost everyone headed to bars or home or wherever, after the boats had mostly dispersed, she had joined the owner in the vessel's stateroom. Actually, the boat belonged to his father. She remembered the guy was a college senior, but couldn't pull his name from the fog of the evening. Hell, couldn't even recall his face. He had seemed nice though.

Tall, good looking, but handsy and all that. She gave in. The sex had been average until he introduced meth to the mix. She refused at first, but he was persuasive. The rush was like nothing she had ever experienced. The sex now electric.

That was the moment her life turned down the steep slope that led her here. She had sought out Tommy Finley, knowing he dealt in all sorts of things. School evaporated, as did her grades, her future, her family and friends. Her everything.

Last night the heroin she'd scored from Jason hadn't helped her sleep and her tossing and turning had left her exhausted. She wanted to fold back into bed and forget everything. But the monster inside had awakened and needed feeding. The anxiety and nausea were mounting, the sweats and panic not far behind. She needed to hit the streets and panhandle enough to hit up Tommy—where the hell was he?—or God forbid Jason, for a fix. Fucking Jason. The last thing she wanted was to see that prick again. Would she have to? Where was Tommy?

She stood on wobbly legs. A wave of dizziness followed. She steadied herself, found her jeans wadded on the floor, and stepped into them.

The bathroom down the hall was empty, not an overly common occurrence, so she took a shower. The first one in two days, maybe longer. She couldn't remember. The hot water made her feel almost human. It had taken a bit of balancing, trying to keep her bandaged arm away from the spray, but she managed. After she dressed, she descended the stairs to the breakfast room. Empty, thank God. She was in no mood for chatter. A pot of coffee and a stack of donuts sat on the table. She poured a cup, sat down, and quickly demolished three donuts, one chocolate, two jelly-filled. The sugar rush struggled, but not very successfully, to settle her nausea and shakiness.

Reverend John walked in. Dammit. She had hoped to slip out without seeing him. It wasn't that she didn't like him. In fact, quite the opposite. He was a good guy and for sure a life saver. A fitful sleep in the bed upstairs was way better then huddling beneath some stairway, or a back alley overhang, or a tree in the park to protect herself from the cold rain. It's just that her head pounded and her stomach felt like it was on fire and she didn't want to make small talk with anyone.

"How's it going?" he asked.

"Fine." She licked red jelly from her fingers.

He grabbed some coffee and settled into a chair across from her. He was tall and lanky, with a full-head of white hair. A matching mustache lay lazily over his lip and draped nearly to his chin on either side.

"You got in late last night," he said. A statement, not a question.

"Yeah. Not sure what time. I was lucky to find a place to sleep."

John nodded. "Did you get your arm looked at?" He had been after her for days to get the infection treated.

"Sure did." She held up her arm.

Should she tell him what she saw? About talking with Cassie? She decided to let that slide. Why invite questions? Besides, had she really seen all that? She was sure she had. Mostly, anyway. It wouldn't surprise her much if none of that had really happened. It certainly wouldn't be the first time she got her two worlds mixed up.

He nodded. "Good, good." He sipped his coffee. "Did you go over and talk with Luke Towry yesterday?"

Luke Towry owned Central Grocery. John had said he was looking for someone to help clean and stock the shelves and had suggested she go check it out.

"I went by, but he wasn't there."

It was a lie. She hadn't felt up to talking to anyone, much less asking for a job. A job? Her? What a joke. Punch in, punch out? She couldn't organize her life, hell, even her backpack, how could she manage an actual schedule?

"I see." His face said he didn't believe her.

It wasn't the first time she had lied to Reverend John and probably not the last. Something else to add to the list of things she hated about her life, and about herself. It seemed she always lied about something.

"I'll stop by today." She looked at him. "After I go by the hospital to get this checked." Again, she raised her arm.

He stood. "You do that. He'll be hiring someone soon and working for him could be good for you. Luke's a decent guy. He'll treat you well." He drained his cup and placed it on the table. He looked at her for a beat, as if expecting some response, but when she sat silently, he walked from the room.

She snatched her backpack from the floor and headed out. Along Main Street, she asked everyone she passed for change. For food, of course. Took less than an hour before she managed to collect two fives, twelve singles, and three or four dollars in change. Time to track down Tommy.

CHAPTER 23

Cassie swung around behind Shaffer's Pharmacy and jerked to a stop near the rear door. Penny Larkin leaned against her car, arms folded over her chest, face pale. Dried tears streaked her cheeks. Penny had worked for Wilbert Shaffer for decades. As long as anyone could remember for sure.

"She don't look so good," Hack said.

"That's an understatement."

They climbed out and walked toward her.

"Penny, are you okay?" Cassie asked.

"No." She sniffed. "He's dead. Wilbert's dead."

"You sure?"

Her face screwed down. "He's all blue. There's blood…and… and…." A sob lurched in her chest.

"Why don't you sit down in your car? We'll go check it out."

Cassie and Hack entered through the open rear door. They found Wilbert Shaffer sprawled on the floor behind the counter. Very dead. He was indeed deeply blue. An entrance wound behind his left ear, the front of his skull blown out. Blood and brain matter fanned out across the floor.

"Good lord," Hack said.

"Check the front," Cassie said.

Hack pulled his weapon and headed around the counter.

Cassie knelt and felt for the pulse she knew wouldn't be

present. She stood and looked around. Along the back wall, the metal-wire door to the controlled-med area stood open. Inside, the shelves were mostly empty and a few plastic bottles lay scattered on the floor. Someone had gone drug shopping.

She drew her Glock and headed out front. Hack was walking up one of the aisles, his gun now holstered.

"All clear," he said. "But a bunch of the shelves have been ravaged."

She put away her weapon and walked up and down several rows. Many of the shelves were in disarray and packages and small boxes littered the floor.

"What do you make of all this?" Hack asked.

She gave a head shake. "I don't know." She jerked her head toward the rear. "They emptied out the drug cabinet."

"Figures," Hack said.

She led the way back to the area and nodded toward the open drug cage. "Looks like they took all the good stuff."

"You think this is somehow connected to the Finley house?"

"Don't you?"

Hack nodded. "Until proven otherwise."

"What the hell is going on?" Cassie asked. "The Finleys? This?"

"I'd say we have a drug problem."

"We've had that for years." She released a long, slow sigh. "But never anything like this."

"I'll call the coroner," Hack said.

Cassie explored the area behind the counter, giving Wilbert Shaffer's corpse a wide berth, taking it all in. Something caught her eye. Something that seemed out of place. A wallet. Peeking from behind the edge of one of the registers. She picked it up.

Hack slid his phone in his pocket. "They're on the way." He nodded toward the wallet. "What's that?"

She flipped it open. A North Carolina driver's license appeared. The face of a handsome man stared back at her. Not a bad picture considering it had been snapped by the DMV. She read the name: Bradley Allen Buckner.

"Why would his wallet be here?" Hack asked.

"I have no idea." She sighed. "This is simply insane."

"Sure is." Hack rubbed his neck. "But I think we should give

Mr. Cain a call."

"Why?"

"He's looking for the doctor. Maybe those two have more insight into this that they're willing to share."

Cassie nodded. "Couldn't hurt."

CHAPTER 24

After leaving Cassie and Hack at the Finley house, Cain and Harper followed the directions Cassie had given them to Reverend John's place. They wanted to talk with Marla Jackson and see if she remembered anything else about the kidnapping.

Harper parked at the curb and shut down the engine. "Looks like a nice place."

"It does," Cain said.

The white with gray trim, two-story house was neat and clean, recently painted, the yard well-tended, the front door standing open. Inside, an empty living room. To the left, the dining area revealed a table that held a tray of donuts and muffins, a coffee maker, and towers of Styrofoam cups.

A man pushed through a door. He stopped when he saw them.

Tall, angular with a narrow face, white hair to his shoulders, droopy white mustache. Sharp, blue eyes.

"Can I help you?" he asked.

"We're looking for Reverend John," Harper said.

"That's me."

"I'm Harper McCoy. This is Bobby Cain."

"Welcome to my humble abode. What can I do for you?"

"We're looking for Marla Jackson."

His posture stiffened. "Why?"

"She witnessed a kidnapping last night."

Confusion settled over this face. "What are you talking about?"

"Dr. Buckner. Over at the hospital. He was apparently kidnapped from the parking lot. According to Chief Crowe, Marla witnessed it."

"I haven't heard anything about that."

"You will," Cain said.

"Who are you?" John asked.

"We were hired by Dr. Buckner's father," Harper said. "To find him."

"Marla didn't say anything about this to me this morning."

"All we know is she called Chief Crowe from the ER and told her she saw it go down. And the doctor is missing."

"Good gracious. That's awful."

"Is Marla here?" Cain asked.

"No. She headed out maybe a half hour ago."

"Any idea where we might find her?"

"The streets. I imagine she's out there panhandling. It's what she does most days."

"To buy drugs?" Harper asked.

He sighed. "Mostly." He looked toward the door. "Marla, what the devil have you gotten into now?"

"Right now, she's a possible witness," Cain said. "Nothing more."

"We know what you do here," Harper said. "Cassie, Chief Crowe, told us. Seems like a good thing."

"I try. Sometimes more successfully than other times."

Harper sensed the pain behind his eyes. Her first impression of Reverend John was that he was a good soul, doing good work. "Marla? She a success story?"

"Marla's special. No doubt about that." He gave a slight shake of his head. "But success might be stretching it. I have a strict no drug policy here. She doesn't always follow the rules. But I can't seem to turn my back on her."

There it was again. That flash of sadness behind his eyes. "Why's that?" Harper asked.

"Do you know her? Ever met her?"

"Not yet."

"You'll see. She was by far the prettiest girl in town. A good student from what I hear. She had a bright future until she went down the wrong road. Still, she has something to her. She's smart, though some of her choices might belie that." A deeper sigh. "But she's worth saving, if that's possible."

That's the tricky part, Harper thought. *Saving the salvageable.* Most drug-addicted kids were salvageable but too few grasped the lifeline. There are only three ways out of addiction: recovery, insanity, and death. Too often the latter two beat out recovery. To Harper, Reverend John seemed like a frontline, in the trenches soldier in that war. She also saw the lines on his face that revealed his work was taking its toll.

After thanking Reverend John, giving him their phone numbers and asking him to call if Marla returned, they walked down Main Street. They didn't have to find Marla, she found them. Stepped from behind a tree and approached.

"Can you spare any change?" she asked.

Harper knew it was her immediately, from the pictures of Marla she had found online; high school yearbook, a couple of Facebook posts, a mug shot from two years ago. Her large, bright blue eyes now tired and dull; her model-like high cheek bones now sentinels over painfully sunken cheeks; her brilliant smile now showing the ravages of meth. But, behind all the damage, her beauty peeked through. No wonder Reverend John couldn't cut her loose. Kept taking her back into the fold. To Harper, Marla looked sad and beaten more than anything else.

"Marla?" Harper asked.

She abruptly stopped.

"I'm Harper McCoy. This is Bobby Cain."

Marla stared at them but said nothing, glancing up the sidewalk as if searching for an escape route.

"Relax," Harper said. "We simply want to ask a couple of questions."

"About what?"

"Last night."

Marla's eyes widened.

"Chief Crowe told us about it," Cain said. "Reverend John suggested we look for you here."

Another look around. Marla seemed to be processing what

they had said. Probably trying to decide if she should run. She didn't, and finally asked, "Who are you?"

Harper explained why they were there and what they were doing.

"Dr. Buck's father hired you?"

"He did."

Her shoulders dropped. Her head, too.

"How about something to eat?" Harper asked.

Marla hesitated, then nodded.

They entered a nearby coffee shop where Cain bought coffee and a ham and cheese croissant for Marla. The girl behind the counter gave the trio a look, glanced hard in Marla's direction. Harper saw disdain on her face. Made her want to slap her or drag her over the counter and punch her teeth into her lungs. She refrained. Wasn't easy.

Cain paid and carried the items to a corner table where they settled. Marla ate like she was starved. Probably was. And was bottoming out. Needing to get well, score a fix. Harper saw all the signs.

"Run us through what you saw," Harper said.

She did. Going to the ER. Dr. Buck treating her infected injection site. Holding up her arm, displaying the bandage. Seeing the black SUV. She didn't know what kind. Just big. The two men. One with a gun. Forcing the doctor into the back. Driving away.

"What did the guys look like?" Cain asked.

"I couldn't see them well. One was tall and had dark hair in a ponytail. The other was smaller and slimmer."

"Where were you?" Harper asked.

"Across the street. In the park."

"Alone?"

She hesitated, then nodded.

"You sure?" Cain asked.

Nothing.

"Look, Marla, we aren't interested in what you were doing, but if we can locate another witness, it might help."

"No, I was alone. He was already gone."

"Who?"

Again, nothing.

"Were you using?" Harper asked.

Marla hugged herself, cupping her elbows with her hands. She nodded.

"What?"

"Meth. Heroin."

"And the guy? He your supplier?"

She nodded, her gaze toward her lap. "Not my usual though."

"Who's your usual?"

"I don't want to say."

"Tommy Finley?"

She looked up, eyes wide.

"We know he deals over there."

"I don't want to get anyone in trouble," Marla said.

Harper leaned forward. "Marla, Tommy was murdered last night."

She recoiled.

"Along with his entire family."

"No, oh no." She rocked back and forth. "Why? Who?"

"That's what we want to find out."

Her eyes glistened. "I don't believe this."

"Unfortunately, it's true," Cain said.

She wiped one eye with the back of her hand. "Did his dealing have anything to do with it?"

"Probably. But we don't know for sure."

"Back to our question," Harper said. "Who did you buy from last night?"

"He couldn't have had anything to do with this." She sniffed. "He and Tommy are friends. Have been for years."

"Let me guess," Cain said. "Jason Epps?"

Even more surprise erupted on her face. "How'd you know?"

"So it was him?" Harper asked.

She stared at her, then slowly nodded.

"Do you know where he is?"

A glance toward the window, a shrug, but no response.

"Look, Marla, all we want to do is talk with him," Harper said. "We can keep you out of it."

Her internal debate lasted less than a half a minute. "Probably over in the park."

CHAPTER 25

For the past couple of hours, Dennie had slept soundly. No murmuring or restlessness, just the soft whispers of his respirations. His vitals had stabilized and now his blood pressure and pulse were normal and steady. No evidence of residual bleeding. The only potential setback was a slight increase in his temperature to 101. The normal post-op elevation, or the first sign of infection?

It was very common for post-op patients to develop a mild fever. Somewhere between 99 and 101 or so. Had to do with the stress response and the bloodstream's reabsorption of the protein-rich body fluids that always leaked into the traumatized tissues. Proteins that worked on the hypothalamus of the brain and stimulated a rise in body temp. No real concern. Common, almost expected.

But the rise could also herald a wound infection. The first sign, well before it became detectable as swelling, redness, and tenderness in and around the surgical site, and well before pus formation could be seen. Gunshots like Dennie had suffered were always dirty. Grime and bacteria from clothing and skin are dragged into the wound by the bullet. Not to mention Dennie had pressed his hands, and a dirty towel, over the wound as he attempted to slow the bleeding. Rolling around in the back of a vehicle hadn't helped either. Plus the location where Buck had performed the surgery wasn't exactly the greatest example of sterile technique. On a dining table, in a cabin—every surface, and even the air, teeming with bacteria. It would be a miracle if Dennie didn't develop an infection given this cascade of events.

But right now, except for the slight fever, all looked good.

Buck was cleaning the incision site with Betadine when Dalton came in.

"How's he doing?" Dalton asked.

"Not bad."

"But not good?"

Buck looked up from his work. "As good as one could expect under the circumstances."

"So he's going to be all right?"

As Buck applied a smear of antibiotic ointment along the suture line his mind raced. What was the right answer here? Say he was going to be okay? Would that make Dalton believe Buck was now expendable? Say that he was in dire danger? Would Dalton read that as overly melodramatic? Truth was, either of those could be correct. Dennie was somewhere between recovery and beginning a downward spiral and it all depended on a bunch of microscopic organisms that might or might not have taken up residence within Dennie. Buck decided middle of the road, the non-answer, was the best answer.

"Maybe. He has a slight fever this morning."

Dalton's eyes narrowed. "That's not good is it?"

Buck shrugged and then explained that the fever could be normal or could be the first sign of an infection. He finished by saying, "His best bet is to be in a hospital."

"So you've said. And as soon as you say he can travel, we can make that happen."

Buck layered several four-by-four gauze squares over the wound as he spoke. "Why would a hospital in Memphis be better than the one down the road?"

A moment of confusion flashed over Dalton's face. Buck could almost see his wheels spinning. Finally Dalton said, "Let me worry about that. We have, uh, uh…someone over there who can take care of him."

Buck caught his gaze and held it. "Timing is important here. The sooner he gets to a proper facility the better his chances are."

"Facility," Dalton said. "That's the word I was looking for. Let's just say I know a facility where he'll get good treatment."

Translation: Dalton had some quack, or maybe a veterinarian, or an old military medic, back on his home turf in Memphis. Someone who helped out Dalton and whoever he worked with in just such situations. Buck knew of a similar set up back in Charlotte. Some vet that did procedures in his clinic for criminal types when they got shot or injured. Apparently it paid well and he had managed to stay off the radar for years until a group of miscreants brought in a cop killer who had caught a slug from the fallen officer. The local PD pulled out all the stops on that one and ultimately—through snitches, if Buck remembered correctly—tracked down the vet turned surgeon, and ended his career. Or began another one. Who knows? He could be a prison doc by now.

Was this situation any different? No doubt Dalton and crew had done something illegal, and probably lethal. Dennie had caught a slug. Now Dalton only wanted to get Dennie to his personal quack.

And clean up the mess, of course. With Buck being part of the mess.

"I assume this facility, as you say, isn't a real hospital?"

"I don't see that that's any concern of yours."

"Actually it is," Buck said. "If he's going to a hospital, he can do so much sooner than if he's going to some back alley butcher."

"Back alley butcher?" Dalton laughed. "You read too many novels. Or watch too much TV. Dennie will have a good doc. As soon as I can get him to Memphis."

Buck stared at him. "Like I said, it'll be a couple of days."

"Not sure we have that kind of time. I'd say you'd better try a little harder."

"Here's the thing, Dalton. You can't bargain with Mother Nature. She has a way of biting your ass if you do."

CHAPTER 26

Cain bought Marla two more ham and cheese croissants before he and Harper walked her out. Marla thanked them and ambled up the street. Cain was sure she'd be looking for Jason Epps. The monkey was biting hard.

Harper apparently had the same thought. "Think we should follow her? See if she tracks down this Jason dude?"

"I do."

They crossed the street, shadowed Marla for the next block until Cain's cell chimed. Cassie. He hoped she had some good news. It wasn't and it moved finding Jason Epps to the back burner.

From the front, Shaffer's Pharmacy appeared normal. Calm and quiet. Not so in back where Cain parked near Cassie's Jeep, two patrol units, and a pair of white vans: the coroner and the crime scene techs. Brought in from Knoxville according to the lettering on the side of each.

Cassie stood just outside the rear door talking with Hack. Cain and Harper walked that way.

"What's the story?" Cain asked.

"Someone murdered Wilbert Shaffer, stole a bunch of stuff," Cassie said.

"Drugs?" Harper asked.

"Mostly. But some other things, too." She glanced back inside.

"Penny Larkin works here. She's the one that found Wilbert. She's trying to make a list of the missing items."

"Is this where they broke in?" Cain asked.

"No sign of forced entry. Preliminary time of death is between seven and ten last night, so I suspect whoever did it caught Wilbert as he was closing up." She hooked a thumb in her service belt. "That'd explain the door being intact and Wilbert being here alone." She jerked her head toward the door. "Penny said she left about seven-thirty. Wilbert was going to finish some inventory stuff and then lock up."

A stretcher carrying a tented body bag nosed through the door. The late Wilbert Shaffer. The two coroner's techs maneuvered it over the gravel to their van and loaded it in the back. One of them walked back toward them.

"You need anything else?" He asked Cassie.

"Just the autopsy report."

He nodded. "Headed that way."

As the van pulled away, Harper asked, "Where do you get your autopsies done?"

"Knoxville. They have a good crew over there. Do all our crime lab stuff, too." She looked at Harper. "Of course we need them like…never."

"Until the past twenty-four hours," Cain said.

"Yeah." She turned, waved them to follow. "Let me show you why I called."

Inside, Cain saw the blood stain where Shaffer had fallen, and the open drug cage, shelves mostly empty. He pointed that way. "Looks like someone filled their prescriptions."

Cassie tossed him a weak smile. "Took everything. According to Penny they had Oxy, codeine, morphine, Versed, and fentanyl. Also Xanax, Valium, Adderall, and Sudafed. The whole enchilada."

"Bet it has some connection to what we saw over at the Finleys," Hack said.

Cain nodded. "Good bet."

"But here's the kicker," Cassie said. She picked up an evidence bag from the counter, handed it to Cain.

Cain saw a wallet. It was opened flat and revealed the driver's license inside. "Where'd this come from?"

"Found it right on the counter." She pointed. "Next to the cash register. Which of course they emptied."

Why would Buck's wallet be here? The answer came immediately. A message. A cry for help. He started to say something but a woman walked up to the counter. She held several pages in one hand, a ballpoint in the other.

"Chief, I think I've got a handle on this. Not sure it's everything but this is what I have so far."

Cassie introduced Cain and Harper to Penny. She then thanked Penny and told her she could head home if she wanted. That if Cassie needed anything else, she'd let her know. She ended with, "Thanks. I know this wasn't easy for you."

Cain thumbed through the pages. The first page listed the drugs. The ones Cassie had mentioned, plus antibiotics, chloral hydrate, and two bottles of betadine solution. The next two pages listed items, such as surgical drapes, gauze, tape, IV fluid bags, surgical instruments like scalpels, scissors, hemostats. An Ambu bag and mask.

Hack, who had been reading over Cain's shoulder, said, "So what do we have? A drug addict who likes to dissect frogs or something?"

"No," Cain said. "What we have is a massacre, an abduction, and a lethal burglary."

"I agree," Harper said.

"Want to explain?" Cassie said.

"Look at the scenes," Cain said. "We have the family of a drug dealer killed. Execution-style. Probably to settle a score, or send a message, or eliminate competition. At the scene we have blood that's not likely from the victims. A discharged weapon, one bullet missing. That suggests one of the killers was hit. Now what to do? Can't go to the ER, so they bring the ER to the injured party by kidnapping a doctor. But a doctor without instruments can't do anything. Like dig out a bullet. Maybe more. So," he waved a hand, "we have this."

Cassie stared at him, then turned and scanned the shelves behind her, shaking her head. "Son-of-a-bitch." She turned back to Cain. "I don't like it but it makes sense."

"Dr. Buckner was smart enough to drop his wallet here and

connect the dots for us," Harper said.

Hack nodded. "He sure did. Which means that Tommy Finley pissed someone off. Probably stepped on their territory. Maybe tried to shortchange a supplier or cut them out of the loop somehow."

Cain shrugged. "Happens all the time. Greed being greed."

"Which means we have a killer, or killers, running around," Cassie said.

"Killers," Harper said. "The duo that grabbed Buck. Bet the injured party was in the back."

"It also means they're probably holed up somewhere," Cain said. "A remote place where surgery can be done."

"I take it there are a few isolated homes and cabins around?" Harper asked.

"Too many to count," Cassie said. "Depends on the radius. But hundreds just within a few miles."

"Mostly inhabited?" Harper asked.

"What do you think?" Cassie asked Hack.

He scratched his chin. "Probably fifty-fifty. Lots of folks from Knoxville, Chattanooga, all over really, have cabins they rarely use."

"It'll be a big job," Cassie said, "but we'll need to expand our search for that SUV, and now include a passel of cabins."

"Follow the drug connection," Cain said.

Cassie nodded. "Jason Epps. He was close to Tommy Finley."

"That's who Marla bought from last night," Harper said.

"You talked to her?"

Harper nodded.

"What'd you think?"

"She's a lost and injured soul."

"That she is."

"My impression is that she was once a very pretty girl. Probably had it together."

Cassie nodded. "Pretty, smart, athletic. The entire package." She sighed. "We were friends. Then, she fell in the drug ditch."

"Which brings us to Tommy Finley and Jason Epps," Cain said.

"He and Tommy always hung in the park. Did much of their business there." She looked at Hack. "Let's round the bastard up."

Cain touched her arm. "Might I make a suggestion?"

"Have at it."

"You and your guys will have your hands full looking for the SUV and the cabin. If that's where they are. You know the area. We don't. We'd just be a fifth wheel."

"Okay."

"Let Harper and me explore the drug angle. Tap some of our resources and take a run at Jason. You already did over at the scene. Maybe we can take a different approach."

"What? Scare the shit out of him?"

Harper smiled. "Something like that."

"What about the guys that apparently did all this?" Cassie asked. "You think Jason might be on their list?"

"I do," Cain said.

"Unless he's part of it," Hack said. "Maybe Jason knew about the hit on Tommy. Saw it as a way to move up the ladder. Maybe helped set it all up."

Cassie seemed to consider that. "Which was good for him until everything went sideways. They just might consider Jason a liability now and might think he knows too much. That it's time to button things up over here."

"Panic tends to change folks' perspective," Hack said. "Killing a dealer and his family's one thing. Grabbing a doctor and doing all this shit," he waved a hand, "takes it up a notch."

"Prior bad acts predict future bad acts," Harper said. "I think Jason Epps should be more than a little concerned."

CHAPTER 27

Marla had already burned through everything she had scored from Jason last night. Amazing how quickly it evaporated up her veins, or nose. Sure it took her away from this shit life, only to slam her back to reality much too quickly. The croissants that couple had bought for her and the donuts at Reverend John's had settled the growls in her stomach, but her nerves were starting that familiar jangle. Like a sputtering electrical current that sizzled through her body. Reminded her of a dying fluorescent light and made her feel as if the cells inside her were suffering a similar fate. They probably were.

True to form in her life, just when she felt as if things couldn't get worse, they did. Tommy was dead. What the fuck was that all about? No Tommy, no reliable connection, would definitely make everything in her world that much more difficult. It meant she'd have to deal with that asshole Jason. One thing for sure, she wasn't going to blow him again. She hoped now that Jason was the top dog he'd be easier to deal with. Hell, she'd pray for that if it helped. But, her prayers were never answered. No one was listening. Reverend John had tried to bring Jesus and all that crap into her life, but she knew better. There was no savior in her future. The truth was there was no future in her future. Only this. Begging, stealing, shooting up.

On the bright side, she'd had a good morning, raking in over forty bucks panhandling. Her usuals, the downtown store owners she could always count on for a few bucks, had been generous. Bev Oakley stood in front of her curio shop smoking and offered Marla a crisp five from the pocket of her jacket. Tilly Watson, who was sweeping the sidewalk in front of her candy shop, Sweet Treats, did the same, and also gave her a small bag of chocolate-coated almonds.

A block later she walked past Central Grocery. She kept her head down, hoping owner Luke Towry wouldn't see her. But he did. He left his post behind the check-out counter and stepped outside, calling to her.

She stopped and turned back toward him. "Mr. Towry."

"How are you doing today, Marla?"

"Fine. Except for this." She raised her bandaged arm.

His brow creased. "Nothing serious I hope."

She shifted her backpack to the other shoulder, tugging her hair from beneath the strap that had trapped it. "Nope."

He nodded, hesitated a beat, and then said, "Reverend John said you might be looking for a job. That right?"

Why did everyone want to save her? Couldn't they just give her a little cash and leave her alone? Not to mention that a job was the last thing she wanted. A schedule? Getting up, showing up on someone else's timetable? How does that work? Most mornings she couldn't get out of bed before ten. And then it took a couple of hours to even feel halfway human. Somehow she couldn't quite picture stocking shelves and shoving groceries into bags, and smiling. She was sure that would be part of the job. Towry smiled all the time. Like it was a company requirement.

She again raised her arm. "As soon as my arm heels I'll stop by and see."

"I need to get someone pretty quick. Any idea how long it'll be?"

"A few days."

He sighed. "Okay. Stop by then and hopefully I'll still have something for you."

"I hope so." That was a lie. She knew if she could string this out long enough he would find someone else and then he and Reverend John might leave her alone.

Towry glanced up the street, then back to her. "I guess you heard about the murders last night?"

She nodded. "Yeah."

"I can't believe it. Here in Tanner's Crossroads?" He sighed. "I guess big city problems are everywhere."

Marla nodded but said nothing.

"The rumor is that it was some drug deal."

Marla felt a knot expand in her stomach. "Why would you think that?"

"I hear that's what Chief Crowe thinks. Tommy apparently dealt drugs. Something I never knew." He sighed. "Sometimes I feel like I'm clueless. Anyway, they think that the killing of his family was related to some drug thing." He gave a head shake. "And then Wilbert Shaffer being murdered this morning. Unbelievable."

"What?" Marla asked. "Mr. Shaffer?"

"Yep. Apparently his place was robbed and he got himself killed in the process. From what I hear, apparently that missing doctor is part of all this. Don't know how, but that's the rumor."

For some reason, put that way, it hit her hard. Sure she had guessed that Tommy might have drawn some evil to his home, but Mr. Shaffer? What the hell was going on? Tommy dealt drugs. Shaffer sold them. She used them. If this was a series of drug world—her world—killings, was she safe? Would whoever it was come for her? Why would they?

Because she saw Dr. Buck's kidnapping. She dealt with Tommy almost daily. Did the killers know that?

The blood seemed to drain from her head and a warm flush filled her chest, followed by a wave of dizziness and a graying at the edges of her vision. Towry's voice sounded tinny and flat.

"Are you okay?" He stepped forward and grabbed her arm.

His voice seemed to waver and crackle, like a distant radio signal shouldering its way through bad weather.

"Here." He led her to the wooden bench that snugged up against the front of his store.

She sat and bent forward, her head hanging between her knees.

"You okay?" he asked again.

She took a deep breath, then another, before straightening and looking into his face. Lines of concern settled in the corners of his eyes.

"Tommy was my friend," Marla said. "One of the few I had left."

"That's right. You two went to school together."

Tears blurred her vision. Her mind struggled to find some order in the thoughts that warred inside. Tommy was her friend. They had known each other since the first grade. She knew his sister, his parents. Now they were all gone.

But, Tommy wasn't just a friend, he was her connection. To pile even more bad luck on her plate that role now fell to Jason. Jason…. Jesus. A wave of guilt settled over her. What was wrong with her? A family killed, a nice man robbed and murdered, and all she could think of was where she'd get her next fix. How sick was that?

She stood. "I have to go."

"You sure you're okay?"

She swiped the back of one hand across her nose and sniffed back her tears. "I'm fine." She looked up and down the street. "I just have to move."

He said something but she wasn't listening. She could barely feel her feet as she walked down the sidewalk. Her backpack now felt as if it was filled with rocks. She needed to get well. She needed to find Jason and then go back to Reverend John's and crawl in bed. Pull the covers over her head and hide from all of this.

CHAPTER 28

Cain and Harper walked out into the pharmacy's rear parking lot, leaving Cassie and Hack to their work: Cassie on the phone gathering the troops to begin the search for the SUV and plotting a strategy for canvasing the myriad houses and cabins where the killers might have landed; Hack rechecking the inventory of stolen items. They climbed in The Rig. The sunshine hadn't lasted long and now misty rain fogged the windshield.

"Hopefully, the rain doesn't dissuade Jason from doing business," Harper said.

"I doubt it will," Cain replied. "Neither snow nor rain nor heat nor gloom of night halts free enterprise."

"Nor postal carriers."

"Them, too." Cain reached for the ignition key but hesitated. "Let's call Dr. Buckner before we head over," Cain said. "Bring him up to date."

"He won't be happy with what we know. Or suspect."

"At least it bodes well for his son still being alive."

"Assuming the wounded bad guy didn't die." Harper pulled out her iPhone and dialed Buckner's number. She placed it on speaker. Buckner answered after a single ring. "Dr. Buckner?"

"Yes."

"Harper McCoy. Bobby Cain is here, too."

"Please tell me you have good news." His voice sounded

strained, thickened with fatigue and fear. "I haven't slept a wink."

"The news is mixed," Cain said.

A deep sigh. "Give it to me straight. Okay? No hedging or sugar-coating."

"The good news is that we have a witness," Harper said. "Someone who saw the abduction."

"Who? What?"

"The what, is that he was taken outside the hospital," Cain said. "The ER parking lot. Two guys in a black SUV."

"I know that. Any idea who?"

"Not yet. The problem is that the witness is a drug addict. She had just used so her story was a bit fuzzy."

"But, I sense you believe her," Buckner said.

"We do," Harper said. "She gave us a vague description of the two bad guys but a pretty good one of their vehicle."

"I see."

"We've already made inroads with the police here. The chief, Cassie Crowe, seems pretty sharp. She has her staff rolling, looking for the SUV right now. We're trying to track down someone who just might be another witness."

"Who?"

"Drug dealer," Cain said. "He had just sold to our witness in a park across from the hospital. She said he had already left but he still might've been in the area."

"Sounds sketchy," Buckner said.

"It is. But hopefully it'll pan out."

"You said the news was mixed. What's the rest of it?"

Buckner had said he wanted it straight, no sugar-coating, so Cain laid it out. The murders of the Finley's and Wilbert Shaffer. The finding of Buck's wallet at the pharmacy scene. His thoughts that Buck had left it behind to show them that all these acts were related. He closed with, "A very clever move on his part."

"He always was a clever young man," Dr. Buckner said. "Why was he at the pharmacy?"

Cain went over what he could remember of the items stolen. "Based on that and the fact that it looks like one of the killers was shot at the original murder scene, I suspect Buck was abducted to deal with the injured man. The pharmacy stop was to get the tools he needed."

"My God," Buckner said. A sob escaped his throat. "Do you think Buck's still alive?"

"We don't know," Harper said. "But probably. If we're correct on all this, he's an asset. They need him and his skills. That's why they took him."

Silence followed as Dr. Buckner seemed to process that. Apparently he came to the same conclusion Cain and Harper had. "Unless the injured man dies."

"Let's assume he doesn't, or didn't, and go with him surviving and Buck still having value."

"But once he doesn't?" Buckner asked. "Doesn't have value?"

"We'll get to that if we need to," Harper said. "Right now we're tracking the drug connection. The police are looking for the vehicle."

"As well as the location where the work could be done," Cain added. "A house or a cabin. Some place off the beaten path."

"Does that mean you think they're still in the area?"

"We do," Cain said. "The guy who caught the gunshot was injured to such a degree that they took a series of very bold moves. Grabbing Buck. Robbing a pharmacy. That indicates a level of panic. So, I suspect the wound is serious enough that a long trek isn't in the cards."

"Which means he might not make it and that would put Buck in great danger."

"It would. Let's hope Buck can save him."

Buckner sighed. "He's good at what he does. He has two years of surgical training so he's seen his share of gunshots."

"That's good," Harper said.

"That's also in a hospital. In some cabin, or wherever, changes things." He sighed. "I wouldn't want to have to do it."

"Hopefully in this situation, Buck's training will make the difference."

"The irony is that he should be here," Buckner said. "Part of the practice and not galivanting all over chasing some...I don't know what he's chasing." Another sigh. "We all come to forks in the road, to crossroads, and we all make choices and have to live with the consequences."

Cain ended the call saying they needed to get moving but that they would call again as soon as they knew more. He cranked The Rig to life and hit the road.

He thought about what Buckner had said. About choices and crossroads. About irony. To Cain, the irony here was that they were in a town called Tanner's Crossroads and were dealing with the aftermath of Buck Buckner's crossroad decision. It was true that had he made a different choice, remained on the path his father, and probably his siblings, wanted, he would be safe. In North Carolina. Not in the hands of guys who seemed to have little compunction about killing.

He flashed on one of the many times Uncle Al had talked about crossroads and choices. Uncle Al and Aunt Dixie had been his and Harper's de facto parents while they roamed the south, putting on shows, hunting and fishing, pulling scams, stealing, whatever was needed to survive. Even though they, and the other kids in the troop, were raised by the entire family, each of the children were taken in by one of the couples who served as their primary guardians. It wasn't a hard and fast, surely not a written, rule, but it worked out that way. He and Harper got lucky. Al and Dixie were good people. It was them, particularly Dixie, who had taught Cain about knives and how to throw them, and created Bobby Blade, Cain's role in the family shows. Actually, the centerpiece of the money-making events.

Al liked his rum, and many evenings after a few nips, while they gathered near a campfire, he would wax philosophical. His topics were wide-ranging but Cain and Harper learned from each.

The ironic point being that Al loved towns called crossroads. Crossroads anything. Like McCullers Crossroads in North Carolina and Owens Cross Roads in North Alabama. They had camped near each more than once.

Uncle Al's take was that crossroads offered options. Forward, right, left, reverse. Each choice possible, each leading to a different outcome. Sometimes the choice was yours, other times events dictated which route you followed. In either case, according to Uncle Al, life changed.

It surely had for Buck Buckner. Big time.

It had for Cain, too.

What if the family hadn't been fractured by the FBI when he was twelve? What if he had been adopted by someone other than the Cains? Or by no one? What if he hadn't stumbled into the military? Hadn't pulled the SERES training stunt that led him to Langley, and beyond?

The permutations were endless. Which is why he rarely dwelled on them, preferring to focus only on the path ahead.

He suspected that the younger Dr. Buckner, if he was still alive, felt the same about now. Not playing the endless '*what-if?*' game, but rather desperately seeking an escape route. Leaving behind his wallet had been ingenious, but now he was engulfed in a criminal world where he had no experience. It didn't bode well.

CHAPTER 29

Cassie sat behind the wheel of her Jeep, while Hack scurried through the drizzle and into Spivey's Coffee Shop. She mentally sorted through the possible scenarios again. The only one that made sense and made all the pieces fit, was exactly what Bobby Cain had said. Bad guys come to town and take out Tommy Finley and his family. Probably a drug war or perhaps a message. The hit doesn't go as planned and one of the bad guys takes a slug. Panic sets in so they grab the good Dr. Buck from the ER and then rob and kill Wilbert Shaffer. Jesus, Wilbert. Now, they must be holed up somewhere. Based on the blood at the Finley's house and the fact they needed a doctor and medical supplies that 'somewhere' was likely nearby. Somewhere in her domain. Lucky her.

Buck leaving his wallet stitched all these events together. One thing was certain: Dr. Buck Buckner could think on his feet and make smart decisions under incredible stress. Good skills for an ER doc. She doubted his training had prepared him for this ordeal, however.

Now the trick was finding him.

Could Buck save the wounded thug? It seemed like a long shot to her. If he managed to pull that off, what then? If the dude died, or even if he got better, Buck would be expendable. That they would kill him was a given. Based on what she had seen, they didn't seem the type that would leave a witness standing. But as long as he was needed, they'd have to keep him above the grass. How long was that? A day? Two?

The clock was ticking and she had no idea how much time was left. Frustration didn't quite cover what she felt. Neither did anger, though both were in the mix. Someone had come into her town, her domain, and killed five people. That made it personal and it was her job to find them. She gripped the steering wheel and stared unfocused through the rain-streaked windshield. The real problem was that they could be anywhere. In any direction. Near or far. Truly a needle in a haystack.

Hack returned with two coffees. The sky to the west had darkened and the wind had ticked up slightly. Real rain, not this misty spitting, was coming, and from what she'd heard on the radio, it would get stormy overnight. She took a sip, then placed the cup in the console cup-holder.

"I think we should swing by Buck's apartment," Cassie said.

"Why?"

"What if they're there?"

"I suspect they bolted out of town," Hack said.

"Probably. But we'd look pretty stupid if we searched everywhere but right under our noses."

"True that."

"They don't know this area. At least, I doubt they do. Probably didn't do a ton of research, thinking they could roll in, whack Tommy, and disappear. But now, they'll be panicked."

Hack nodded, then took a sip of coffee. "Buck don't know the area none too well either."

"So what do panicked folks do?" Cassie asked. "They head for the familiar."

"You're a pretty good cop."

Cassie smiled. "I had good teachers."

Next stop, the Greenwood Apartments where Dr. Buckner was staying during his tenure here. She didn't expect to find him, no way, but maybe there was something to be learned. Something that might make the haystack a little more manageable. She didn't hold high hopes for that either.

The complex was older but well-maintained. Four two-story,

six unit, dark brown wooden buildings, three up and three down, shingled roofs, squared around a central garden area. Cassie gave it a drive by. It looked quiet.

"You don't really think this's where they're hiding out, do you?" Hack asked.

"I don't. I'd suspect they'd want to put some distance between them and the crime scenes."

"Probably," Hack said. "Then again, this is familiar territory. For the doc, anyway. Might figure it's better than driving around looking for a place."

"Maybe. But if it was me, I'd book it out of town as fast and as far as possible."

"But you're rational. These guys probably aren't."

"Glad you think I'm rational." She smiled at him.

"Always were. Even as a kid."

She pulled a U-turn and then rolled through the parking area, which extended across the front of the complex. No black SUV visible.

"They could've dumped it," Hack said.

"Sure could have." She pulled another U-turn at the end of the lot and backtracked, parking in front of the manager's office.

"If they're here, they're armed," Hack said. "From what we've seen, they ain't too bashful about shooting folks."

"True."

"Maybe we should call in some backup just in case."

"They ain't here," Cassie said.

"I suspect that's true but do you want to bet your life on it?" Cassie considered that. "Nope."

Hack tugged his cell from his pocket and called the station, putting it on speaker.

"Poppy," he said, when the answer came, "round up Fowler and Duckworth. Get them rolling over to the Greenwood Apartments."

"Something going on?" Poppy asked.

"Don't know yet. But tell them to keep their eyes open and come in quietly."

"I'm on it." Poppy hung up.

Hugh Janssen, owner and manager, wasn't happy about handing over his master keys to anyone, even the chief of police.

But after Cassie explained that the situation just might turn messy and that he should remain in his own home, door closed, he relented. Not before saying he didn't want any trouble. Cassie assured him that she didn't either.

Fowler and Duckworth pulled up, parked, and climbed out.

"What's going on?" Duckworth asked.

"This is where Buckner lives," Cassie said. "It could be where the bad guys are holed up."

"Here?" Fowler asked. "I figured they'd be long gone."

"They probably are, but let's not assume anything," Cassie said.

"How do you want to play it?" Duckworth asked.

"We'll knock, you guys stay back and cover."

Buck Buckner's apartment was number 21, ground floor on the end of building 2. They approached with caution, flanking the door, guns out. Hack knocked, then banged, and shouted "Police" a couple of times. No response. Cassie keyed opened the door.

"Police," she shouted. "If anyone's in here, make yourself known."

No response, or sounds of movement. She entered the living room. Hack, Fowler, and Duckworth followed.

The apartment was neat and orderly, and sparsely furnished. Cassie suspected there was no need to do much decorating or add any personal touches if your stay was going to be short. After they cleared each room and searched the bedroom closet and drawers, finding only a few clothes and several pairs of surgery scrubs, they stood in the kitchen. Buckner had apparently set up the kitchen table as his home office. On its surface sat a laptop and a stack of medical books, including "Harrison's Textbook of Medicine," "Grey's Anatomy," and a couple of tomes on emergency medicine.

"What do you think?" Cassie asked.

"Don't look like anyone did any surgery here," Hack said.

"Unless they cleaned up and are in the wind."

Hack nodded. "You don't believe that."

"Nope," Cassie said.

"What are you guys talking about?" Fowler asked. "Surgery?"

Cassie explained their current thinking on the subject.

"Since they couldn't take the dude that got shot over at the Finley's place to the hospital, they brought the surgeon to the victim?" Duckworth asked. "Something like that?"

"Exactly," Cassie said.

"That's actually pretty smart," Fowler said.

"It is. If that's the deal, we have a multiple murder, a kidnapping, and a robbery-slash-murder."

"The trifecta," Fowler said.

Cassie massaged one temple. "Just what we need."

Hack offered her a smile. "See why I turned the chief job over to you?"

She raised an eyebrow. "Want it back?"

"Not a chance."

"What now?" Duckworth asked.

Hack hooked his thumbs beneath his belt. "They aren't here, and it doesn't look like they ever were. That means they're somewhere else."

"We have to find them," Cassie said. "Soon. I think the doctor is an expendable item. Once he's done all he can do, or the bad guy with a hole in him dies, they'll kill him for sure."

Silence reigned for a full minute, everyone letting that fact sink in.

CHAPTER 30

Marla—shoulders hunched forward, head down—hugged herself as she walked up the street. She felt a deep chill, not from the cold drizzle, but rather from her fast-approaching crash. She waited for two cars to pass, scurried across the street, and turned toward the park. She actually prayed Jason would be there. Who knows, maybe the Holy Ghost was listening today.

As if to answer her prayers, she saw Jason. Leaning against the tree where he always hung out. He held his phone to one ear, but lowered it and slid it into his jean's pocket as she approached.

"Well, well," he said, "if it isn't my new girlfriend."

Prick.

"What can I do you for?" He looked her up and down. "I'd say you need to get well."

"What the hell is wrong with you?" Marla said. "Tommy was murdered and here you are being all jerky."

"Look, I'm as freaked by this as you are. It wasn't just Tommy. It was also Jennifer and their parents."

"I know." Marla swiped a sleeve across her nose. "Who could have done that?"

"I don't know."

"Fuck me." Her face screwed down as she tried to hold back her tears. "What am I going to do?"

"You look a little strung out. Need anything?"

She sniffed. "You holding?"

"What do you need?"

"The usual."

He smiled. "Same deal as last time."

She slugged his shoulder. "Fuck you, asshole. I'm not going to blow you again."

"If you don't want my services, you can haul your ass on down the road."

God, she wished she could. But Jason was now her only hook up. Did she have a choice here? Either deal with him, or crawl back over to Reverend John's and ride out the pain. She couldn't do that right now. She just couldn't.

"I got money," Marla said.

Jason gave her a smirky smile. "Then I've got what you need." He touched her cheek. She flinched. "If you're a little short again, we'll work something out." His thumb trailed across her lips.

She pulled away, wiped a sleeve across her mouth as if to remove any residue of his touch. "I got the cash."

"Too bad."

"Twenty of meth. Twenty of heroin."

"My, you have had a good morning."

She dug a wad of bills, mostly singles and a few fives, from her pocket. "Let's get this done."

He looked around, glanced back toward the parking area and the road beyond, then gave a quick nod. He unzipped his backpack and rummaged inside, coming out with two small baggies. She reached for them but he pulled them away.

"You got the forty?"

"Yeah."

"Or we could still work out a discount."

"Fuck you, Jason. I got it covered."

She flattened the bills into a disordered stack, extracted the needed amount, and shoved the remainder in her pocket. She held the cash toward him. He counted the bills and stuffed them in his own pocket before handing her the baggies.

"I'll be here later tonight," he said. "When you use this up, come find me." He actually laughed. "Who knows? Maybe you'll be a little short on cash."

She wanted to punch his face but knew she couldn't. If he cut her off, things could get ugly. She clenched her teeth, and turned toward the park entrance.

That's when she saw a large black SUV turn into the parking area. Dark windows so she couldn't see who was inside. Was that the same one she had seen last night? The one that took the doctor? She veered to her right and melted into the trees, taking the long way back through town.

CHAPTER 31

At Cassie's suggestion, Cain and Harper had grabbed rooms at the Beverley B&B, a converted two-story, white frame house, two blocks off Main Street. The tree-lined neighborhood was quiet, classic small-town America. The inn was in its third generation of ownership, having been founded by Beverley Whitelaw some fifty years earlier and now run by her granddaughter, Julia Mackey. Thirty-something and pleasant. She showed them to a pair of rooms across from each other on the second floor and gave them the lay of the land. The morning breakfast hours, the Wi-Fi password, the essentials.

To Cain, the bed looked inviting. After a night of poor, basically nonexistent sleep, a drive halfway across the state, and all they had seen and done this morning, a brief nap would be nice. Wasn't going to happen. Buck was missing, the bad guys were out there planning something, and the clock was ticking. Fortunately, he, Harper too, was no stranger to sleep deprivation. Many of his missions had required being "in the field" for days. Hunkering down in the desert or some shithole village, waiting and watching before acting and then humping it to some secret extraction point. Sleep was either never, or in twenty minute bites here and there. So, they settled in quickly and headed out to track down Jason Epps.

Cain crunched The Rig to a stop in the park's empty gravel lot. Harper pointed through the rain-misted windshield. Marla was walking their way, her hoodie pulled up over her head against the light drizzle. She apparently saw them, hesitated, cut right into the trees, and disappeared. About thirty yards beyond her, Cain saw Jason standing beneath a tree. He looked directly at them, then with forced casualness slid behind the trunk.

"I'd say Marla just scored," Harper said.

"Looks that way."

"Which means Jason is probably holding. That might give us some leverage."

"Or we could just break his arms."

Harper gave a quick laugh. "Yeah, I don't care much for him either."

They stepped out and headed Jason's way. He peeked around the tree as they approached.

"How're you doing, Jason?" Cain asked.

"What's it to you?"

Jason the tough guy. This was going to be fun.

"We weren't formally introduced this morning. Over at the Finleys. I'm Cain. This is Harper."

"That supposed to mean something to me?" Jason said, chin up, wearing an arrogant smirk.

"We're looking into the murder of Tommy Finley and his family and the abduction of Dr. Buckner from the ER."

"Ain't that Chief Crowe's job?"

"Ours, too," Harper said. "We were hired by Dr. Buckner's father to find him."

Jason gave her a blank stare. Water drops plunked the leaves overhead. "So what? You think he's here in the park?" He slouched against the tree trunk, cigarette dangling from one corner of his mouth. Playing it cool, unconcerned.

Maybe too cool. Cain knew that most folks, even innocent folks, got nervous when talking to an investigator. Any type of investigator. Cops, private types, each raised the tension. Most guilty folks become hyper-alert, fidgety, dilated pupils, gaze unable to settle on anything, speech too fast, too flighty. All the signs of stress, or guilt. But some, even the guiltiest, remain calm and composed. Or at least able to present that face.

Which was Jason? Innocent and calm, or guilty and a good

actor?

"We came to the park to find you," Harper said.

"Why'd you think I'd be here?" Now questions appeared behind his eyes, stress lines at the corners.

"It's where you do business," Cain said.

"I ain't doing no business. Even if I was, it ain't no bother to you."

Cain slid his hands in his pockets, nodded. "You see, Jason, we've got a problem here. An entire family was executed last night. A cold blooded killing."

"Don't see how that's got anything to do with me."

"That's part of my problem. I know Tommy and you were friends, and business associates. Yet his murder, his family's murder, doesn't seem to have had any effect on you. Not this morning at the scene and not now."

Jason dropped the cigarette to the ground and crushed it with his shoe. "You don't know nothing about me."

"We only know what we know," Harper said. "And what you tell us. So let's start with you and Tommy. What's the story?"

"I don't have to talk to you."

Harper sighed. "No, Jason, you don't. You could try to simply walk away and I could slap you to the ground."

"You can't threaten me."

Harper smiled but said nothing.

"I've got rights." Stress tightened Jason's voice, pitched it higher.

"Yes, you do," Cain said. "But since you just made a deal with Marla, you're probably holding."

"So after I whack you in the face," Harper said, "we could call Chief Crowe and let her dig around in your pockets. How about that?"

Jason hesitated, glanced toward the trees where Marla had disappeared, buying time. Probably deciding if it was best to talk or flee. Finally, he spoke. "Not much to tell. We'd known each other since we were kids. We've been friends forever."

"Now he's gone. How do you feel about that?"

"How do you think I feel?"

"I honestly don't know," Harper said. "That's why I'm asking."

"I feel bad."

"Bad? That's it? You feel bad?"

He shrugged and looked past her toward the trees again. "Don't know what else to tell you."

"How about who you think might have done this?" Cain said.

"I don't know nothing about it."

"What about the robbery over at Shaffer's Pharmacy? Where Mr. Shaffer was killed? Know anything about that?"

Jason looked directly at Cain. "What? I didn't know about that. Someone robbed Shaffer's?"

Harper nodded. "Sure did. Shot Mr. Shaffer in the head."

Cain could almost hear the hum and crackle of Jason's nerves. His gaze bounced here and there, eyes wider, face muscles tense.

"You saying it was me?" Jason asked. "That's what you're saying?"

"Are we?" Cain asked.

His jaw set. "Sounds that way to me."

"If we were saying that, would we be wrong?" Harper asked.

"Absolutely." His fists balled at his sides. "I don't like any of this. You're accusing me of killing Mr. Shaffer. Tommy and his family."

"We haven't accused you of anything," Cain said. "We're just asking. Doing our job."

"I don't know nothing about any of that. All I know is that here you are going all Gestapo on me."

"Gestapo?" Harper asked.

"Yeah. Accusing me of all sorts of things. Murders, robberies. It ain't right. Whatever happened to innocent until proven guilty?"

"I'll let you in on a little secret," Cain said. "That all sounds good to John Q. Public. But, the truth is that folks like us, cops, too, don't really think that way. We usually start with guilty and look for evidence to prove us wrong. Seems to work better that way."

Jason shook his head. "Why do I get to be the focus of your delusion?"

"Let's see. You show up at the crime scene. Unsolicited. You and Tommy deal drugs." Jason started to say something but Cain stopped him with a raised hand. "The Finley killings smell like a drug hit. Over at Shaffer's some pretty potent narcotics were part of the haul. Add to that the fact that you don't seem overly torn up over a multiple murder where your supposed friend and his family were massacred." He shrugged, opening his palms toward Jason. "Sort of makes me wonder why all this looks like it could revolve around you."

"I didn't have nothing to do with it."

"But you know who did?" Cain said. "And why?"

"No, I don't. It was a big shock to me."

"Let me offer you another shock," Cain said. "One you can take to the bank." He had slid one of his blades from its secret pant-leg compartment and now aimed it at Jason's eye. Only a couple of inches away.

Jason flinched. "What the hell?"

"You see, Jason, we aren't constrained by laws and rules and crap like that. We each have a considerable body count and aren't bashful about moving that needle north. So, I can either gouge your eye out, or you can cut the BS and tell us the truth."

Jason's face was now slick with sweat, his breathing deep and fast.

"Who the hell did this?" Harper asked.

"I don't know."

Cain moved the knife point closer to Jason's eye. "Not the right answer."

"Okay, okay. I'll tell you what I know. Just get that thing away from me."

Cain lowered the knife. "Talk."

"I have no idea who did any of this. I swear. Tommy handled all the supplies. I know he got everything out of Memphis. I don't know from who. I was never in on any of that. I only helped him sell."

"Okay, so far, so good," Harper said. "The rest of it."

"Tommy had found another guy over in Knoxville. Better prices, he told me, and closer by so easier to get supplies."

Supplies. Sounded so innocuous. Sort of like typing paper, rubber bands, and number two yellow pencils.

"The guys in Memphis?" Cain asked. "How'd they feel about that?"

Jason shook his head. "Tommy said they didn't know nothing about it."

"I'd say current events suggests that they did. So they settled his account."

Jason's shoulders sagged. "After what happened, I figured they must've. You know, killed Tommy and his family."

"That's what happens in the world you decided to inhabit," Cain said.

"These people you don't know from Memphis?" Harper said. "Sounds like convenient forgetfulness."

"I don't know them. Never met or talked to them or anything." He glanced toward Harper, Cain, back to Harper. "That's the truth."

"You will get to meet them," Cain said. "Up close and personal. You do know that, don't you?"

"What?"

"You think they don't know about you? That you worked with Tommy?" Cain smiled. "You don't think they have eyes and ears everywhere they ship product? That they would kill off a supply line unless they had another one already in place? Not sure that would be a smart business decision."

"So?"

"So, tag, you're it. The next man up."

"I won't do it."

"Will you have a choice?" Harper said. "I don't think the guys who did what I've seen in the past few hours are good at accepting no."

Jason wavered, flattened a palm against the tree for support.

"We don't really care what you decide," Cain said. "Or better, what they decide. But when they contact you, and they will, I want to know about it."

Jason said nothing. His brain apparently on overload.

"What's your phone number?" Cain asked.

"Why?"

"I'll text you my contact info. You'll need it to call me as soon as you hear anything."

"Why would I do that?"

Cain caught his gaze, held it. "So we won't have to visit you in the dead of night."

Jason recited the number and Cain shot him a text. And just like that, they were in his phone. Or, Mama B was anyway.

CHAPTER 32

"Mr. Greene came by to see you," Poppy said from her perch behind the PD's reception desk.

"Where is he?" Cassie said, looking around.

"He went across the street to grab a coffee. He said he'd drop back by."

"Thanks." Cassie tapped a knuckle on the desktop. "I'll be in my office."

She sat behind her desk. The stack of papers she had neglected for a few days glared at her. She knew most would be inane memos and forms but she still needed to weed the wheat from the chaff. She dug in, tossing the first three into the blue trash bin. The one that held documents to be shredded.

Hack stuck his head around the door jamb. "Anything new?"

"Nada."

"Duckworth and Fowler laid out a search plan. Kind of spreading out from The Crossroads."

"If they went that way," Cassie said.

"That's where most of the cabins and stuff are but that's why I'm headed east. See what's in the hills that way."

Cassie swiped her hair back. "Hell, they could be in Montana by now."

Hack scratched one cheek. "Probably not with one of them shot."

147

Cassie shrugged. "Probably not."

"Before I head out, you need me to do anything?"

She picked up a stack of papers. "Maybe go through these."

He laughed. "Another reason I got tired of playing chief." He waved and headed down the hallway.

Wasn't that the truth. It seemed she spent more time pushing paper around than she did actually doing cop work. Bureaucracies kill more trees than forest fires and she had a good sized sapling on her desk right now. She began the sorting again, assigning each to one of three fates: trashcan, shred can, or a stack that she would have to actually deal with. Unfortunately, most ended up in the latter.

Her intercom button buzzed and flashed. She punched it to open the line.

"Mr. Greene is here."

"Send him back."

She and Simon Greene had a history that reached back to grammar school. He was two years older and for some reason glommed on to her as a love interest in her sixth grade year. He never let go of that desire either. They actually had one date. His senior prom. She a sophomore and his second choice; Marla Jackson was the first. She didn't uncover that little fact until much later, however. Marla had been dating one of the football players then. Simon wasn't an athlete. He was smart though. Smart enough to win a full-ride scholarship to Ole Miss and then another to Yale Law. Then he returned to Tanner's Crossroads and built the largest law practice in a hundred-mile radius.

He also picked up his pursuit of Cassie. So far she had batted away all his advances and didn't see any way that would ever change.

"How's your day going?" Simon said as he came in and dropped into one of the chairs that faced her desk.

"Been better."

One thing you could say for Simon is that he had model good looks. Tall, thin, blond hair that fell easily across his forehead, and deeply blue eyes. His smile was electric and the tiny crow's feet at the corner of his eyes only added to his charm. As did his chin dimple. Today he wore a tan suit, Armani no doubt, a crisp white shirt, and a yellow silk tie. Lawyer dripped from his pores.

"I imagine so," Simon said. "I hear the Finley murders were pretty gruesome."

She nodded. "Very. Add in the murder and robbery over at Shaffer's and a missing doctor, and my day has been delightful."

"I heard about those. What's the story on the doctor? I don't know him. Is he new?"

"He's temporary. One of those locum things."

"*Locum tenens.*" He smiled.

"Yeah, that." She shrugged. "Anyway, he was apparently grabbed outside the ER."

"How do you know that?" Simon asked.

"Marla Jackson. She saw it go down."

"And you believe her? Her brain makes up all kinds of stuff. What's left of it."

Cassie sensed her blood pressure rise. She had always felt protective of Marla even back in school. Maybe even more so now that Marla was vulnerable and apparently spiraling toward total destruction. From drugs or from something even more painful, she didn't see Marla being around long. So, when a prick like Simon piled on, her hackles elevated. She considered hurling her desk phone at him but refrained.

"I do believe her. She saw two guys, a black SUV, and a gun. They shoved Dr. Buckner in the back and took off." Cassie opened her palms. "She seemed pretty clear on what she saw."

"She recognize the guys?"

Cassie gave a head shake. "One tall with a ponytail, the other shorter. That's about it."

Simon seemed to mull that over. "I hear there're a couple of private types here looking for him," Simon said. "The doctor."

"Hired by his father. A doc over in North Carolina."

"That didn't take long. What, it's only been a day, actually less, since all this happened?"

"Apparently the father had some military connections that led him to Bobby Cain and Harper McCoy. That's the two you're referring to."

"Bet that makes you happy. Having a couple of interlopers sniffing around your case."

"I'll take all the help I can get on this mess. Besides, I get the impression these two are pretty clever."

"Where're they from? North Carolina?"

"Nashville. Apparently they have some spook-world military background."

Simon shifted forward in the chair, stared at his clasped hands for a few seconds, then looked up. "What actually happened over at the Finleys?"

"Looks like an execution more than anything else. They lined them up in the living room and shot them on the sofa. Sort of looked like the Brady Bunch, only with bullet holes and blood."

Simon smiled. "You sure paint a picture."

"Trust me, that doesn't do it justice." She shrugged. "But they didn't exactly get away unscathed."

"Oh?"

"One of the bad guys apparently caught a bullet from Tommy."

Simon leaned back, smoothed his tie. "You're thinking all these are connected? I mean, someone kills the Finleys, one gets shot, they grab the doctor, hit the pharmacy to get whatever they might need to fix things? Something like that?"

"You're pretty smart for an attorney."

He shook his head. "You're funny."

"I try."

"Tommy's my client," Simon said.

"Really? I didn't know that." She made no attempt to hide the sarcasm in her voice.

Truth was Tommy Finley had been a sore spot between them for a while now. She had popped Tommy for possession a couple of times and a third for distribution. Simon had gotten him off. The first two were small fines, easily paid from his drug proceeds; the latter, the distribution, led to Simon humiliating her before the judge. Illegal search and seizure crap. The fact that Tommy had tried to sell his poison to a couple of sixteen-year-old high school girls on school property didn't seem to bother Simon. Judge William Hauser either, for that matter. Simon and Hauser went way back and were a bit too cozy for Cassie's tastes. Their relationship smacked of bribery, or payola, or whatever the hell you wanted to call it. Something else she could never prove.

He raised his hands. "Let's not get into that again."

"Wouldn't dream of it." She leaned back in her chair. "But this time your client just might have gotten his entire family murdered."

"So this wasn't just a crazy random thing? The Finleys?"

"Still won't admit your client was into the drug scene?"

"Not my place to judge."

Her smile was not a friendly one. "You have Hauser for that."

He leaned forward, elbows on his knees, and seemed to examine his shoes. His expensive Italian shoes. "John and Martha were clients, too."

"I didn't know that."

"Nothing big. Just wills and estate stuff."

"Sorry for your loss."

"That's not what I meant."

"I'm sure your practice can take the hit. No pun intended."

"Aren't we in a pissy mood today?"

"Pissy hardly seems strong enough." She forked her fingers through her hair. "Actually, I'm furious. To think that Tommy, a scumbag that should have been in jail, brought this horror to his family is beyond anything I could even consider forgiving."

"Forgiving? You're laying this at my feet?"

She shrugged. "From where I sit you're the reason Tommy was still in business."

Another shake of his head and he stood. "I hope your day gets better."

"It won't."

He hesitated as if searching for a comeback but apparently found none, so he left.

She leaned back again and stared at the ceiling. Why did she let him get to her? She knew better than to engage but he always seemed to push the wrong buttons. Something about his good looks that gave him special privileges. The fact that he was smart and a good attorney and had smacked her upside the head a few times in court certainly didn't help. Stir all that into the soup of a shitty day and, well...yes, she was in a pissy mood.

Still, she needed to learn to keep her goddamn mouth shut. Why provoke a snake? Except that viscerally it felt good and made her smile inside. Take that, Simon.

She sat up and eyed the stack of papers before her. She was in no mood to tackle them right now but a couple of things couldn't wait. She dug back in.

Ten minutes later, Poppy looked in. "A Bobby Cain just called. Said he had some info for you."

She glanced at her phone. None of the lights were blinking. "He's not on the phone?"

"Said they were on the way over. He just wanted to make sure you were here."

CHAPTER 33

Buck removed the bandage from Dennie's wound. Thankfully, it still looked clean. A little redness, slight swelling, but no true evidence of infection. A borderline miracle considering the situation.

"I'll clean this again," Buck said. Dennie gave him a groggy nod. "Might hurt a little but I'll get it done as quickly as possible."

"Go ahead," Dennie said. "I can handle it." His lips were dry, his tongue thick from the pain meds and sedatives.

Buck worked quickly, finally applying a fresh bandage. "All done."

Dennie had dozed, so he said nothing.

"What's the story, Doc?" Dalton asked as he walked in the room. He held a cup of coffee. "He doing okay?"

"Better. But not out of the woods by any stretch."

"When can we move him?"

"If you mean all the way to Memphis, it'll be a while yet."

"Seems to me he did okay rambling around the hills. Now that you've fixed him up, I'd think traveling would be safer."

"Yeah, well, that was then, this is now. He's been opened up and has had a kidney taken out. Moving him could lead to significant bleeding and he's lost a lot of blood already. Here, unlike in a hospital, I don't have anything to replace it with." Buck waved a hand. "Bottom line is that he can't really afford to lose any more."

"So, when?"

"It's like I said before. A couple of days at best," Buck said. "That's if all goes well."

Dalton's expression reflected his exasperation, and anger. "Are you pulling my chain?"

"What do you mean?"

"Dragging your feet on all this. Trying to buy time."

"Why would I need to buy time?" That rocked Dalton back a bit. Good. Buck continued, "You brought me here to help Dennie and that's what I'm doing. As best I can under the circumstances. If you think you can do a better job, then go ahead." Buck nodded toward Dennie. Dalton's eyes narrowed; his jaw pumped. "Dennie's best chance to get through this is to let me do what I'm good at and for you not to make any rash decisions that could put him in jeopardy."

Dalton hesitated as if considering what Buck had said. He probably wasn't used to being told what to do. Wasn't he always the guy in charge? But right now, Buck could sense his uncertainty. Something that made Dalton uncomfortable and something Buck might be able to use to his advantage.

Finally, Dalton spoke. "I'm heading into town. You need anything else? For Dennie?"

"An ambulance to take him to the hospital."

"You're a funny guy." Dalton stepped closer, now next to Dennie's bed, his dark eyes almost physically piercing. "But don't try anything funny while I'm gone. Jessie might seem nice and all but trust me, he'll do what's necessary."

"I'm sure he will." Buck didn't break away from Dalton's gaze, refusing to give him the ground between them. "Besides, what could I possibly do? He has a gun and I have no idea where I am."

"This is a small town. Bet you know your way around pretty good."

"I've been here barely a week. I haven't even figured out where to take my laundry yet."

Dalton hesitated, and then nodded. "I won't be gone long. Make sure my brother's okay." He walked out of the room.

A minute later, Buck could hear Dalton talking to Jessie. Their voices filtered through the AC duct. Buck had used this before to eavesdrop and when he inspected the layout earlier he saw that the grate, high up near the ceiling in the bedroom, was directly across from a similar one in the kitchen. This connection made their conversation amazingly clear. He moved closer.

Dalton: "I'm going to call our guy and bring him up to speed. See what he can do to help here."

Jessie: "Our guy in Memphis or the one local?"

Dalton: "Both. We need to know what the cops around here know, what they're doing, and get things set up in Memphis for when Dennie can travel."

Jessie: "Sounds good."

Dalton: "Not sure how far I'll have to go to find a signal."

Jessie: "There'll be one in town."

Dalton: "Yeah. But I need to talk with our guy before I go rolling in there. You just never know what the cops know."

Jessie: "How could they know anything? I mean, we didn't run across no one."

Dalton: "Problem is, witnesses pop up in the strangest places."

Jessie: "I guess."

Dalton: "But if all is okay I'll slide into town and get supplies."

Jessie: "We got lots of food. The cupboards are full of all kinds of stuff."

Dalton: "Couldn't hurt to have more. The doc said we'll be here a couple more days."

Jessie: "Get me some Cheetos. I love Cheetos."

Dalton: "I'll take care of the supplies. You stay focused on the situation. Don't let your guard down. I think our doc is craftier than he seems."

Jessie: "Don't worry. I got this covered."

Dalton: "Keep it all calm. But if he tries anything, don't hesitate to kill him."

Jessie: "What about Dennie? If I have to shoot the doc, what happens to him?"

Dalton: "We'll cross that bridge when and if we have to."

Jessie: "Okay."

Dalton: "I mean it. Don't take this guy lightly. Don't blink if push comes to shove. Take him down."

CHAPTER 34

Dalton climbed in the SUV and cranked it. He sat, staring through the rain-slicked windshield. His mind sorted through everything that had happened over the past 24 hours, trying to make some sense of it. It should have gone smoothly. In and out. Done deal. But Tommy Finley had altered the script by playing the hero. Did he honestly think he could win a gun fight against him and Jessie and Dennie? Why couldn't he simply have died like a soldier? Take the hit he deserved?

Desperate people do desperate things. Now he had to deal with the fallout.

He looked back toward the house. He could see Jessie through the window, pouring a cup of coffee. He had mixed feelings about leaving Jessie in charge. Dennie he would have trusted, but Jessie? Not all that bright. To Dalton, the wrong guy got shot. Had it been Jessie things would have been much simpler. Put a bullet in his head and dump him in a ravine. Another done deal. But, Dennie? Dennie's family.

He also had concerns about the doc: Was he lying about Dennie's condition? Was he buying time? Did he suspect he wasn't going to survive this? Probably. He knew their names, what they looked like. He was a smart kid. He'd have to know what was what. Which would make him desperate and maybe make him consider some unpredicted stuff. Like Tommy had done.

He sighed. He had no choice. He had to make these calls. Jessie couldn't do that. Only he could. Which meant leaving Jessie in charge was the only option.

At least the place they had found was perfect. High up the slopes, deep into the forest, and several turns from any major road. The house was well hidden by a thick stand of pines and gums and other trees he had no name for. Plus, it sat at the end of a long gravel and dirt path that was so overgrown with weeds and Johnson's grass that it looked more like an abandoned trail than the entrance to someone's home. Obviously, the owners wanted privacy. So did Dalton.

He put the SUV in gear and headed down the drive. The central strip of ragged grass scraped against the undercarriage. Drizzle peppered the windshield. He flicked on the wipers.

Took two miles to find a signal that was usable. Three bars should be enough. He pulled off the road into a rectangular graveled area that served as an overlook for the deep forested valley. The area was small and ended at a grassy strip that sloped gently downward to where the terrain dropped precipitously. He tugged his cap down, and climbed out. He dialed the first number.

"Speak to me."

Frankie Campanella was a man of few words. He also was not someone to fuck with. No hedging things. Straight up true story was the only thing that worked.

"We got problems," Dalton said.

"Spell it out."

Dalton paced, the gravel crunching beneath his shoes. "Things started out good at Finley's place. All the targets eliminated. But then Dennie got shot."

"How?"

"Tommy had a gun hidden in the sofa. He got off a single round. His last ever, but it caught Dennie in the gut."

"He alive?"

"Yeah." Dalton told him of kidnapping Dr. Buck, visiting the pharmacy, finding the secluded house, the surgery on Dennie.

"Pretty clever move."

"It's all we had."

"Dennie going to make it?" Frankie asked.

"Looks like it."

"The doc? He still with us?"

"He is. I think Dennie'll need him another day or so."

"I take it that means you aren't rolling this way."

"The doc says two more days. At least. But he might be gaming me. Hard to tell."

"Maybe simply take him out and roll."

Fuck you, Frankie. It ain't your brother the doc is keeping alive. That's what Dalton thought. What he said was, "Maybe. Not sure yet. Don't want to jeopardize Dennie."

"It's your call."

"Right now, I think we're tucked in pretty good. Definitely off the radar. But I'll talk to our guy over here. He'll be in the loop and know what the story in town is."

"Keep me posted." Frankie disconnected the call.

Dalton tugged down his cap and zipped his jacket. He dialed the next number. The man answered on the third ring.

"It's Dalton."

"You responsible for this shit storm?"

"Unavoidable."

"What the hell happened?"

Dalton went through the highlights.

"Jesus, the Finleys, Shaffer, a doctor kidnapped. You're like a rolling plague."

"Like I said, unavoidable," Dalton said. "Shit happens. Now we have to get out of it."

"Where are you?"

"In the hills holed up in a secluded cabin."

"They're looking everywhere for you."

"What do they know?" Dalton asked.

"Let's see. A big black SUV grabbed the doc. Two men. One with a ponytail. That enough for you?"

"A witness?"

"Yeah. A druggie named Marla Jackson. She was shooting up in the park across the street and saw the whole thing."

"Shit."

"Oh, at least that."

A pair of crows dropped into a nearby pine tree and began

fussing and cawing. Dalton glanced their way. "I was going to drive in for some supplies. I guess that's off the table."

"Don't even be on the road. They're literally searching the entire county."

"Unfortunately, I'm sitting on the side of the road right now. I had to move down the hill to get cell service."

"Crawl back underground. If you need supplies, I can get some to you."

"We're good," Dalton said.

"What's the plan?"

"Lay low a couple more days and then cut and run to Memphis."

"If they don't find you first."

"The cops aren't all that good, are they?" Dalton asked.

"Good enough. And a couple of P.I. types are snooping around, too."

"Who?"

"Someone the doc's father hired. Bobby Cain and Harper McCoy. Seem to have some sort of military background. Exactly what, I'm not sure."

Dalton didn't know what to make of that except that the posse was growing. Never a good thing.

"I'm starting to regret ever opening up a shop over here," Dalton said.

"Except the money's been good, hasn't it?"

"Not this good." Dalton sighed. "With Tommy gone, I guess it's a moot point now."

"What about his partner?"

"Jason Epps?"

"Yeah."

"Never met him," Dalton said. "Just know he exists. Don't really know anything about him."

"He'll be okay. He's more or less like Tommy, but less ambitious. I'll talk with him. See where his head's at."

"Sit back for right now," Dalton said. "I'll have to talk to Memphis before we move on that."

"He'll be looking for supplies."

"He'll have to make do for now."

"Might press him to look elsewhere. Like Tommy's contact

over in Knoxville."

Dalton considered that. Frankie just might be willing to let that happen. Close up over here in this shitty little village. Let this Epps dude go his own way. But Frankie hated to lose. Especially to snot-nosed punks. He'd seen it before. Hell, he'd done it before. Whacked that kid that tried to push meth from an alley near Beale Street. Frankie's turf.

"If I get the go ahead from Memphis, I'll have a chat with him," Dalton said. "Impress on him the wisdom of not doing a fucking thing. Maybe paint a picture for him. One where he has a bunch of bullet holes in his lungs."

"Don't do anything that'll drag me into this."

"You're already in it."

An exasperated sigh. "Don't I know it."

"Just deposit your cash and keep your mouth shut. And your eyes and ears open."

"Don't I always?"

"For now, sit tight. Give me the Epps guy's number. I'll handle him."

CHAPTER 35

"Mama B's amazing," Harper said as she ended her call.

"She is all that and more."

Beatrice Baker, affectionately known as Mama B. US Naval Intelligence icon. Now retired, she still held a host of dark alley connections, meaning she was able to look under rugs others didn't even know existed. Like someone's cell phone, social media, entire life. The 'someone' in question here: Jason Epps.

"What'd she find?" Cain asked.

"Unfortunately, not much. She dug into both Tommy Finley's and Jason Epp's phones. Similar vanilla picture for each. Family, friends, Facebook, Twitter, Instagram, Snapchat. The usual mindless stuff. And of course each other. Both buy a lot of music on iTunes."

"Got to spend all that drug money on something."

"No calls to Memphis or Knoxville," Harper said.

"Means Jason just might have been telling us the truth. That Tommy Finley handled the business and Jason simply distributed for him."

"That's what it smells like." Harper slid her phone into her jacket pocket. "I'd bet Tommy had another phone. A burner. His business connection."

"I'd be surprised if he didn't."

"Where is it?" Harper asked.

"I suspect the bad guys took it and destroyed it," Cain said. "Only thing that makes sense."

"But things have morphed with Tommy gone. The operation just might fall to Jason."

"Which means more communication. Maybe with the guys upstream."

"Maybe Jason isn't bright enough to use a safe phone," Harper said.

"Let's hope." Cain turned into the police station's parking lot. "He doesn't impress me as a rocket scientist."

"I suspect the only rocket he rides is the crystal meth in his pocket."

They climbed out and hurried inside through the misty rain. Harper saw a young woman sitting behind the reception desk. Dark hair, middle part, large eyes. Her name tag read "Poppy." She looked up and smiled.

"Can I help you?"

Harper gave her their names, saying they were there to see Chief Crowe. She responded that she was Poppy Phelps.

"You the two looking for Dr. Buckner?" Poppy asked.

Harper nodded. "That's us."

"It's just awful." She gave a head shake. "Things like this don't happen around here."

"They unfortunately happen everywhere."

"Is Chief Crowe here?" Cain asked.

"Oh yes, she's expecting you." She picked up the phone and punched the com line. "Chief, they're here." Pause. "Okay." She pointed toward the hallway to her left. "Right down that way."

Once they were seated, Cassie spoke, "You said you had something for me."

"Jason Epps," Harper said. "We found him over in the park."

"His office."

"We saw Marla making a buy."

"Oh?" Cassie asked.

"She scurried into the trees when she saw us pull up," Cain said.

"And Jason? What'd he have to say?"

"He was reluctant," Harper said, "at first. Until Bobby convinced him otherwise."

"Not sure I want to know how that went down," Cassie said.

"Let's just say Bobby can be convincing."

"I was very polite," Cain said.

"Yeah. Right up until you threatened to cut his eye out." Cassie's eyes widened.

"I didn't touch him," Cain said with raised hands.

"It's the thought that counts," Harper said. "But in the end, I think we have a motive for all this. It's just as we thought. Tommy and Jason are hooked up with someone out of Memphis. But Tommy got clever. Found a better bargain over in Knoxville."

"The Memphis folks took offense," Cassie said.

"Big time," Cain said.

"Memphis is a shithole," Cassie said. "Used to be a fine city. Now? It's a criminal cesspool." She picked up a ballpoint, clicked it a couple of times. "Wish they'd keep their miscreants over there."

"Apparently at least three of them came here," Harper said. "The two kidnappers Marla saw, and the one that caught a bullet. Unfortunately, the clock is ticking on Dr. Buckner."

Cassie nodded. "Yep. They'll kill him for sure once he's no longer needed."

"Which means we have to find them," Harper said. "Pronto."

Cassie sighed. "I got folks out everywhere. It's a tough slog. Too many places to look." She clicked the ballpoint again. "How'd you find out all this? About Jason Epp's phone?"

Harper smiled. "We have resources."

"Care to elaborate?"

"Someone who has access."

"Access?"

"To anything and everything."

Cassie clicked the pen a couple of more times, tossed it on her desk. "Who are you guys exactly?"

"We told you," Cain said. "Private investigators."

"Yeah right. I've known a few P.I.s in my career. You two don't exactly fit the mold. So tell me, what's your real background?"

"Can't say."

"Just a thumbnail would help."

Cain glanced at Harper, shrugged.

"Okay," Harper said. "Bobby was regular Army. Sort of. More

a Ranger than anything else. He did special ops for every branch. Things off the books. Things that required getting into and out of places, completing a mission, and leaving behind no footprints."

"What kind of missions?" Cassie asked.

"That's the part we can't talk about," Cain said.

Cassie leaned back in her chair and laced her fingers over her abdomen. "The kind where the target was less healthy when you left than when you arrived?"

"It's a big bad world out there," Cain said.

"Particularly in some of the world's desert communities," Harper added.

Cassie nodded, considered that. Looked a Harper. "What about you?"

"I ran some of the ops."

"Sounds like the CIA to me."

Harper shrugged.

Cain leaned forward. "This is what we do. We track people. We find them. We solve issues like this."

"It's the solving that could be problematic," Cassie said.

"Nothing that'll blow back on you," Cain said.

Cassie gave a half-smile. "I will say that confidence isn't one of your shortcomings."

"We've done this in environments much more hostile than Tanner's Crossroads."

"Against guys much more skilled and better trained than a handful of drug dealers," Harper added.

"But aren't the amateurs the ones who always screw things up?" Cassie asked.

"That's true," Harper said. "That's why missions have to be fluid and adaptable."

"Let me ask you something," Cain said. "You didn't find a second phone on Tommy, did you?"

"No, just the one he had in his pocket. An iPhone."

"The one we know about," Harper said. "But we suspect he had a second one. A burner most likely."

"And you're thinking the killers took it?" Cassie said.

Harper nodded. "It would be a connection to them, and they'd of course know about it, so...."

Cassie sighed again. "I'm thinking these guys are pretty clever."

"They are," Cain said. "Let's hope they think they're smarter than they are."

Cassie forked the fingers of one hand through her short-cropped, blonde hair. "So, what's your next move?"

"Jason Epps might be the key to finding these guys," Cain said.

"We've got a track on him," Harper said.

"How so?"

"We're in his phone."

"That makes no sense."

Harper smiled. "We hacked it with a text. Over in the park. In the, what...twenty minutes it took to get from there to here, we found out what I told you about his phone. Tommy's, too."

"Your mysterious source?" Cassie asked.

Harper nodded.

"Okay, but if his phone is clean and has no odd communications, how does that help?"

"The Memphis boys came here to deliver a message," Harper said. "They did. But they also severed their distribution line over here. They'll want to reestablish it. Money is money. That puts Jason in the middle of it."

"You think they'll contact him?"

"Probably."

Cassie leaned forward. "They might just kill him."

"They might." Cain nodded. "Unless the money here is good. Then they'd want to keep it going."

Using an index finger, Cassie gave the pen a couple of spins. "The heat this has generated might make them shy."

"It might," Harper said.

"Sounds like I need to have a sit down with young Jason Epps," Cassie said.

"Any pressure on him would be good. Make him nervous. Make him do something stupid."

"If I can find him."

Cain smiled and pulled out his cell. He punched in a number and placed it on speaker. It was answered after two rings.

"Yeah."

"Jason. Bobby Cain here. Chief Crowe wants to see you."

"Yeah, right. Like I'm going to put up with her BS."

"BS?" Cassie said.

Silence.

"Yeah, we're in her office," Cain said. "Now get moving."

"I'm busy. Got things to do."

"It wasn't a request," Harper said. More silence. "Don't make us drag your sorry ass over here."

"You can't do that. I have rights."

"Actually, you don't," Harper said. "Not in our world."

"Chief?" Jason said. "They can't do this."

"Twenty minutes," Cassie said. "That should give you enough time."

Cain disconnected the call.

"That broke about a dozen laws," Cassie said.

Cain shrugged.

"But it sure felt good." Cassie smiled. "You guys want to hang around for the show?"

"Should be fun," Harper said.

"Good. I want to make him squirm."

CHAPTER 36

The drizzly rain intensified. Water dripped from the bill of Dalton's cap as he walked around the SUV to the driver's side. He slammed a fist against the roof.

"Goddammit."

This was becoming a true clusterfuck. A witness. Now the cops were looking for him and the SUV. Time to get undercover before another clueless citizen saw him. He scanned the road, forward and back. All clear. He yanked open the door but before he could step in, he heard the unmistakable rumble of a car engine and the whine of tires on wet pavement, coming up the hill toward him. A black sedan rounded the corner. He tilted his head downward, shielding his face with the cap's bill.

The car slowed.

Keep going, he thought.

It didn't. The vehicle pulled across the road and stopped twenty feet from where he stood. The door creaked open and a man stepped out, rounding the front of the car.

A cop.

Fuck me.

"How you doing?" the man said.

"Fine."

He noticed the officer's hand rested on the service revolver on his right hip. Dalton felt the weight of his own weapon tucked into the small of his back.

"I'm Officer Duckworth. And you?"

"Sammy. Sammy Foster."

"Where you headed?"

"Looking for a friend's place. Got a little lost."

The officer nodded. "Easy to do up here." He took a few steps but stopped fifteen feet away. A cop move. Never get too close.

"Is there a problem, Officer?" Dalton asked.

"Don't know. Is there?"

"Not that I see."

"Good, good. Mind if I see your license?"

"What for?" Dalton asked.

"We're looking for a car. One like yours."

"Mine? Really? Why?"

"Just something we're investigating." He nodded again. "Your license?"

"It's in my vehicle."

"Why don't you get it for me? I'll run your plates in the meantime." He turned toward his cruiser.

"You don't need to do that."

The cop stopped, turned back. "It's just routine." He gave a quick nod.

"I don't think so." Dalton withdrew his Glock and shot the man in the right side of his forehead. The cop dropped like a stringless marionette.

"Fuck, fuck, fuck." Dalton scanned the road again. Up and down. Quiet.

He dragged the dead man off the road and dumped him in the backseat of his sedan. He searched his pockets, found what he was looking for. His cell phone. He dropped it on the gravel and crushed it with his boot. He picked up the fractured device and tossed it into the backseat, where Duckworth lay. He climbed behind the wheel, spun it around and drove it to the edge of the gravel where the grassy strip sloped downwards, only the deep valley beyond.

Cop cars have radios, GPS, all kinds of tracking crap. Probably even in this Podunk town. Dalton lifted the hood and disconnected the battery. That should take care of that.

He reached through the open driver's door, released the emergency brake, and settled the gear shift into neutral. He grasped the windshield frame and, using his weight, rolled it forward. It picked up speed until it tipped over the edge and disappeared into the valley. He heard the crashing of trees and shrubs, the scraping of metal. It seemed to go on forever but ended with a sudden loud bang. He walked to the edge and looked down. A couple of saplings were down, several shrubs trashed, but the car wasn't visible. The silence was heavy, only the sound of tumbling water far below.

He hurried back to his SUV and climbed in. The rain was now harder. He called Frankie Campanella again.

"Change of plans," Dalton said.

"Tell me."

"A cop. He saw me on the roadside making calls. I had to take care of him."

"And?"

"His corpse is currently residing in his cruiser at the bottom of a ravine."

"They can track cop cars."

"Taken care of," Dalton said.

"What's your plan?"

"We have to move. Get the fuck back to Memphis."

"Dennie okay to travel?"

Now he's concerned?

"No choice," Dalton said. "We'll have to risk it. I need a couple of guys to transport Dennie."

"Why not simply leave? Now?"

"There was apparently a witness to us taking the doc. She saw the SUV. They're out looking for it. That's why the cop stopped and asked questions. So, we'll have to wait for night to run."

"Why do I need to send other guys over?"

"I think we should take care of the witness. I also want to have a little chat with this Jason Epps guy. See if we can stay up and running over here or if dear old Jason's another liability."

"This is starting to slide downhill."

As far as Dalton saw it, things were well down the hill and picking up speed. Case in point: the parallel depressions the cop's car had mashed into the parking area's grass perimeter, pointing toward the ravine where a dead cop now lay. A fucking cop. That ramped things up considerably and for sure made Frankie nervous. The last thing Dalton needed was to piss off Frankie. Worse, have him lose confidence. What should have been a simple hit had gone to shit because of Tommy Finley. A fucking gun in a sofa for Christ's sake.

"It's covered," Dalton said. "I can't drive this SUV around in daylight any longer. I've already attracted one cop. We'll hunker down until nightfall and then we'll be ready to move."

"Okay."

"Give me a safe number. Tell them I'll call at nine."

"Why not give me the address?"

"Don't know it. I just know where the cabin is. I had to drive a couple of miles to get a signal. I'll call at nine and hook up with them. Just have them hang somewhere near Tanner's Crossroads."

"Got it," Frankie said.

"Not in town. Somewhere west of it. One of the guys can then run to Memphis with Dennie. Me, Jessie, and whoever you send can hang around and take care of things."

"I'll send your crew. Myrick, Harris, and Navarro."

"Not sure I'll need all of them."

"Call it overkill. I don't think you can have too many hands on deck. With the way this little adventure has played out so far, further complications aren't exactly out of the question."

Frankie was pissed. Never a good thing. "Okay," Dalton said.

"What about the doc?" Frankie asked.

"Won't need him any longer."

"Might be wise to bring him along. In case something medical comes up with Dennie. We can take care of his disposal here."

"Good idea."

"I have one every now and again," Frankie said, no attempt to hide his sarcasm.

CHAPTER 37

Dennie was restless. His fever had jumped to 102 and he appeared flushed, even through his anemic pallor. His lungs were clear and his breathing comfortable and unlabored. Buck continued to hope it was a simple post-op fever and not the early signs of an infection. Not that an infection would be a surprise given the slap-dash nature of the surgery he had performed.

What if Dennie slid into shock? Buck had no real way to handle that. He didn't have the vasopressors or the steroids or the spectrum of antibiotics he would need to turn such a tide. A rampant infection, sepsis, would take Dennie out in short order.

Where would that leave Buck? The answer to that was clear. Dalton had all but said so to Jessie earlier. What were his words? "Take him down." No ambiguity there.

Which meant that escape was his only option. The how and when were guesswork, and a matter of opportunity. Not to mention luck, lots of luck.

Buck had a plan. Not much of one, and it had a razor-thin margin for error. The first step was isolating Jessie. No doubt the weak link in the duo. But was he weak enough?

Buck gave Dennie another two milligrams of morphine to settle him and then walked into the kitchen. Jessie sat at the table, eating an apple.

"How's he doing?" Jessie asked.

"Not bad, not good."

"What does that mean?"

"It means he needs to be in an ICU."

"Yeah, well, that ain't going to happen." Jessie took the final bite off the apple, stood, and walked to the sink. He opened the cabinet beneath and tossed the core into the waste basket.

"Look, Jessie, I know he isn't your brother, but I suspect he's your friend. It's up to you to help me help him."

Jessie poured a cup of coffee and returned to his seat at the table. "That's Dalton's call."

Of course it was. Everything was Dalton's call. So common sense and decency wasn't working. Time for another approach.

"How'd you guys get in this mess?" Buck asked.

Jessie stared at him over the rim of the cup he cradled. "Don't matter. Why're you asking?"

"I'm just curious."

"Be curious about something else."

"My feeling is that you got yourself into something more than you anticipated," Buck said. "Like maybe you had a job to do and it all went wrong."

Jessie nodded.

Well, that was something.

Buck continued, "Did anyone else get shot?"

"You ask a lot of questions."

Buck smiled. As friendly as he could. "My father says that all the time."

"He a doc, too?"

"He is. Over in North Carolina."

"And you're here. Didn't want to stay under Daddy's wing."

"Very good," Buck said. "You read it correctly."

"So, what? You came here to this little dead end town to practice?"

"Not exactly. I work with a *locum tenens* outfit."

Jessie took a sip. "What the hell is that?"

"It's Latin," Buck said. "Basically, I travel around covering practices temporarily. Mostly ER work. Here one of the physicians is out on maternity leave so I'm filling in for a couple of months until she returns."

Jessie smiled. "Sort of a traveling salvation show."

Buck laughed. Keep it light and friendly. "You might say."

Jessie placed the cup on the table. He ran a finger around the rim. "I've got to say…what you did, operating on Dennie, that was impressive."

"As was your help. You did good. Very good."

Another smile. "Just glad I didn't throw up."

"You wouldn't be the first med student that did."

"Except I ain't no student."

Buck shrugged. "Could've fooled me. You did better than most."

Jessie leaned back, stretched, extending his arms over his head. "Maybe I should go to medical school."

"Maybe. But first you'll have to learn to focus on the patient's well-being and not your own."

Jessie flashed a look. "What the hell does that mean?"

"It means doctors don't hang around and wait for patients to die. They do things to prevent that."

"If he does, it's on you, not me."

Buck nodded. "You really believe that?"

"What the hell else should I believe?"

"Look, Jessie. You did a great job. You jumped right in, put aside all your fears and anxieties, and helped save Dennie. I couldn't have done it without you. That's the truth. But now? Taking it to the next step; getting Dennie where he needs to be? You're blocking the road to that."

"Not me. It's Dalton's call."

"He's gone. You're in charge."

"So what? You expect me to load up Dennie on my back and run him down the hill?"

"I'm sure there're other cabins not far from here. Ones where the phones still work."

Jessie glanced toward the window, the world beyond. "Like I said, that's up to Dalton."

"But he isn't here."

Then Buck heard the unmistakable sound of a car engine coming up the drive. The SUV swung past the windows and into the backyard.

"He is now."

CHAPTER 38

After ending the call with Jason, Cain, Harper, and Cassie walked over to Spivey's Coffee Shop to grab a cup before jumping in Jason's face. The rain more a light shower than the earlier drizzle. Spivey's was quiet, two people in line, a couple at one table, and at another near the window, a blond man in a stylish tan suit and yellow tie, newspaper open in front of him. Cain could only see half his profile but when he turned the page his full face came into view.

Cain did a double take, his gait faltering. Harper, too. They glanced at each other. She had also seen it. The unsettling resemblance to a man they'd crossed paths with many years ago. Not so much a crossing as an invasion. Of his home. By them.

It was nearly a year before the family was taken down by the FBI and Cain and Harper were hauled off to the orphanage. Cain had been eleven, Harper twelve. The scam, hatched and planned by Uncle Mo, had unfolded in two parts. First, the theft of a dozen cases of Girl Scout cookies from the residential home of the den mother, troop leader, whatever she had been called. Uncle Mo had discovered that she took in the shipments and then the girls would come by and collect boxes of mints and shortbreads and whatever before hitting the streets to make sales. While Harper stood in the front door, asking question after question about maybe joining the troop, Cain and Uncle Mo hauled the cases from the screened-in back porch to the van idling in the alley,

Aunt Dixie behind the wheel.

Phase one complete.

Then the sales scam, as Uncle Mo called it, rolled into motion. After purchasing an old Girl Scout uniform, complete with badges, from a discount store, Harper dressed for her part. Innocently selling cookies at the front door while Cain came through the back and feasted on the spoils. Jewelry, cash, whatever he could quickly find and carry away. The third town and thirteenth home they had visited was where the man lived. The one whose doppelgänger sat in Spivey's Coffee Shop. Harper had seen him face to face, Cain in a framed picture in his master bedroom. While Harper performed her routine, acting all flustered, confused, bordering on tears because she didn't "know how to do this," the man and his wife comforted her, and bought a dozen boxes.

After a bird-call whistle from Aunt Dixie, Cain ascended a rose trellis to the second floor and entered the bedroom through an open French door. Ten minutes later he descended with four watches, including two gold Rolexes, a pocket full of rings and necklaces, one with a nice emerald, another a string of pearls, and over eight hundred dollars from the man's wallet. That's where the photo was. Above the dresser. The man and his wife smiling at him as he folded the cash into his back pocket.

"Cassie," the man said, folding his newspaper.

"Simon."

"Anything new?"

"You mean in the last hour?"

The man shrugged.

"This is Simon Greene," Cassie said. "Our local big-shot barrister." She nodded toward Cain and Harper. "Bobby Cain and Harper McCoy."

Simon stood. They shook hands. Even close up, the resemblance was uncanny.

"You must be the investigators who're looking for Dr. Buckner," Greene said.

"We are," Harper said.

"I take it you haven't found him yet."

"We're working on it."

Greene gave a quick nod, then said to Cassie, "Anything new

on the Finley murders?"

"Not much."

He examined her. "There is but you're not going to tell me, are you?"

"Probably not. It being an ongoing investigation and all." Cassie shrugged. "Call it killer-victim privilege."

"She can be difficult," Greene said, glancing at Cain. "In case you haven't figured that out yet."

"Just using language you'll understand." Cassie yanked her head toward Greene. "Simon's an attorney. Tommy Finley's attorney in fact," Cassie said. "The one that's kept him out of jail all these years."

"She never misses an opportunity to jab me about it."

"You're lucky I haven't jabbed you with a sharp stick."

Greene smiled. "That would be police brutality."

Cassie raised an eyebrow. "I'd take off my badge first." She smiled. "So it'd simply be a civil issue."

"You see what I have to put up with?" Greene said. "And we're not even in a courtroom." He glanced at his watch. A gold Rolex. "Speaking of court." He nodded. "Nice meeting you both." Another nod. "Cassie." He lifted his briefcase and the folded newspaper, tucking it beneath one arm, and he was gone.

"That was weird," Harper said. She spoke softly but apparently not softly enough.

"What was?" Cassie asked.

"He reminds me of someone we knew when we were kids."

"A family friend?"

"More a client," Cain said. He looked at Harper.

"Of our Uncle Mo's," Harper added. "Handsome guy."

"He is," Cassie said. "If you don't believe it, just ask him."

"Yeah, I know the type," Harper said.

"He seemed nice enough to me," Cain said.

"Of course he did," Harper said. "You're a guy." She punched his arm, laughed.

"He's not all that nice," Cassie said. "He's a defense attorney, which makes him more reptile than mammal."

"He likes you," Harper said.

Cassie's brow furrowed. "How do you figure that?"

"Eyes, facial expression, body language. A few other tells."

"You conducting PsyOps here?"

Harper smiled. "Always."

"The truth is that Simon and I go way back. I was his senior prom date. My sophomore year."

"See, you make a cute couple," Harper said.

"I was his second choice. Marla Jackson was his first."

"Ouch."

Cassie smiled. "Back then, yeah. Now, not so much."

"There's a story there," Cain said.

"Mostly he keeps pursuing and I keep stiff arming."

CHAPTER 39

Earlier, after she had scored from Jason, Marla had hidden among the trees in the park. She found a spot, shielded by the sagging branches of a pine, from which she could see the black SUV. Where was Jason? Still beneath the tree where she had exchanged her forty bucks for the drugs that were now secreted in her backpack? Had he seen the SUV? More importantly, were the killers inside, hidden behind the tinted windows? Had they come to kill Jason? Or her? As she watched, the SUV sat, unmoving, like some mechanical creature. When the doors finally opened, she recognized the people who got out. Those two investigators who were looking for Dr. Buck. The ones who had bought her food.

She realized she'd been holding her breath and now exhaled sharply. Thank God it was them and not the pair that grabbed Dr. Buck. She never wanted to see them again but these two had seemed nice.

She crept forward toward the edge of the trees and watched the couple approach Jason. The conversation that followed seemed tense; the couple in charge, Jason appearing cowed. She felt good about that. Jason was an ass after all. But what was going on? What were they pressuring him about? Did Jason even know Dr. Buck? Did he have anything to do with his disappearance? Surely not.

But she couldn't think on that. Not when she needed to get well. She had melted deeper into the trees, settled against a tree trunk, spiked herself with a fix, and let the world fade away.

Now, back down to ground level, Marla ambled up Main Street, the afterglow of the smack still warming her veins. She collected a few bucks here and there before she ran into Jason. He came from the alley he often used for business. She stopped. Should she ask about what she had seen in the park? Curiosity ate at her, but she decided to wait and see if he would bring it up.

He did. "Those two people looking for the doctor harassed me in the park," he said.

"About what?"

"Everything. What happened with Tommy and his family. Mr. Shaffer." He looked at his shoes. "Like they thought I had something to do with it."

"Did you?" Marla asked.

"Fuck you, bitch." His eyes narrowed. "I don't know anything about it."

"Okay. Don't get all agro on me."

"But they think I know something. They also think that the whole thing was over drugs. Tommy and me selling. They think they'll reach out to me."

"Why?"

He shrugged. "Maybe so I can take over for Tommy."

"Would you do that? I mean, after what happened?"

He gave a head shake. "I don't know. They might not be none too happy if I don't."

"Couldn't you just say no? That you're quitting the business?"

She immediately regretted putting that idea in his head. If he did walk away, what would she do? He was now her only supply. Could she find another one? Who? Where? Why was this happening to her?

"Maybe," Jason said. "Or maybe they wouldn't accept that."

Marla considered that. Not that she felt sorry for Jason, but if he was in a bind she was too. "Where're you headed now?"

"Over to see the chief."

"Cassie? Why?"

"She wants to talk to me again. I already told her I didn't know anything but she wants to talk."

Was he lying? Something about his expression, his stance, his eyes darting away from her, suggested guilt. Did he kill Tommy and his family? Somehow she didn't think Jason had the balls for that. But could he have been involved on some level? He and Tommy worked together. She wasn't stupid. She knew drug dealers got killed all the time. And that's what Tommy and Jason were. Dealers.

"Is that true?" she asked. "You don't know who did this?"

"Why would you ask me that? You know I don't know nothing about it."

She shifted her backpack to a better position on her shoulder. "You and Tommy work together. I just thought…maybe…"

"Well, think something else. I don't know who or why or anything. Okay?"

"You never made any of the buys?"

"Tommy handled all that. I never met the guys who brought it over. That satisfy you?"

"I'm sorry. I was just wondering why you have to talk to Cassie again is all."

"It's what cops do. Ask the same shitty questions over and over. Like the answers will be different." He stepped near her. "So, if you need anything else, now would be a good time. I've got to drop by my place and empty things out before I stroll into the police station."

She still had a couple of rides left. But what if things went badly with Cassie? What if Jason was arrested? "Yeah," she said. "I could use some more."

"You got any money?"

"Thirty."

"Tell you what, I have a bit more than that on hand but I'll let you have it for the thirty."

"What's the catch?"

"Not that." He smiled. "Unless you want to."

She glared at him.

"It'll save me a trip by home. So, you want it? Bargain price?"

She nodded.

"Okay. Follow me."

They slipped between two stores and entered the alley behind Tish Sabbatini's dress shop. How many nights had she spent in this very spot? Huddled in the shrubbery or beneath the steps or behind the trash bin of one of the businesses that lined Main Street? This alley had been where she bought drugs, shot up, sold her body, and had been her home until Reverend John gave her a place with a roof, a heater, and a real bed.

"Let's have it," Jason said, his head swiveling back and forth, making sure no one was coming.

She handed him the thirty and he passed her two small plastic bags. He stuffed the bills in his pocket.

"Got to bounce," he said. "I'll see you later. Maybe in the park."

Marla entered Reverend John's, hoping to get up to her room for a taste of the meth. Maybe get some of the smack up inside and slide away into that wonderful oblivion. But when she walked through the front door, she saw John. His brow furrowed as he looked at her.

"What's the matter?" he asked.

"Nothing."

"You look like you saw a ghost."

"It's nothing."

He offered her a paternal smile. "Marla, you know you can't bullshit an old bullshitter. What's the problem?"

"Tommy Finley and his family." She shook her head. "I can't believe it."

John took a step forward. "Was he your supplier?"

"I don't do that stuff anymore."

"Marla, what am I going to do with you? You've bombed out of rehab, what, three times now? And as a former addict, I know what folks look and act like when they're using. So, was Tommy your dealer?"

She didn't respond because she didn't really know what to say. Her mind was locked on getting upstairs. Getting well.

"Okay," John said. "You don't have to tell me. Just don't bring any of that shit in here. You know the rules."

She nodded.

He sighed and massaged one temple. "City seems to be going to hell in a hand basket. Five folks murdered, a doctor missing. Did you talk with Luke Towry?"

"I did."

"And?"

"Looks like I might have a job," she lied. "As soon as my arm's better."

"Good."

She nodded and headed for the stairs. A job? She didn't see that happening. She hated lying to Reverend John, but really, was it a lie? She hadn't told Towry no. Not totally. Not yet.

CHAPTER 40

Buck saw the Navigator roll past the window and into the backyard, wipers churning against the increased rainfall. A minute later, Dalton came through the kitchen door and into the living/dining area, his jacket dripping on the hardwood floor. He looked at Buck, then Jessie, where he held his gaze for an extra beat. Back to Buck.

"How's my brother?" Dalton asked.

"Same as before. Sleeping right now."

Dalton jerked his head toward the bedroom. "Go check on him."

"I just did."

Dalton's eyes narrowed. "Do it again."

Buck raised his hands defensively. "No problem."

Inside the room, he saw Dennie, still asleep. He heard the door close behind him.

What was up? Dalton's face, his stance, his ushering Buck into this room, suggested that something had changed. Drastically so. But, what? Had he been seen in town? Recognized? Were the police on the way? If so, would this turn into a shootout, or a standoff? Either way Buck could become a hostage. But then, wasn't he already?

Buck positioned himself beneath the vent again. He could easily hear the rumble of Dalton's voice.

Jessie: "What are you saying? You shot a cop?"

Buck recoiled with a sharp intake of breath. He closed a hand over his mouth, fearing they had heard his gasp. Sound would travel both ways though the ducts. Apparently neither had as the conversation continued.

Dalton: "I had no choice. I think he made me. Or at least suspected the Navigator might be the SUV they're looking for. He was going to run my plates and I couldn't let that happen."

Jessie: "Jesus. Where'd this take place?"

Dalton: "Just down the hill a couple of miles."

Jessie: "When they find him they'll be all over this area."

Dalton: "They won't. At least not for a while. I dumped his car into a ravine so it's completely out of sight."

Jessie: "But they'll know where he was searching and start looking around here."

Dalton: "Probably."

Jessie: "Don't those cars have GPS stuff in them?"

Dalton: "Taken care of. His cell phone, too."

Jessie: "What are we going to do?"

Dalton: "As soon as it gets dark, we're out of here."

Buck felt his heart tick up a notch. If they were leaving, he was done. They'd kill him for sure. He looked toward the bedroom window. Was it time to run?

Footsteps approached. Buck stepped toward the bed, facing Dennie. The door opened.

"Get your ass out here," Dalton said.

Buck followed him. Dalton closed the door again.

"We got a problem," Dalton said, "and the solution is we're leaving tonight."

"I told you…" Buck began.

"Yeah, I know what you've been saying but I'm telling you how it is. Get my brother ready to move. Tonight."

"It's not safe," Buck said. "Not yet."

"It'll have to be. Do whatever you need to do but we're out of here."

"Okay," Buck said. "What about this? You guys go and leave me here with Dennie. I'll make sure he gets the care he needs."

Dalton's stare hardened. "This isn't a negotiation." His Glock appeared and he nestled the muzzle against Buck's chin. "Are you ready to listen?"

Buck nodded.

"Good." He lowered the weapon. "Let's all have a seat."

They gathered around the dining room table. Dalton placed the Glock on its surface, pointed in Buck's direction. He laid it all out. Backup was coming. Should be around nine. One of those guys, Dennie, and Buck would take the SUV and run for Memphis.

"What about us?" Jessie asked.

"We got business to tend to."

"What?"

Dalton stared at him. "You want me to tell you right here in front of the doc?"

"I guess not."

"All the doc needs to know is that Dennie's got to be ready to travel by nine, ten at the latest." Buck started to say that wasn't smart but Dalton waved him to silence. "That's a hard deadline and it isn't up for debate. Clear?"

Anger flashed in Dalton's eyes. Dark, threatening. Buck wanted to argue, to buy more time, but sensed that flaming Dalton's ire could prove dangerous. He simply nodded. "Crystal."

"Then get in there and get things ready."

Buck pulled the door closed behind him but paused near the vent.

"Who's coming?" Jessie asked.

"Three guys. The boss's sending them."

"They'll never find this place."

"I'll head back down the hill and call them at nine. I'll hook up with them and lead them back here. Then, we'll get Dennie on the road to Memphis and the rest of us can clean up this mess."

Buck walked to the window and pulled back the curtain. Rain streaked the glass. Open the two twist latches, raise the window, and run. Those were his first thoughts. But then what? Nothing nearby as far as he could tell. When they had arrived—when was that?—he had lost track of time—he had seen nothing for at least a mile. Of course, it was dark and his attention had been on Dennie, but surely he would have seen another house or store or something if it had been there.

If he ran, where would he go? Which direction? To what?

They'd be on him in no time. And Dalton would kill him. He had no doubt about that now. If he killed a cop, Buck would get no quarter.

But, Dalton said he had to call them. Whoever they were. To do that, he'd have to head out again. What had he said? A couple of miles? That would leave Buck here, alone with Jessie. That would be his only reasonable opportunity. Not a great one, but a better one.

Fortunately, he had planned for that possibility. Of course, he had assumed he'd have to deal with both men but with only Jessie it would be easier. Except for the rapidly ticking clock. How long would Dalton be gone? Would he have to wait for the others or would they be nearby already? Would he have fifteen minutes, an hour, longer?

He turned from the window and looked at Dennie. Maybe he had another option. Maybe Dennie could buy him time.

He touched Dennie's arm. The young man stirred, his eyes flitted open, and he blinked. Finally, his wavering gaze found Buck.

"What's going on?" Dennie asked. His voice raspy, tongue thick. Still sedated.

"I need to get you ready to travel."

Dennie smacked his lips. Buck picked up the plastic cup of water from the bedside table and tilted it toward Dennie's lips. "Small sip. Don't try to swallow. Just wet your mouth."

Dennie, of course, swallowed, causing him to choke and cough. He clutched his stomach, moaning.

"I told you. Small sips and let it sit a few seconds."

This time Dennie did. He took a few more sips. "That's better."

Buck used a towel to wipe Dennie's chin.

"Where're we going?" His gaze was now sharper, his voice less raspy. "To the hospital?"

"No. Dalton said to Memphis, I think."

Dennie glanced toward the door. "I thought you said that'd be dangerous."

Buck shrugged. "It's not ideal for sure. But, it's not my decision."

"Get him in here."

So far, so good. If Dennie could buy time, one more day even, who knew? Maybe the calvary would arrive. Of course, that might mean a shootout or worse, but at least then Buck might have a reasonable chance of surviving this. On his own, he had his doubts.

Buck found Dalton and Jessie still sitting at the kitchen table. They fell silent when he entered.

"Dennie's awake. He wants to talk with you," Buck said to Dalton.

Dalton headed that way. Buck followed.

"How're you doing, brother?" Dalton asked.

"Hurting like a bitch."

"The doc says you're doing okay." Dalton glanced at Buck. "Ain't that right, Doc?"

Buck shrugged. "Not too bad all things considered, but definitely not out of the woods."

"What's this about getting out of here?" Dennie asked.

"Yep. We got to roll."

"I ain't ready to move," Dennie said. "Doc, tell him."

Before Buck could respond, Dalton did.

"We don't have much choice. Things have changed. We've got to hit the road."

"What happened?"

Dalton glanced at Buck, back to Dennie. "Can't say. All you need to know right now is that we're leaving."

"Jesus, Dalton, are you trying to kill me or something?"

"You'll be fine."

"That's easy for you to say. You ain't the one that got gut shot."

Dalton balled his fists at his sides, twisted his head to one side as if working out a kink. "Listen to me. Come nightfall the boss is sending some guys. You'll be back in the SUV and headed out of here. The back way. The doc here will be with you and he'll get you back home so our doc can see you."

"The one that took that bullet out of my arm last year?"

Dalton nodded.

"Jesus Christ. This ain't no flesh wound. He's not even a real doctor. He's a fucking vet."

"But he's discrete and he can handle this now. The doc here did all the hard part." Dalton shrugged. "I'm sure he'll gladly stay around and take care of you until you're up and moving."

Translation: Buck would be headed to Memphis as a captive,

and he'd never leave Memphis alive. No way he could crawl in that SUV, leave this area, and expect any other outcome. That meant his plan—his only plan—had better work.

CHAPTER 41

Cassie, Harper, and Cain walked out of Spivey's with three large cups of dark roast and a handful of granola bars. Cain unwrapped one and took a bite. He couldn't remember his last meal. What or where. Was it even today? He finished the bar in three bites, tossed the wrapper in a street side trash container.

"You think Jason really knows anything?" Cassie asked. "About the murders?"

"Based on what we found in his phone," Harper said, "he plays second fiddle. Tommy ran the show."

"But he knows something," Cain said. "I got that feeling when we talked with him. Seemed he gave up just enough for us to go away."

"You think he'll be more forthcoming now?" Cassie said.

"With your powers of persuasion?" Cain said. "Definitely."

She laughed. "And if I fail, you can always threaten to cut his eyes out again."

"Or turn Harper loose on him."

"Me?" Harper said.

"She's much more dangerous than I am," Cain said. "She just looks innocent."

As they entered the PD, Poppy smiled from behind the welcome desk.

"Anything new?" Cassie asked.

"Not that I've heard."

Cassie glanced toward Cain and Harper. "Poppy actually runs everything around here. If she doesn't know something, there's nothing to know."

"She's just being nice," Poppy said. "I mostly push papers around and answer the phone."

"Which makes you the hub," Cain said.

Another smile from Poppy. "I like that."

"Okay, Captain Hub," Cassie said, "we'll be down in the conference room. Jason Epps is coming in. At least he better. Let me know when he does."

They barely got settled around the long wooden table that dominated the room when the com-line of the phone near where Cassie sat buzzed. She answered, said, "Send him back." She looked at Cain. "It seems you got his attention."

Jason appeared at the open doorway, slid to a stop. "I'm only going to talk to Chief Crowe."

Cain kicked a chair back from the table. "Take a seat."

Jason hesitated, then sat. "Okay, what do you want?"

"Tell me again," Cassie said. "Where exactly were you when Tommy Finley and his family were murdered?"

Good move, Cain thought. Knock him off-balance. Put him on the defensive. Make him reconsider lying.

"Like I said, over at Big Bill's. Go talk to Mr. Keener. He'll tell you."

"I did. He says you were there until one. Just like you said."

"Okay. So why am I here?"

"Here's what this smells like," Cain said. "You and Tommy Finley do business with a group over in Memphis." Jason started to say something but Cain raised a hand. "Tommy, or maybe both of you, decided you could do better. Hooked up with someone over in Knoxville. Memphis decided that poaching their business wasn't allowable so they sent a crew over to send a message."

"I told you, I didn't know much about any of that. It was all Tommy."

"That's what you said earlier over in the park." Cain removed one of his throwing knives from its secret leg compartment. He flipped it and snatched it from the air by the handle. Repeated the maneuver. "Remember what I said would happen if you lied?"

Jason scraped his chair back. "He threatened me, Chief. Said he'd cut my eye out."

"You've got another one," Cassie said.

Cain liked Chief Cassie Crowe more and more. She had guts. No love lost for dirt bags like Jason.

"You ain't going to do nothing about it?" Jason asked.

"I'm more curious about your answers than I am any perceived threat."

"You see, Jason," Harper said, "the murder of the Finley family, and Mr. Shaffer, and the abduction of Dr. Buckner are all part of the same package. What we want to know is who did it, and we think you know the answer."

"I don't."

"Then you're the most clueless individual on the planet."

"Listen, I'm telling the truth," Jason said, now talking faster, tension in his voice. "Tommy ran everything. I simply worked with him. He's the only one that ever talked with anyone from Memphis. I never did. I never met them."

"You never received any supplies?" Cain asked.

"Never." He swallowed hard. Sweat formed on his upper lip. "They wouldn't allow it. At least, that's what Tommy said. He said they'd only deal with him."

"And who are they?" Cassie asked.

"Aren't you listening? I told you, I don't know any of them."

"And they haven't contacted you?" Cain said.

"No."

"Like I told you earlier, they will."

"Well, I won't talk to them. I'm done with all this."

Cain leaned back, examined Jason. He was scared. Terrified about now. Time to crank it up.

"You do see that you'll have no option, don't you?"

Jason stared at him.

"They'll need a new boy over here. It'll either be you or someone else. If it's not you, you're a liability. A source of exposure. You see where this is going?"

Jason's head dropped. "Jesus."

"Did you ever hear any names?" Harper asked. "Did Tommy

ever let one slip?"

Jason looked up. The internal war waging in his head was evident on his face.

Cain flipped and caught the knife again. "Let me remind you, you're under oath here."

Jason sighed; his shoulders sagged. "I don't want anything to do with this."

Cain placed the knife on the table, the point directed at Jason. "Here's the problem. Life choices always have consequences. You chose to enter this world and here you are. It's all on you. They know who you are, where you live, probably a lot more than you can imagine. You've seen firsthand what they're capable of. You're only way out of this is if we can find them and take them off the board. Understand?"

Jason took a couple of deep breaths, trying to settle his nerves no doubt. Gather the spine to cross a threshold. His personal Rubicon, as it were. "Tommy mentioned two names. Jessie and Dalton. I don't know any last names. That's all I know."

"They're his Memphis suppliers?" Harper asked.

"As far as I know."

Cain reiterated that Jason could expect them to contact him and if they did he should agree to whatever they said and then call him immediately. He finished with, "We just might be your new best friends."

"And the only ones that can get you out of this in one piece," Harper added.

After Jason left, Cain asked Cassie, "You know anything about these guys? Jessie and Dalton?"

"Never heard of them."

Cain looked at Harper. "Time to dig in."

She nodded. "Mama B."

"Mama B?" Cassie asked.

"Our source," Harper said.

"The one that dug up the phone info?"

Cain nodded. "She can get into places most people don't know exist."

"She sounds sinister."

"She's actually old enough to be your grandmother. But, the

Navy trained her well."

"And she'll be able to find out who these guys are?" Cassie asked.

Harper raised one shoulder. "Maybe. Probably."

Cassie considered that for a few seconds. "Okay. Let me know what you find. I'm going to hit the road and help hunt down the SUV. Or the cabin. Right now, I'll take anything."

CHAPTER 42

Cassie drove through town, toward the hospital and the park. The ER looked quiet as she rolled by, no ambulances, only a few cars in the lot. The park was the same. Only one car, a couple inside who appeared to be eating fast-food burgers. She rolled on east and then north, following the county road that would eventually plug into I-75 much farther north than she was going. She looped left and wound through the forested hills, turning off on a number of side roads, climbing a few gravel and dirt drives. Some muddy enough to make traction less than ideal. She encountered a few clusters of homes and isolated cabins. Most were quiet and uninhabited since they were owned by folks over in Knoxville, maybe even Nashville, who came here for R&R when time permitted. She stopped and chatted with a few folks, mostly pulled near the front porch, talking through her lowered window to stay out of the rain.

No one had seen a black SUV, at least not one they didn't know. No strangers. No unusual traffic. All quiet.

The rain kicked up as she ascended a slope, now almost directly north of town. Thick woods on either side, ratty Johnson's grass and other weeds edging the pavement, scattered water-filled potholes in the road. Not like she hadn't complained to the county about the condition of the roadways up this way, but they did nothing. The truth was that they didn't have the budget and probably weren't all that interested. Frustrating.

But not as frustrating as trying to find the SUV. Maybe they were wasting their time. Maybe the killer/kidnappers were far away. Knoxville, Nashville, Kentucky. Hell, they could be in Deadwood, South Dakota for that matter. She was beginning to lose confidence in her initial assessment—that they would go to ground nearby, with one of them hit and obviously in trouble, enough to take a doctor hostage right from the ER. Ballsy move. Desperate for sure. To her that meant the victim was seriously damaged. Not a mere flesh wound as they say. This belief was underscored by the considerable blood she found on the floor at the Finleys.

If they were still in the neighborhood, how hard should they be to find? They'd have to come out of their hole sooner or later, wouldn't they? For supplies, if nothing else. If not, it meant they were well-supplied. Which was a direction Cassie didn't want to go.

Had they invaded someone's home? An occupied residence? One that was well stocked because the owners were there? That would mean they had taken hostages and that would up the ante considerably.

The other possibility that popped into her head was just as dark. What if the bad guy is dead? Killed by Tommy Finley's single gunshot? That just might mean that the killers were long gone and they should be searching for Dr. Buck Buckner's body in a ditch somewhere.

Frustration didn't seem strong enough to cover what she felt. Anger, fear, a sense of personal violation. This was her town after all, and her responsibility. She had somehow failed. At least, that's what it felt like.

Her cell buzzed. Fowler. Maybe he had found something. A little sliver of sunshine would be welcome about now.

"What's up?" Cassie asked when she answered. The signal was weak, Fowler's voice static-filled. She couldn't make out what he said. She slowed, diminishing the tire noise. "Say that again."

"I can't find Duckworth."

"What do you mean?"

"We been talking every half hour or so. Sort of coordinating things, but it's been an hour. Actually a little longer and his phone goes over to voicemail."

"Maybe he doesn't have a signal."

"Could be, I guess."

"Maybe he's talking to someone."

"Chief, are you serious? Ever known anyone who hated to talk on the phone more than Scotty?"

That was true. Scotty Duckworth made no bones about that. He hated phone calls. Despised texts. Always went out of his way to talk face to face. "The way folks was meant to communicate," was his belief.

"I take it his radio doesn't work either."

"Nope. I got Poppy working on contacting him but so far she says there's no signal."

Another source of frustration. Only her SUV and Duckworth's sedan were actual police vehicles and the city groused about buying those two. Fowler and everyone else drove their personal rides and got reimbursed for the miles. Sort of. But it meant that their radio network consisted of two, everyone else relying on their cell phones as the primary means of communication. Most of the time that was sufficient but not always. Like now. Up here, in the hills, miles from town, the service was weak, spotty, or nonexistent.

"I hope he didn't slide off the road somewhere," Cassie said. "Down some ravine."

"Today would be the day for it. Pretty slippery out here."

"Where was he, last you heard?"

"Up north of The Crossroads. Zigzagging through the hills."

"He hadn't found anything, I take it."

"No. None of us have."

"Where are you?"

"Out west a few miles. Not far from Joe Curtis' and Guy Richland's places. They ain't seen anything. No one else either, so I'm headed back and then up toward where Duckworth was searching."

"Okay. I'm up north. I'll swing down that way, too."

"I'll look for you," Fowler said. "Poppy's notifying everyone to keep an eye out for him."

"Good."

"Chief?" Fowler asked.

"Yeah."

"You don't think he ran across these guys do you? Got all sideways with them?"

"I hope not."

CHAPTER 43

The plan was that while Cassie and her crew searched for the elusive SUV and canvassed as many cabins as they could, Cain and Harper would dig into the two that Jason said supplied the late Tommy Finley with drugs. Dalton and Jessie whoever. The earlier drizzle had morphed into a full-on rain. According to Harper's weather app a storm brewed to the west and was headed their way. This was the leading edge it seemed.

They grabbed some coffee at Spivey's and were now sitting in the parking lot, watching people dart in and out of the coffee shop, umbrellas deployed. Harper called Mama B and gave her the names—Dalton and Jessie, adding that they were probably embedded in the Memphis drug world.

"Last names?" Mama B asked.

"Don't know."

"You aren't making this easy."

Cain laughed. "Somehow I think you'll manage."

Mama B agreed, said she'd have something soon. Of course she would.

"The guy in the coffee shop?" Harper said. "Simon Greene? The attorney?"

"Weird, huh?" Cain said.

"I swear I thought he was that guy over in Georgia."

"Me, too," Cain said. "Of course I realized that the dude in

Georgia would've aged a couple of decades by now so he wouldn't look the same. Still, the similarity was unnerving."

Harper nodded. "Made my heart bounce a couple of times."

"What was that town? Where he lived?"

"Dahlonega."

"Yeah. Cute place."

"And profitable."

Cain smiled. "That it was."

Cain cranked up The Rig and pulled from the lot.

"I had an odd feeling about him," Harper said. "Not just because he looked like Mr. Georgia."

"It was the gold Rolex," Cain said.

"Yeah, that must be it. My memory is you snagged a couple of them that day."

"And some jewelry and cash."

"I don't know," Harper said, "Greene seemed shady to me."

"He's an attorney. They're all shady."

"No argument there."

Cain waited for a woman, three kids bouncing in the backseat, to make a left turn, then proceeded down Main Street. "He's connected with Tommy Finley. Maybe Jason, too."

"We going to have a chat with him?" Harper asked.

"We are."

Simon Greene's office was in a residential setting. A red brick house, corner lot, a block off Main. Neat, with white trim. A sign that hung above the front door, white with black lettering, indicated this was the office of "Simon Greene, Esq., Attorney At Law." Inside, the small waiting room was empty. A pleasant receptionist said Mr. Greene was with a client but should be finished "soon." They sat and waited.

Ten minutes later, Greene appeared. He escorted a middle-aged woman to the door, holding it open for her, adding that he'd call her when whatever documents she needed were ready. He then smiled and welcomed Cain and Harper. They followed him to his office. Also, small and neat. A large window to the right, the left and rear walls filled with thick law books.

"What can I do for you?" Greene asked as he sat behind his desk.

"A few questions about Tommy Finley."

He gave a half-nod. "I could invoke lawyer-client privilege, but given the circumstances I'm not inclined to stand on protocol."

"We'd appreciate it," Harper said. "You defended him on distribution charges."

"Yes. Also possession a couple of times. Those were misdemeanors so no big deal."

"He could afford you?" Cain asked.

Greene smiled. "It was more or less *pro bono*."

"Generous," Harper said.

"Tommy wasn't big on saving money. He spent his ill-gotten gains on stupid stuff."

"So, he was guilty?"

Greene folded his hands on the desktop. "Of course he was. Doesn't mean he didn't deserve an effective defense."

"And it was effective, true?" Cain asked.

"It was."

"What made him a candidate for *pro bono* work?" Harper asked.

"Tommy wasn't a bad kid. Screwed up, but not bad."

"Just dealt drugs?"

"It wasn't like he was a kingpin or anything like that. Very small time." He smiled. His teeth were perfect. "Besides, his parents were clients and good people. They were at wit's end with Tommy. They tried though. Did everything they could for him, but like so many his age, he thought he was smarter than they were."

Cain nodded. "A common disease."

"It was more a favor for his parents than anything."

"In your discovery, did you run across his suppliers?" Cain asked.

Greene hesitated, as if deciding how to answer. "No. He never told me."

"Ever hear the names Dalton or Jessie?" Harper asked.

Another hesitation. "Not that I recall. Who are they?"

"According to Jason Epps, they were the ones who supplied Tommy. Might be from Memphis."

Greene shook his head. "Don't know anything about that." He opened his palms, flashed that perfect smile. "Like I said, Tommy wasn't very forthcoming with that kind of information."

"But, you asked?"

"I did. Told him that one approach would be to give them up. Maybe the judge would go easy on him if he did."

"The judge went easy anyway?" Harper said.

"After Tommy agreed to a treatment program and some community service."

"Did he do that?"

"Mostly. I think he spent a few weeks in counseling and did most of his hours over at the park, picking up trash."

"The park where he did business?" Harper said.

Greene shrugged but said nothing.

"What about Jason?" Cain said. "You ever represent him?"

"No. Never had to." He lifted a cuff and glanced at his gold Rolex. "I have to head out for a meeting. Is there anything else I can do for you?"

"No. Thanks for your time."

Greene stood. "Sorry I couldn't help more."

CHAPTER 44

Buck worked on his second bowl of soup. Jessie had opened several cans he found in the pantry—vegetable beef and tomato—and heated the mixture in an over-sized pot. They sat at the table while they ate the concoction along with saltine crackers. Buck wolfed down the first bowl but took his time with the second. Not that he was all that hungry but he knew calories might be the advantage he needed. Not much of one, though. If he was going to run for it, he had no idea how far that would be. Or for how long. If he got out of the yard and into the trees at all.

It was dusk and night was falling rapidly. As was the rain that peppered the roof. Not a good night to be out in the elements but Buck saw it differently. If he could make the trees, the rain and wind would be his ally. Cover his sounds and movements and make him more difficult to track.

"When you headed out?" Jessie asked.

Dalton glanced at his watch. "Maybe half an hour."

Jessie looked at Buck. "You got everything ready to go?"

"Mostly. I've got all the materials I'll need stuffed into plastic trash bags. It'll just be a matter of getting Dennie wrapped up and protected from the rain."

"When we get back," Dalton said, "it should be a quick deal to get him loaded up and hit the road."

"This still isn't a good idea," Buck said. "All that movement and bouncing could make him bleed again."

"Then you'll have to be ready to fix it."

Buck locked gazes with him. "Why not leave us here? Let me get him to the hospital? You guys can take off."

Dalton took a deep breath and let it out slowly. "We've been through this. My brother ain't going to prison and I ain't leaving him behind."

Buck hadn't expected any other response but felt he should take one more shot at reasoning with Dalton. "So, if we're heading out, why do you need these other guys? Why not just cut and run?"

"That's what you and Dennie and one of the guys are going to do. I got some business to take care of around here."

"Like what?"

"That ain't none of your concern." Dalton gave him a hard look. "Stick to your own business. I'll take care of mine."

Buck gave a quick nod, and stood. He rinsed his bowl and spoon in the sink and then began looking through the cabinets until he found what he wanted. Things he had seen earlier. Time to get the ball rolling, and set the stage. He removed the bottles of whiskey, vermouth, and bitters he had seen earlier and placed them on the counter.

"What're you doing?" Dalton asked.

Buck opened the refrigerator and lifted a small jar of maraschino cherries from one of the door shelves. "Making a drink. I need one."

"You think that's smart?"

Buck turned toward him. "Nothing the last two days has been smart. Now I'm making a drink, unless you want to shoot me." He stared at Dalton. "Or you could join me."

"Sounds good to me," Jessie said.

Dalton shrugged. "Why not."

Buck removed three glasses and filled them with ice. He added the bourbon, the vermouth, and a splash of bitters.

"What's that?" Jessie asked.

"A Manhattan. Sort of. This is bourbon and not rye, which I think makes a better one, and I don't have any orange peel. But it should work."

"I ain't never had no Manhattan," Jessie said.

"You'll like it." Buck added some cherry juice and a single cherry to each. He walked two of them to the table and placed one in front of each of them. "Enjoy."

He then lifted his from the counter and took a swig. "Not bad."

Dalton took a sip. "Interesting." He took another. "Actually, it's pretty good."

"I saw some chicken broth in the cabinet," Buck said. "I'm going to heat a little for Dennie."

"I thought he couldn't eat nothing," Jessie said.

"He can't. Not yet. But this is how we progress things after surgery. First sips of water and then broth. I'd give him Jell-O if we had any, but he needs the calories. He's got a hard trip ahead of him."

Dalton took another sip and leaned back in the chair. "I bet you're a pretty good doctor."

"I hope so," Buck said. "For Dennie's sake."

CHAPTER 45

Cain and Harper returned to the Beverley B&B. It was eight, now dark outside. The rain continued, mostly light, punctuated with more intense waves. They each downed a couple of granola bars and a bottle of water while Cain called Mama B. His phone lay on the bed with the speaker function activated.

"You must be clairvoyant," Mama B said. "I was getting ready to give you a call."

"We must have sensed your bat signal was coming," Harper said.

"You always seem to."

"What've you got for us?" Cain asked.

"These hombres you asked about. They the ones who snatched the doctor and did all the killing down there?"

"Looks that way."

"Well, they're surely the type. Dalton Southwell seems to head the crew over in Memphis. He has a fairly long record. Multiple arrests for assault, a couple for possession, meth, and one rape allegation. Most got tossed. He did two months a few years back but that hardly seems much for a career like his."

"I was afraid of that," Cain said. "A guy with a violent history."

"Of course, we expected that," Harper added.

"It gets stickier," Mama B said. "He's apparently hooked up with a guy named Frank Campanella. Folks call him Frankie the

Finger. Apparently if old Frankie fingers you, they never find your body. Suspected in a number of hits but none ever stuck. Seems he has a couple of judges in his pocket."

"You thinking he might have had the Finley boy targeted?"

"I'm getting to that," Mama B said. "Southwell's crew consists of a half-dozen guys. Mainly his brother, Dennie Southwell, and another fine citizen named Jessie Parker. The trio supplies meth and marijuana, and some Oxy and black tar to several small-time dealers in central and eastern Tennessee. Including Tommy Finley, it seems."

"And Tommy crossed the boss, Frankie, somehow?" Harper asked.

"I reached out to a friend at the DEA. She said she'd heard some chatter about a couple of Frankie's dealers going rogue and hooking up with another supplier. She didn't know who but the trail seemed to lead to the Knoxville area."

"That fits with what we've uncovered here," Cain said. "Our witness saw two men take the doctor. I suspect there was a third and he was the one that got shot at Finley's place. From what you've told us, smart money would bet they're the Southwell brothers and this Jessie character."

"Bad news always comes in threes."

"It does that. Anything else?"

"That's it for now but I'm not finished."

Of course she wasn't. If Cain knew anything about Mama B, once she got her teeth into something she shook it like a rabid pit bull.

"While you're snooping around," Harper said, "can you take a look at an attorney over here? Name's Simon Greene. He defended Tommy Finley a couple of times."

"Will do."

Cain then called Chief Cassie Crowe. When she answered, he said, "I've got some information for you."

"Yeah, well, we've got a problem."

"What's that?"

"Scotty Duckworth's missing."

"What do you mean?"

"He's been out of pocket for nearly three hours now. Doesn't answer his phone or his radio. I've got everyone out looking for him."

"Where was he last you knew?"

"Roaming around the backwoods north of The Crossroads. Doing what we've been doing for what seems like forever."

"We'll head that way."

"Much appreciated. What do you have for me?"

"It'll wait. Let us get rolling and then I'll call back."

"Okay."

Cain looked at Harper. "Time to saddle up."

"You thinking he found our bad guys?"

"Or they found him."

"He could've simply had a wreck. Slid off the road and is injured. It's nasty out, and those roads in the hills aren't the best."

Cain looked at her.

Harper shrugged. "Yeah. I don't believe that either."

They scurried out into the rain, retrieved a pair of duffles from The Rig, and returned to their respective rooms. Cain changed into his real combat gear, sturdier and more functional than the lighter weight gear he had been wearing. Tactical pants and shirt, pocketed jacket, multiple knives onboard. You could never have too many blades. Most were of his own design. His combat readiness consisted of a throwing knife in each boot sole, others strapped to each ankle, one in each secret compartment sewed into his pant seams along his thighs, and two T-bar stabbing weapons disguised as part of his belt buckle. A final one secreted in another sheath in the back of his shirt, high, just beneath the collar, easily reached. Standard for him when a mission loomed.

As he grabbed his combat jacket, Harper appeared in the doorway. Similarly dressed, her Glock 17-40 hanging from her right hip. Cain knew she had a smaller Walther strapped to her ankle.

"Let's roll," she said.

CHAPTER 46

Buck changed Dennie's dressings, reinforcing each with extra padding and tape. He'd need that for the trip. The truth was that Dennie's wounds were healing nicely and there was no evidence of infection. He should be able to make the trip to Memphis without problems. Buck had painted a more ominous picture for Dalton, but what the hell. He had to play the cards on hand.

Dalton came in. "You about ready?" he asked Buck.

"As ready as we'll ever be." He glanced at Dennie, then back to Dalton. "You sure I can't talk you out of this move?"

"You can't."

"Well, if we're going to do it," Dennie said, "let's get it done and over with."

"I'm heading out now," Dalton said.

"How long?" Dennie asked.

"Not sure. Depends on exactly where they are. They're going to stop just west of town and wait for my call. So by the time they get up the hill and we hook up, I suspect a half-hour or so."

Dalton looked at Buck. "So get ready to roll. As soon as we're back, we hit the road."

Dalton left the bedroom. Buck knelt near the two trash bags of supplies just inside the door. He pretended to be checking on things but his attention was on Dalton and Jessie as they walked toward the back door.

"Keep an eye on him," Dalton said. "Anything funny, don't hesitate. Kill his ass."

"You got it."

The kitchen door opened and closed. The SUV's door did the same and the engine cranked to life. He peered through a narrow crack between the curtains. Dalton spun the SUV around and crunched down the drive. The rain had lightened. At least it wasn't windblown and hammering the window.

Buck might not know where he was or which direction would lead him to safety, but he knew one thing for sure—he had to be gone before Dalton and his guys returned.

Time to roll the dice.

Buck walked out of the bedroom.

Jessie stood at the front window, curtain peeled back, looking out. He turned toward Buck. "You ready to go?"

"I guess. I changed his bandages and gave him some more morphine. It'll help with any discomfort during the ride."

"He going to be okay?"

"He either will or he won't. It could go either way. What he needs is a hospital."

"That ain't going to happen."

Buck walked to the kitchen, filled a glass with ice from the fridge.

"What are you doing?" Jessie asked.

"Having another."

"Not sure that's a good idea."

Buck smiled, trying to look casual. "Actually, it's a great idea." He poured in some whiskey. "Want one?"

Jessie hesitated, glanced toward the door. "It was good."

"I'll make it light," Buck said.

"That'd be good."

Buck filled another glass with ice and splashed in some bourbon. As he added the other ingredients he slipped the small bottle of Noctec Syrup from his pocket. The one he had added to the trash bag at the pharmacy as they loaded up drugs and surgical supplies. The one he grabbed just in case the opportunity arose. Now it had, but the window was narrow.

Noctec. Liquid chloral hydrate. The original Mickey Finn.

This version was cherry flavored because it was made for pediatric use. Hopefully sweet enough to meld with the Manhattan's flavor. He added a healthy amount to each drink as a substitute for the maraschino juice. No dose calculation here. Only too much was enough. He said a silent prayer this would work. Quickly.

He stirred the two drinks and carried them to the table where Jessie sat. He slid one toward him. Jessie lifted it and examined it.

"How do I know you didn't do something to it?" Jessie asked.

Buck had read Jessie right. Not as clever as he thought he was. Probably watched too much TV.

Buck shrugged. "Don't drink it then."

"Here," Jessie said. He slid the drink toward Buck. "I'll drink yours."

"Fine."

They swapped drinks.

Buck pretended to take a sip. "Good."

Jessie followed suit. He nodded. "You're getting better at this." Another sip. "I could get used to these. You'll have to share your recipe."

"It's pretty easy," Buck said. "I'll write it down for you."

He walked to the counter where he had seen a pad and pen near the kitchen wall phone. The dead wall phone. He returned to the table and began writing down the ingredients.

"I got to piss," Jessie said. He headed toward the nearest bathroom. The one in the room where Dennie now slept a peaceful morphine sleep.

Buck worked quickly. He dumped his drink, refilled the glass with tea from the fridge, tossed in a cherry, and was seated by the time Jessie returned. Jessie's gait already a bit unsteady.

Jessie giggled. "Old Dennie's out like a light."

"Morphine will do that."

Jessie took a sip. "Man these are good." Another sip. His head gave a slow nod. "You know what I think?"

Did he know? Did he sense something was wrong? The signs were evident. To Buck anyway. His walk a bit off, his speech thicker, his eyes headed toward glassy. "What?"

"I think you're probably a good guy. And a good doctor."

"Tell my father."

"Oh?"

"He thinks I'm wasting my career out here doing ER work."

"Yeah, well, my father thought I'd never amount to nothing neither. But I've done all right."

Buck refrained from saying that Jessie's father was probably more correct than Jessie's own self-image. Instead he said, "You like working with Dalton?"

"I do." More Manhattan. "And Dennie. Dennie's a real good guy. Like a brother to me."

"It's good to have friends."

Jessie laughed and slapped the table. "Ain't that the truth." He eyed Buck. "Maybe under other circumstances me and you would've been friends."

"I agree."

Jessie drained his drink. "Man that was good."

"Want another?"

He considered that a beat. "Maybe so." He stood, one hand flattened against the tabletop for support. "I wish Dalton would hurry up." He moved in the direction of the front window but only managed three steps before he wavered and fell to his knees. "Whoa." His face twisted toward Buck. "What the—?" Now even his knees wouldn't support him and he lurched forward on all fours. His shirt road up, exposing the weapon tucked beneath his belt in the small of his back.

Buck jumped to his feet, rounded the table. He jerked the weapon free. Jessie toppled to his side, his gaze sweeping toward Buck. Unable to lock on anything, his eyes wavered, glassed over, and he exhaled heavily. He rolled to his back as sleep smothered him.

Buck moved quickly now. He wore only the surgical scrubs he had on when captured and his athletic shoes. He had seen clothing in the closet so he headed that way. A hunting jacket hung to one side. He grabbed it and tugged it on. A little large but it would do. He stuffed Jessie's gun in the pocket.

Now where was the shotgun? He had seen a dozen shells in one of the kitchen drawers so there should be one somewhere. He shoved the clothes aside, hoping to find it leaning against one corner. Nothing. Nor was it on the closet shelf. He saw a cardboard box on the floor and lifted the lid. Two dolls and a teddy bear. Whoever lived here had kids. Or more likely grandkids that visited from time to time. Nothing in the house told him kids lived there but these toys just might mean they visited.

So if a shotgun existed, it would be in a safe place. Where kids who liked dolls and teddy bears couldn't reach it. He checked the closet in the other bedroom before returning to the living room. He scanned everything, his gaze finally resting on the hutch that stood against the wall. Filled with plates and cups. He stood on tip toes and ran his hand over the top. There. The shotgun. He lifted it.

Dusty, the twelve-gauge pump otherwise looked to be in good working order. He racked it a couple of times. So far, so good. Back in the kitchen, he shoved three shells into the shotgun, stuffed the others in a jacket pocket. Then, he was out the back door. The rain was lighter. It had been coming in waves and the current lull was welcome.

Which way to go? The trees, then downhill. He moved that way. He passed the garage. Did they have a car? The side door wasn't locked. He pushed it open. A white Toyota Celica sat inside. Could it be his path to freedom? He rounded it, tripped, nearly fell. As he grabbed the car's fender for support, he looked down. Two bodies. An elderly couple.

Dalton had taken care of the owners. That's what took him so long to return the night they located this cabin. That's how he knew they wouldn't return and surprise them.

Time to get the hell out.

Before he could move headlights swept across the garage and leaked through the edges of the door. The sound of an engine and gravel crunching followed. Dalton and his crew were headed up the drive.

He eased out the door and slid behind the garage. Another set of headlamps swept over the yard and lit up the trees.

He had only one choice.

Run!

CHAPTER 47

At The Crossroads, Harper turned The Rig north, uphill. Rain, now heavier, battered the windshield and the wipers fought to keep their path visible. Harper held her pace down and the vehicle gripped the slick road well.

"Conditions like this, he could've easily slid off the road," Harper said.

"Could have," Cain said.

"But, he didn't."

"No, he didn't."

"If he did get sideways with our bad guys, and he was searching up this way, their hidey-hole must be in this direction, too."

"Also means they haven't cut and run yet," Cain said.

"Which might or might not bode well for Dr. Buck."

"I'd say his fuse is down to the wick. If these guys killed a cop, or kidnapped one, as soon as the doc's usefulness has reached its expiration date, he'll be history."

"Did you call his father?" Harper asked.

"Yeah. While we were getting ready. Tough conversation since I had little to offer."

"Did you tell him about the Memphis crew?"

Cain glanced at her, she at him. Cain shook his head. "Not really. I simply said we had a line on some guys who might be involved. I didn't give him any details. Better he envisions an anonymous someone than a pack of professional criminals."

Harper negotiated a tight chicane of rights and lefts. "That kind of news would only add to his angst. He's dealing with enough already."

"Take the next right," Cain said. "Cassie said she'd be out that way. I'll give her a call."

They met Cassie a mile ahead, her vehicle pulled to the shoulder of the rural road. Harper slid up behind the police SUV. Cassie hopped out and walked toward them. The rain slanted through the headlamp beams. Cassie climbed in the backseat.

"Anything new?" Cain asked, twisting in his seat to partially face her.

"Nothing. Just checked in with everyone. At least, everyone I could reach. Cell service is sketchy at best in these parts."

"And only you and Duckworth have radios. Right?" Harper asked.

"Yep. No money, I'm afraid. At least that's what they tell me over at city hall."

"Not uncommon for a town this size," Cain said.

"Yeah well, most of the time it's not an issue. About now, it is." She forked back her hair, wiping the dampness off her hand on her pant leg. "You said you had some news."

"Not good, I'm afraid," Cain said. He told her what they knew about the Memphis crew. About the Southwell brothers, Jessie Parker, and Frankie "The Finger" Campanella. "Seems that Campanella runs the fiefdom and the others are his capos."

"This is from the mysterious Mama B?" Cassie asked.

"It is." Cain expanded on what they knew and how they knew it. "Jason remembered two names: Dalton and Jessie. Said they were the suppliers for Tommy Finley. He never met them, just heard the names. So, Mama B dug into the drug world in Memphis and in this area. Contacts with the DEA and others. Long story short, she found the Southwell brothers and this Jessie dude."

"Never heard of them," Cassie said. "Not that Frankie the Finger guy either." She shook her head. "Where do they get these names? The freaking Finger?"

"In Frankie's case, he earned it," Cain said. "Maybe many times over."

"Just great." Cassie gave a head shake. "These clowns had to invade my world."

"That'd be my guess," Harper said.

"So, you're thinking this trio came over to whack Tommy?" Cassie said. "Because he was painting outside the lines? And in the process one of them got shot?"

"That's what started the cascade," Cain said. "They then grabbed the doc, robbed the pharmacy, and headed to the hills."

"That's more than a cascade. That's a torrent."

"And maybe, just maybe," Cain said, "Duckworth found them."

Cassie's pain was almost palpable. Cain could see it in the lines around her eyes and lips, feel it like an electric current in the air. This was small town stuff. Not like the big city. Here, everyone knew everyone. The police force was small, like family. He imagined they had barbecues together, knocked back a few beers together, raised their families together and now one of the family was missing. Maybe worse.

"You sure he was up this way?" Harper asked.

"Yes. We had divided the area into quadrants. This was his."

"Then I suggest we concentrate up here. Get everyone back this way."

"Already on it," Cassie said.

Harper climbed from The Rig, circled to the back, and lifted the rear gate. She moved around a few duffles, finding the small one that held all their electronics. She carried it back inside and settled behind the wheel once again, passing the bag to Cain. He zipped it open and tugged out three phones. He handed one to Cassie, another to Harper.

"What are these?" Cassie asked.

"How we'll communicate," Cain said. "With only your radio in service, apparently, and with cell service spotty at best, these will work."

Cassie examined it. Looked like a standard flip phone.

"Satellite," Harper said.

"Really?" Cassie asked. "Where do you guys get this stuff?"

Cain smiled. "Here and there."

"All you have to do is flip it open," Harper said. "It'll automatically connect to and vibrate the other two phones. No ring. Keep it where you'll feel it."

Cassie nodded. "Got it." She slipped it into her shirt pocket.

CHAPTER 48

Dalton had wanted to lay low until Dennie was able to travel. Then make a night-time run for Memphis. Leave this little corner of the world behind. For now. He had delivered the needed message with the killing of Tommy Finley and his family. Though he hadn't yet talked with Jason Epps, he believed Tommy's demise would essentially guarantee that Epps wouldn't follow a similar path. He wouldn't try to go out on his own, and steal money from him and from Frankie the Finger. But, if Epps didn't hear so well, Dalton would handle him the same way.

The killing of the cop had changed everything. It couldn't be helped but it altered his path considerably. Before, business as usual was a reasonable outcome. Jason stepping in, the supply line reopened, the cash flow to Memphis pumping along. But now…. A dead cop? The heat would be intense. Frankie agreed. After Dalton had contacted his crew and got them rolling his way, he had called Frankie. He had asked Frankie about Epps and the future of the business over here. Frankie's take was that shutting down in the area for a while would be best. Draw less attention. That the death of the cop would indeed crank up the heat and Frankie wanted no part of that. Not for such a small slice of profit. They could always nose back in later if need be.

Which made Epps a liability and placed him on the agenda. So, help was on the way and the clean-up could begin.

Hopefully dumping the cop's car and body into the ravine would buy the time he needed. Twenty-four hours was all he asked. That should be enough time to get Dennie on the road and clean up the loose ends.

Fortunately, he had rolled back down the hill, made the call, hooked up with the rest of his crew without incident. Not a cop in sight. Now, he turned back up the cabin's drive, sliding past and into the trees as before. Mission accomplished.

His crew consisted of five men. Dennie and Jessie and the three that pulled up behind his SUV in a similar, but metallic gray, Navigator. He trusted the three men inside. Bud Myrick had been with him from the beginning, the two, plus Dennie, pulling odd jobs for a few years and then joining up with Frankie. A big jump in cash flow followed that move. They had gone from local, small-time, hand-to-hand dealers to a more regional distribution. They added Jessie almost immediately. Dennie had known him for years. Then came Dale Harris, a whiz with weapons of all types, and Chris Navarro, who had a couple of cousins hooked into the cartels. Cousins known well to Frankie.

The plan was simple. Jessie, Dennie, and the doc would head north in Dalton's vehicle and loop back toward Memphis. The doc driving, Jessie holding the gun. The rain and the darkness would help. Dalton figured all they needed was twenty lucky miles to be out of the circle that the local PD was likely searching. Then, he and the others could take care of business. Clip all the now frayed edges of their Tanner's Crossroads business.

Dalton stepped from his vehicle, the rain now light, tapping the overhead leaves. Above, it seemed that the clouds were beginning to break. The moon peeked through, slivering everything. Time to get Dennie loaded up and on the road.

As he rounded the SUV and stepped past the concealing tree, his senses ramped up. Something was off. What? It was a feeling more than anything. Then he saw it. The side garage door was open. He pulled his weapon as the other three clambered out of their vehicle followed by Harris's pit bull Rocco.

Dalton raised a hand and waved his weapon toward the garage. They fell silent, and their weapons appeared. Harris snapped a finger and Rocco dropped to his belly, haunches flexed for action, ears up, on alert.

Dalton angled away from the open door, to the rear edge of the garage. The other three arrayed themselves where they possessed unobstructed shooting angles. Rocco moved to Harris's side.

Dalton eased to the door. "Who's in there?" he said. "Come out now." Silence. "We have a dog. We'll send him in and he will bite you." Silence.

Dalton glanced at Harris and nodded.

Harris snapped his fingers again. "Find the man."

Rocco lurched forward, flew by Dalton, and into the garage. Dalton could hear him grunting, rooting around, no barking. Harris had trained him well.

Rocco found no one; neither did Dalton when he circled the car inside the garage. Except for the two bodies he had left behind earlier. Otherwise, nothing looked out of place.

"Maybe it was the wind," Navarro said. "That pushed the door open."

"Maybe." Dalton waved his weapon toward the house. "Better to assume we have visitors."

Dalton now saw that the cabin's rear door stood ajar. He shouldered it open and stepped inside. Harris and Rocco behind him, Navarro and Myrick lagging, providing cover from the doorway. Rocco charged ahead, veered right, let go a few yelps. Dalton followed.

Jessie. Sprawled on the floor, motionless, eyes half-open, glazed.

Dalton waved to Harris, pointed toward Jessie. Then he and Navarro cleared the two bedrooms. Dennie asleep, no sign of the doc.

"Son-of-a-bitch," Dalton said as he returned to the living area. Harris squatted next to Jessie.

"He ain't dead," Harris said. "But he ain't responding either."

Dalton knelt beside Jessie and checked his pulse. It seemed normal. He examined him for injuries, finding none. He stood and walked to the kitchen table. Two glasses, one half-full, one empty except for a couple of half-melted ice cubes. His teeth ground. "He drugged him." Dalton spun back toward Jessie. "You stupid fuck," he shouted at the unconscious man.

This had now become a true clusterfuck. First, Dennie getting shot by that little shit Tommy. The doc, the pharmacy, and holing up here when they should have been back in Memphis long ago. Free and clear. Now, a dead cop, Jessie out of commission, and the doc in the wind. What the hell else could go wrong?

Dalton looked toward the rear door. "He's running."

"He wasn't on the road," Navarro said. "He probably took to the woods."

"We have to find him," Dalton said. He looked at Myrick. "You stay here. Start getting ready to roll."

"Roll?" Myrick asked.

"We'll have to get my brother and Jessie out of here. After we take down the doc."

Dalton, Harris, Navarro, and Rocco hit the door running. They flew past the garage and into the trees. They stopped and listened but heard nothing. No sound of someone crashing through the trees or stumbling over rocks. Dalton heard only the tapping of rain against the overhead leaves and his own breathing.

"If he's smart, he'll head downhill," Dalton said. "And he's smart."

"No problem," Harris said. "Rocco'll find him." He snapped his fingers. "Find the man."

Rocco was off. They followed as best they could, pushing through the water-soaked trees, following the soft grunts and yelps from Rocco.

CHAPTER 49

Downhill. The only direction that made sense. Buck had no idea where he was but from the trip up, even though he was occupied with Dennie and it was dark and raining, he knew they went north, uphill from The Crossroads. If he made it down to the valley floor he would find help, but getting there was the trick.

Dalton would no doubt pursue him. He couldn't allow Buck to survive. How much of a head start did he have? How long would it take Dalton to find Jessie and assess the situation? Probably not long. He had barely gotten away before they pulled up. So, what? Maybe five, ten minutes?

He saw the softening rain and clearing sky as a double-edged sword. He could see better, but so could they. With the lack of heavy rain, he would be able to hear his pursuers better. And they him.

The terrain sloped this way and that, the ground and the rock formations slippery, the tree limbs biting. He attempted to weave among the trees, making as little noise as possible, while keeping his speed up as best he could.

The worse news was that Dalton had reinforcements. How many, he had no way of knowing for sure, but from what he managed to overhear, Dalton had said his boss, whoever the hell that was, was sending three men. Made it four to one. At least Jessie was out of the picture. Buck's only advantage was that he had somewhat of a head start. A slim one, but every second counted. He picked up his pace, weaving through the trees. Downward, always downward. As he cut between two trees, his feet slipped and he tumbled to the ground. Air exploded from his lungs. He managed to maintain his grip on the shotgun, but his head bounced against a tree. Light flashed behind his eyes. He struggled to his feet, sensing pain along his left ribs. He touched them. Tender. *Great, just great.*

He pressed on, watching more carefully where his feet landed. The moonlight stabbed through the tree canopy, making picking a path easier. Not less slippery though. His footfalls betrayed him a few times but he managed to stay on his feet and continue forward.

Another couple of hundred yards and he stopped, listened. What was that? Did he hear something? Was it his imagination? *Move.* He sidestepped down a slope and into a shallow depression that diagonaled downhill. He quickened his pace. After a few minutes he halted and listened. No doubt. He heard something moving through the brush. Whoever it was, they weren't far behind. He circled a rock formation, and squatted. Run or make a stand right here? Neither choice seemed a good one.

He had Jessie's handgun and the shotgun. But there were four of them, and they were trained for killing. Sure he had hunted as a kid. Rabbits and squirrels. Not humans, like Dalton and his crew.

The sounds of brush being pushed aside grew closer. But Buck heard something else. Grunts and a soft yelp.

A dog?

Jesus.

He peered over the rock, looking for movement. Nothing. Then, he saw it. A nasty looking pit bull. He slowly racked a shell into the shotgun's chamber, trying as best he could to muffle the sound. Not very successfully. The dog stopped. Now only thirty yards away, its muscular shoulders twisted in his direction.

The pit bull lowered its head; a deep growl came from its throat. The beast locked on Buck and moved forward and to the left, as if triangulating its target. Another guttural groan, mouth slightly open, teeth now visible. Buck and the animal stared at each other for what seemed like forever.

This dog was trained for this, Buck thought. Knew exactly what it was doing. Its hesitation more planning than fear.

Then, it moved. Fast. Head low, shoulders forward, it hurtled toward him, teeth bared, snarling.

Buck raised the shotgun and pointed it toward the animal, now fifteen yards and closing. He squeezed the trigger.

The discharge was deafening among the trees. The dog yelped, fell. Its paws churned the air for a few seconds and then it fell still.

No doubt Dalton and his crew weren't far behind and now they knew exactly where he was.

Run. No need for stealth. Speed was everything now.

CHAPTER 50

Cain was an excellent hunter. He had been trained in the art since childhood, mostly by Uncle Al and Uncle Mo. Typically employing bows and knives; occasionally shotguns. The family refrained from guns when near towns or farms. Didn't want to alert or annoy the locals. Preferring to do their hunting off the radar. Throughout the South there are large swaths of forested land; some far from civilization, others butted up against towns and farms. Finding truly isolated hunting grounds wasn't always easy.

As an itinerant group, they were outsiders and constantly raised suspicions. Rural folks rarely trusted strangers. Particularly a group of travelers. No roots, no connections to the local community. They were viewed as scavengers at best, thieves at worst. The family was both.

Sure they shopped at markets like everyone else. When they could afford it. But, when necessary, as was often the case, they would scour the woods in search of meat for the nightly meal. Mostly rabbits, squirrels, deer, and wild hogs—those that escaped from farms and became feral packs. The farmers actually appreciated them taking down feral pigs since they were extremely destructive—eating through gardens, devastating chicken coops, and even taking down young calves. When they became nuisance enough, the farmers would band together and go hunting. If someone else was willing to do that, and they didn't have to take time and energy away from their farming, so much the better.

A real treat was when they managed to bag a turkey. Most people think of turkeys as big, dumb birds that magically appear on the Thanksgiving Day table. In the wild, nothing could be further from the truth. Smart, tough, and very wary, they could settle in brush, unmoving, their coloring allowing them to melt into the environment and render them invisible. They could run through brush with amazing speed and agility and fly, hugging the ground, through even the densest forest, like a jet fighter along a narrow valley—something Cain had witnessed more than a few times in Afghanistan. Usually from some mountain crevice where he had hunkered down with a couple of Navy Seals on his way to or from an elimination mission. Missions that were no small feat to successfully complete. Same was true of a turkey hunt.

Movement is the hunter's friend. Whether it was a well-concealed pig or turkey, or one of the many human targets Cain had stalked in the Middle East. Even the smallest movement would lift the prey from the background, revealing its location and direction of travel. Cain was well schooled in this.

Harper, on the other hand, saw more. She saw patterns with amazing clarity. More to the point, breaks in the pattern. That's why Cain always took her with him on turkey hunts. She didn't need for the bird to make a move. She could distinguish its form from even the best camouflage.

Like now.

They had zigzagged though several neighborhoods, even some that had already been searched. No black SUV, most houses and cabins dark and quiet. Then they headed back down the hill, toward The Crossroads.

"Stop," Harper said.

"What?" Cain, who had taken over the driving, braked The Rig and eased to the shoulder.

"Turn around. Go back to that turnout."

Cain did. He pulled into the gravel area, obviously a place to overlook one of the many valleys. He stopped.

"There." Harper pointed.

"What?"

"The tracks."

Cain looked where she pointed. The angle of the headlamps revealed parallel depressions in the gravel and the grass beyond.

They climbed out and followed the path, careful to stay to one side. Cain directed his mini Maglite along the ground ahead of them. The grass wasn't disrupted or gouged, but rather compressed into two strips that angled down the gentle slope and over the edge. That's what Harper had seen.

"A vehicle came through here," Harper said.

"An accident?" Cain asked.

"Maybe. But, these don't look like skid marks. Too clean."

They reached the edge, where the ground fell away. A snapped sapling and several mangled shrubs were visible a few feet down. Cain moved to his left and directed the Maglite beam along the slope. Something reflective caught his attention. Maybe fifty feet down.

"There's something down there."

"What?"

"Can't tell for sure but I suspect it's the vehicle that did this. I'm going down."

Cain slipped his flashlight into his pocket, tightened his jacket, and tugged on his gloves. He side-stepped down the incline, digging his boot soles in to keep from slipping. He used the trees for handholds. Only took a few minutes and he arrived at a black sedan, its front end mashed against a pine tree, hood crumpled and bowed upward, windshield spiderwebbed. Twenty feet further down the slope an active creek cascaded over rocky shallows and continued downhill.

"Got a vehicle," he shouted back up to Harper. He pulled out his Maglite and scanned the windows. No one seated inside. He moved along the driver's side. When he reached the rear window he angled the beam inside. A body.

He yanked open the door. The man was face down. He rolled him over. Duckworth. Entry wound to his right forehead. Cold to the touch, no carotid pulse.

He straightened, pulled out the satellite phone, and flipped it open.

"Yeah," Harper said.

"This is Cassie," Cassie said.

"I found Duckworth. He's dead. Gunshot."

He heard an intake of breath from Cassie. "Oh no," she said. "Where?"

"In his car. Looks like someone shot him, then rolled his car down a ravine. It smashed into a tree near a creek."

"We're at the turnout along Highway 43," Harper said. "Just past Aspen Road. You'll see our rig."

"I know where you are. On my way."

That's when Cain heard the shotgun discharge.

CHAPTER 51

Fury. That's what rippled through Dalton's veins. Water dripped from his clothing as he stood over Jessie, now laying on the sofa where Myrick had placed him. He paced, marking the floor with his muddy boot prints.

"Worthless son-of-a-bitch." He whirled back toward the motionless Jessie, snatched his Glock from the small of his back, and pressed it against Jessie's cheek. "I should kill your stupid ass." He ground his teeth until they hurt. He spun and stomped away.

They had chased Buck for a mile, maybe more. After the shotgun blast that killed Rocco, Dalton thought they had him. Based on the sound of the gun's discharge, they knew where he was and it wasn't far away. But then, he seemed to evaporate. Buck's good luck was that another band of heavy showers swept through, making hearing his footfalls impossible and plunging the forest back into darkness. Worse, the clock was now ticking. If he made it to help, they would come this way and sooner or later find the cabin. As isolated as it was, it was findable. For sure, the roads up this way would be crawling with cops, which meant he had to get Dennie on the road to Memphis and he and the others had to disappear and find another hole to hide in. Reluctantly, Dalton gave up the chase. They trudged back up the hill.

Dalton returned to where Jessie lay and again nudged his face with the gun muzzle. No response. "I'd love to shoot his ass and leave him here."

"Better to let Frankie handle him, don't you think?" Navarro said.

Dalton nodded. "It won't be pretty."

"Nothing he don't deserve."

"What about that asshole doctor? He killed my dog," Harris said.

"What?" Dalton said, turning toward him. "You're worried about a fucking dog?"

"But Rocco…"

"You can get another dog for Christ's sake." Dalton scratched his chin with the gun muzzle. "We got bigger problems. We have to assume he'll find help and will do that pretty quickly. They'll be coming."

"Does he know how to find this place?" Harris asked.

"Maybe. He can at least get them in the right neighborhood. Before that happens, we need to get the fuck out of here."

"What about the others? Jason and the girl?"

"Let's get Dennie and Jessie in the SUV. Myrick will head for Memphis with them. We'll get down the hill, find another place to hang, and then plan what's next."

"Which is?" Navarro asked.

"Getting rid of Jason and the girl. Finding that doctor and doing the same."

"They'll have him under wraps."

"Ain't no wraps tight enough. We'll find him."

It took a good ten minutes to get Dennie and Jessie into the back of Dalton's SUV. They watched as Myrick drove down the drive and out of sight.

"We going to wipe the house?" Navarro said.

"Don't have time for that," Dalton said.

"You guys have prints all over it, I imagine. Not to mention all that other shit."

Dalton turned back toward the structure. "I thought we'd have more time." He gave a head shake. "Only thing to do is cut and run. Or burn it."

"That'd attract some attention, don't you think?" Harris said.

Dalton considered that. "Probably would."

"But that'd take care of the prints," Navarro said.

Dalton turned the options over in his mind and came to a decision. "Let's get out of here. Distance is our friend right now. Once we clean house, we can come back by and torch it on the way out. If it attracts attention then, who cares?"

"What if they find it before that?"

"We'll deal with that when and if we have to."

CHAPTER 52

"Did you hear that?" Harper said.

Cain, Harper, and Cassie were still connected via the satellite phones.

"I did," Cain replied.

"Hear what?" Cassie asked.

"Shotgun," Cain said. The discharge had been muffled by the trees and the rain, but remained unmistakable. "Nothing else makes that sound."

"Where?" Cassie said.

"North of my position. I'm headed that way."

"Want me to come down?" Harper asked.

"Stand in place. Let me see what's what."

"I'm on the way," Cassie said. "Maybe you should wait until I get there."

"This is what Bobby's good at," Harper said. "Let us handle this."

"But I'm the chief of police."

"We're here to help," Harper said.

"Where are you?" Cain asked.

"North of you. Coming around the county highway. Maybe five miles away."

"Round up your crew," Cain said. "Keep your eyes open in case I spook whoever it is back to the road."

"So, you're not waiting?"

"Nope. If this is related to whoever killed Duckworth, time is critical."

Cassie hesitated a few seconds, then said, "Okay. Be careful."

"Always."

Cain closed the phone and slipped it into one of the many zippered jacket pockets. He removed one of his throwing knives from its sheath along his right thigh. Quickly, quietly, senses on edge, he moved uphill, in the direction of the shotgun blast. The rain strengthened, hammered the trees overhead, and splattered the water in the creek, now wider, slower moving.

Who had fired the shotgun? Who was he stalking? Did this person have anything to do with the killing of Scotty Duckworth? If so, who the hell was he shooting at? Made no sense. But then, shotguns didn't have to make sense. They just had to be avoided.

Cain worked his way upstream through the thick growth of trees and shrubs, remaining a good thirty feet away from the creek, where the cover was less dense. Still able to catch glimpses of it through gaps in the trees, he paralleled the ribbon of water. He twisted and side-stepped his lean frame between the foliage, pausing every few yards to listen.

After he had covered a hundred yards or so, a sound caught his attention. He squatted near the trunk of a pine tree, its water-logged limbs providing cover. At first he heard nothing, then there it was again. Someone was coming toward him. He fisted the knife, ready for close-quarter combat if needed.

The sounds increased. Whoever it was wasn't in stealth mode. They were moving quickly, sacrificing stealth for speed. He scanned the trees. Movement. Near the creek. A man came into view. He carried a shotgun in one hand. He stopped, looked back uphill. He cocked his head as though listening. He moved on, hugging the edge of the creek.

Cain followed, taking a somewhat parallel and down-angling path that would eventually intersect with the man's route, and bring Cain up behind him.

The man stopped, turned, looked back. Cain froze. The man continued forward, downward. The pursuit continued for only a couple of minutes before things came together in Cain's favor.

The rain increased, as did the breeze. The creek narrowed and its floor elevated, adding turbulence. And noise. Cain took advantage.

Now only yards behind the man, he pushed between two trees and was on him before he knew Cain was there. He clutched the man's hair and brought the blade to his throat.

"Drop the weapon," Cain said.

The man stiffened but did not release the shotgun.

"Now."

The shotgun struck the rocks and clattered to the water's edge.

"Please," the man said.

"Who are you?"

"Buck. My name's Buck."

Cain let go of his hair, grasped his arm, spinning him around. He lowered the knife to his side. "I'm Bobby Cain. We've been looking for you."

"What?"

"Your father hired me and my partner to find you."

Buck staggered. Cain thought he might fall but he recovered his footing.

"My father?"

"Yes." Cain looked back up the hill. "Are they behind you?"

"They were. I think I lost them."

Cain pulled him into the trees. "Sit."

"What?"

"We wait."

Buck wanted to talk, but Cain waved him into silence. After ten minutes, no one appeared. Cain stood. "Let's go."

As they ascended the slope, where Duckworth's car was, Buck asked, "What's all this?"

"The bad guys killed a cop, I suspect."

"They did. I overheard Dalton telling Jessie about it."

"So it was Dalton Southwell that killed Officer Duckworth?"

"How'd you know that name?"

"That's what we do."

"It's his brother Dennie that got shot. Jessie is one of Dalton's men."

"How's he doing? Dennie?"

"Actually, better than he should, given the circumstances."

"Your father said you were a pretty good surgeon," Cain said.

"More lucky than good."

"Somehow, I think not."

They rose up to the parking area. Wasn't easy. The ground wet, the slope steep, but they made it. Buck with a helping hand from Cain.

Cain introduced Harper.

"You can't imagine how good it is to see you guys," Buck said. "Even if I don't know who the hell you are." He smiled.

Harper explained. Sort of. Merely repeating the same speech that they "find people" and "fix problems."

Buck considered that, nodded. "There are others. Dalton brought in some help."

"How many?"

"I don't know for sure, but from what he told Jessie, three guys. They showed up just as I was running away." He swiped water and grime from his face with the towel Harper had retrieved from the back of The Rig.

"What kind of vehicle?"

"Didn't see. I ran."

"Smart move."

"They had a pit bull. Son-of-a-bitch ran me down. I shot it."

"The blast I heard," Cain said.

"That's how you knew I was down there?"

Cain nodded. "Where were you all this time?"

"In a cabin. Up that way somewhere." He pointed up the road. "I think so anyway."

"Think you can find it?"

"Maybe. It was dark and we twisted and turned a lot. And I was a little occupied with preventing Dennie from bleeding to death."

Cain nodded.

"I can tell you it was deep in the woods. Set back from the road a long way. Surrounded by trees and brush."

Cain pulled his phone from his pocket. "We'll see if we can find it, but the first order of business is to call your father."

CHAPTER 53

Cassie rolled down a narrow farm road toward Highway 43. Rain hammered her windshield and she clicked the wipers to a faster level. She splashed through several water-filled ruts, but the Jeep handled them well. The satellite phone Cain and Harper had given her vibrated. She answered.

"We have Buck," Cain said.

"Is he okay?"

"Tired and dirty but overall fine. He's talking to his father right now."

"The gunshot?"

"That was him. They turned a dog loose on him. He shot it and ran."

"Where'd he get a shotgun?" Cassie asked.

"We haven't gotten that far yet. Figured we'd wait on you to ask him."

"Where are you?"

"Same place. The turnout where we found Duckworth."

"On the way." She checked her cell phone, surprised to find two bars of signal strength. Not bad for up here. She called Hack. He answered quickly. She had talked with him maybe twenty minutes earlier to tell him about Duckworth. Hack had been out east of town searching the area for the SUV. "Where are you?" she asked.

"Don't tell me you have more bad news."

"I don't."

"I'm just about back into town. Headed your way."

"They found Buck," Cassie said.

"Who did?"

"Cain and Harper. He's okay. Looks like he escaped. The bad guys turned a dog on him but he shot it and got away."

"Shot it?"

"Apparently he had a shotgun. Don't know the details yet but they're all waiting for us at the turnout I told you about earlier."

"Okay. I'll pick up the pace."

She closed her phone and dropped it in the center console tray. She turned left onto Highway 43 and gunned the engine. The rain slacked to a drizzle.

Okay, so Dr. Buckner escaped, apparently in one piece. Right now, that seemed a bit of a miracle. Hopefully, he could lead them to where the killers were hiding out. Unless they'd run for it, which was likely the case. If he got away, they were no longer safe wherever they had been before. Time to cut and run.

A half-mile down the road, she blew past an SUV. A black one. Single driver. Male. She didn't recognize him. Could it be? With only the driver? No passengers?

She continued. But something dug at her. What if? If she let them slip by her, she'd lay awake too many nights chairing the 'what-if' committee meeting in her head. She braked, found a shoulder broad enough to make a U-turn.

The SUV, a Lincoln Navigator, rolled along well under the speed limit. Casual. Too casual? She slipped in behind it. No way the driver wouldn't know she was a cop. The light bar and the larger grill headlamps were a dead giveaway. Not to mention he must have noticed the black and white paint job and the door decals as she went by earlier.

She half-expected him to run. He didn't but rather maintained his speed. Ten miles per hour below the 50 MPH limit. No one drove that slow around here.

It crossed her mind that this was likely a waste of time but she lit him up anyway. Better to be sure. The Navigator eased off the road onto a grassy shoulder. She pulled in twenty feet behind it and stepped out.

The driver did, too.

"Stay in the car, sir," she said.

Her headlights bathed him. The strobing blue lights from her light bar reflected off the Navigator's rear window and pulsed against the surrounding trees. Her right hand reflexively fell to her service weapon on her right hip, her fingers curled around the grip. She lifted it an inch. Not clearing the holster but elevating it just enough so that she could do so quickly.

"What's the problem, Officer?" the man asked.

He held his position, unmoving. Right hand at his side, left behind his leg, out of sight. He was maybe mid-thirties, five-ten, lean, thick black hair. Jeans, white tee shirt, a Corona beer logo front and center. He didn't appear scared, or concerned, or anything. Flat eyes stared at her.

"Let me see your hands," Cassie ordered.

He raised his right hand. Chest high. Showing her his open palm. "Did I do something wrong?"

"Both hands."

He hesitated. She slid her weapon free, muzzle directed at the ground.

"Sir, show me both hands. Now."

He did. But his left hand came up with a Glock. Cassie raised her weapon. He fired once; her, three times. The sounds echoed among the surrounding trees.

His bullet whizzed by her left ear. So close she felt it. Hers? One cracked the car door window behind the man, the other two punched him in the chest. His eyes snapped wide and he looked down, momentarily confused. His weapon clattered to the pavement. He wavered, one hand rising to clutch his chest, smearing the blossoms of blood on his shirt. He looked back up at her. His eyes rolled white and he folded to the ground. Sitting position, one leg twisted beneath him, the other splayed to the side, his torso slumping against the open door.

She approached, led by her own Glock. She kicked his weapon away. She squatted, felt for a carotid pulse but found nothing. She stood, lifted her mini Maglite from its case on her service belt, and flicked it on. No one in the passenger seat. She swept the beam through the vehicle. Two men sprawled in the rear compartment, neither moving. *Dead?*

"You. Inside. Let me see your hands."

No response.

She rounded to the rear of the SUV and lifted the gate. The backseat had been folded forward and two men lay side by side. Still, neither moved nor reacted to the light she aimed at their faces. She nudged one leg. A soft groan. The guy on the left. His eyes opened, glassy, unfocused, then closed again.

Took her a couple of minutes to decipher what she saw. Both men out. One, the guy on the right, wore pale blue boxers, an oversized gray tee shirt, barefoot. She saw a smear of blood along the left side of the shirt.

What the hell?

She needed backup.

CHAPTER 54

"We're on the way," Cain said, the satellite phone to his ear.

"So is Hack," Cassie said. "Up 43. Maybe three or four miles."

Harper now drove, Cain shotgun, Buck in back. A mile up the road, Buck said, "Those mailboxes. I remember them."

Cain saw them. A row of seven or eight boxes, lined up along the left side of the road near a gravel road that spurred off. For the cabins that were up that way, no doubt.

"From that night?" Cain asked.

"Yes, we came this way."

"Makes sense given where I found you."

"I remember because of the bright red one on one end and the white one with that oil-rig-looking stand."

"That might help us find the cabin."

"We turned right up here. Maybe another half-mile."

They flew past a paved road.

"Right there," Buck said.

"You sure?"

"Mostly. It was dark and I was busy with Dennie, but it sure looks like what I remember."

"Once we see what's what with Cassie, we'll head back this way."

Flashing blue lights painted Cassie as she stood near the rear of a black Lincoln Navigator. The driver's door stood open and a man sat crumpled against it in the roadway. As Harper parked on the opposite shoulder, Cain saw two forms in the SUV's rear compartment.

"He drew on me," Cassie said as they walked up. She pointed toward the front. "Didn't leave me much choice."

"Good shooting," Cain said, eyeing the corpse.

"I don't know how. My hand was shaking so badly I thought might shoot my own foot."

"But you didn't," Cain said.

"He almost took care of that himself. He got off one round. Missed my ear by a gnat's ass."

Cain looked toward the two men in back. "Who're these guys?"

"That's Dennie and Jessie," Buck said.

Hack rolled up and climbed out.

Over the next twenty minutes a lot happened. The dead man's wallet revealed he was Robert Buddy Myrick. Memphis address. Buck didn't know him. Had never seen him. One of Dalton's crew, no doubt.

Buck examined the two men.

"How're they doing?" Cassie asked.

"Dennie's wound's still intact. Only a little bleeding along the suture line. Jessie will be out for a while yet."

"What'd you do to them?" Harper asked.

"The miracles of modern medicine," Buck said. He smiled. He told of Dalton going to meet the other guys. "I knew that if I was going to escape it had to be while Dalton was gone. I gave Dennie a little morphine and Versed. Then I managed to get Jessie to drink a Manhattan with me. Of course, I added a little chloral hydrate." He shrugged. "The original Mickey Finn."

"Where'd you get that?" Cassie asked.

"At the pharmacy. While I was gathering everything I might need to patch up Dennie, I ran across it in the narcotics cabinet. Thought if I was truly lucky, I'd get a chance to use it."

"Clever," Harper said.

"Or desperate."

An ambulance pulled in behind them followed by another vehicle. Officer Rick Fowler stepped out. While the medics loaded

Dennie and Jessie, Cassie brought Fowler up to date.

"You ride back with the medics," she said to Fowler. "In case these clowns wake up and get antsy." She looked at Buck. "You think you can find this cabin?"

"Maybe."

She nodded. "All right. Let's take a crack at it."

Hack and Fowler pulled their cars well off the road and locked them. Harper rode with Cassie, Cain took The Rig—Buck up front, Hack in the rear seat.

CHAPTER 55

Buck's recall proved to be spot on. Particularly given the circumstances last time he was up this way. Probably explained how he got through med school. Cain turned up the road they had seen earlier, just short of where Buck had pointed out the collection of mailboxes. Buck asked him to slow down and after a half-mile or so told him to stop.

"I think this is it."

"The dirt road?" Cain asked.

"It sure looks like it."

Cain continued another hundred feet and pulled to the shoulder. Cassie eased up behind him. Everyone stepped out.

"You think this is the place?" Cassie asked.

"That's my best guess." Buck looked back that way. "If so, that road or drive or whatever it is, is barely passable. It winds a couple of hundred yards up into the trees. Like I said, the house is well hidden."

"I don't know this place," Cassie said. "Didn't even know anything was up that way. Didn't see a mailbox either." She rubbed her neck. "Maybe it's abandoned."

"It's not," Buck said. "Older couple. You'll find their bodies in the garage."

"Really?"

Buck nodded.

Cassie sighed. "These are very bad actors."

"Dalton is, for sure," Buck said. "Scary as hell."

Cassie looked at Cain. "You think they're still in there?"

"Probably not. With Dennie packed up and sent off and Buck getting away, they'd have to assume we'd find this place."

Cassie glanced up the dirt pathway. "Maybe they're on the way to Memphis."

Cain gave her a look.

"You don't think so?" Cassie asked.

"He doesn't," Harper said. "I don't either. If the plan was to cut and run, why bring in others? Just hit the road and disappear."

Cassie hooked a thumb in her belt. "I agree."

"Which means they have something else on their agenda," Cain said.

"Dalton had some business to take care of," Buck said. "I don't know what. He never said specifically."

"Take out a couple of witnesses," Harper said.

Cain nodded. "Unless Jason is helping them."

Harper shrugged. "They'll get around to him sooner or later. Maybe, after he helps."

"They wouldn't know this area well," Cassie said. "But Jason would and he'd know how to find Marla."

"Might be a good idea to warn her."

Cassie pulled out her cell. "No service."

"Use the satellite phone," Cain said.

She called Fowler, brought him up to speed, and told him to work on finding Marla and Jason. She closed the phone, saying, "Let's get this done and get back to town."

"Let us do this," Cain said.

Cassie shook her head. "This is my job."

"But it's what we do," Harper said.

Cassie didn't seem convinced. "Maybe, but I'm in charge."

It took Cain a couple of minutes to convince Cassie he had a plan. Vague and fluid, but a good one given the situation. Cain and Harper would go first, work around to the rear of the cabin. If there was one. If Buck was right. Cassie and Hack would follow, cover the front. Buck insisted on going. Cassie hesitated but agreed when Buck added that standing out here on the side of the road could make him a target and that he'd stay well out of the way and behind them.

Harper removed her Glock, checked it, held it to her side. Cain pulled out one of his knives. They melted into the trees.

Cain and Harper were in their element. The terrain densely forested, steep and uneven. They moved quickly through the trees, paralleling the drive. The rain had slackened to a drizzle once again and there was little wind. The soaked ground and wet foliage helped muffle their approach. Wasn't long before they saw the cabin. Weak light pushed against the closed curtains. No movement.

Exchanging hand signals, they split, each flanking the structure, using the trees for cover. Cain came out near the garage. No vehicles. No activity. The rear door stood open. Harper slipped from the trees and joined him.

"They're in the wind," she said.

They were. Inside, Cain and Harper cleared each room. Both beds rumpled, slept in. The kitchen messy. Two glasses sat on the dining table—one empty, the other filled with a dark liquid.

Harper nodded toward them. "That was a clever move."

"Risky. Could've backfired."

"Guess he saw that as his best shot."

"Maybe his only shot."

Cain cracked open the front door, standing to one side in case either Cassie or Hack got trigger happy. Through the gap he shouted, "All clear." Then pushed the door open.

Cassie and Hack entered. Buck followed.

"This is it," Buck said. He looked around. "I take it they've gone."

Cain nodded. "Where'd you do the surgery?"

Buck pointed toward the dining room table. "Right there." He walked around it. "Not exactly like med school."

"I'd say you did a good job."

"More luck than anything. No major blood vessels and the bullet missed the bowel. Either would have been a complication that I couldn't have handled here. As it was, he lost a kidney and a lot of blood."

"He going to make it?" Harper asked.

Buck considered that for a beat. "Probably. He made it through the hard part. If he manages to dodge a major infection he should do okay." Buck led them into the bedroom. "This was our ICU." He pointed to a pair of large trash bags in one corner. "That's mostly biohazard stuff, so whoever comes to look for evidence or clean up should handle it carefully."

"I'll make sure," Cassie said. She looked around the room. "Let's get to the ER. I want to have a chat with those two."

CHAPTER 56

"Quit looking out the fucking window," Dalton said.

Dale Harris released the curtain he had peeled back. "Just checking."

"Don't. Someone peeking through a motel curtain looks suspicious."

"To who? Did you see anybody out there?"

After Buck's escape, the cabin was no longer safe. If he got to help, they would saddle up and be back. In force. So they packed up and headed east, then south on a ratty county blacktop. Looking for an out of the way place to reorganize and plan. Dalton didn't want to be on the road or anywhere in public. Not until he had sorted things out and plotted his next move.

They'd be looking for two, three, maybe four men in a car. The doc and the cops would have to figure that out. The doc knew he and some of his crew were staying in the area to take care of business. He, of course, wouldn't know the details, but really, how hard would that be to figure out? Silencing the witnesses, and the doc, would be the only thing that made sense. Surely the cops weren't so clueless they wouldn't see that.

With Dennie injured, and Jessie not able to drive—the doc would've told them about that—they'd have to know that Dalton would be forced to send one of his guys to take Dennie, and that fuck up Jessie, back to Memphis. So, they might not know exactly how many guys they were looking for, but they'd for sure be sniffing around for strangers in a strange vehicle. It was time to go to ground and let things cool off for a few hours.

The detail that bothered Dalton most was whether Buck had seen Myrick's Navigator. Was he already down the hill, or did he see them drive up? He hadn't gotten very far by the time they caught up to him, and he killed Harris's dog, so he guessed it could go either way. But, what could he do about it? Nothing, and that's what grated on his nerves.

Dalton had to admit, it was a ballsy move on Buck's part. From the beginning, he had thought Buck was cleverer than he let on. Maybe even not as afraid as he should have been. That was on Dalton. He should've pounded the fear of God into him more forcefully. Too late now. But not too late to settle the account.

That would be the hard part. Getting to him. Surely he had been found and was now under the wing of the cops. Taking care of Jason and the girl would be a snap. Dealers and users weren't usually genius-level thinkers. Just greedy and needy, which made them vulnerable. But, Buck? It might take days before the lid was lifted on him. After the cops figured that Dalton and his guys were long gone and no longer a threat. But hanging around and waiting carried more risk than was acceptable. He wanted to button all this up and get back across the state.

They found this seedy little motel five miles out of Tanner's Crossroads. A thirty-five-dollar-a-night, eight-unit dump with only two other cars in the lot, the red neon vacancy sign sputtering toward death. Harris got the room, acting like a lone traveler. Three guys this time of night might have ramped up the manager's radar. Fortunately, according to Harris, the man behind the counter was old, sleepy, and engrossed in some stupid laugh-tracked show on the wall-mounted TV behind the counter. Hardly gave Harris a second look. Didn't even ask for ID. Simply took the money and handed him the key, mumbling, "Number eight, down at the end."

Navarro flopped on one of the two single beds. "What's the plan?"

"I need to call Frankie," Dalton said. "Bring him up to speed."

Harris dropped in a chair. "He'll blow a freaking gasket."

"I know. But I need to see how he wants to handle things now."

"I say we take care of business and get the hell out of here."
Navarro gave a grunt. "I sort of agree with Dale."

"Good thing it isn't your decision." Dalton looked from
Navarro to Harris. "I need to check in with Frankie. Get some
information. Info only Frankie can get right now, and not jump
into something until we have a plan. We don't know all the players
involved. All the moving parts. We don't know the town. So, first
order of business is to call Frankie. See how he wants it to go
down." He again looked back and forth between the two men.
"Unless you think we should bypass Frankie and go our own way."

Neither Navarro nor Harris responded.

"Didn't think so."

"I just want to get this done," Navarro said.

"I do, too," Dalton said. "I also want to make sure my brother
makes it to Memphis."

"And Jessie?" Navarro asked. "What're you going to do about
that douche bag?"

"Drop him in Frankie's hands. I'm sure he'll have some creative
ideas along that line."

"Which means we can write his sorry ass off."

"Probably."

"No probably about it," Harris said. "Frankie won't put up
with this shit."

Dalton nodded his agreement. "It's possible Frankie will want
us to cut our losses and clear out. I doubt it, but it's possible. If he
wants us to clean up things around here, we'll have our work cut
out," Dalton said. "Three targets, maybe four. None likely in the
same place. In a town we don't know."

"Jason and the girl should be easy," Navarro said. "They'll have
the doc on lock down."

"And he's the one that can do the most harm," Dalton said.
"He's seen me. Dennie and Jessie, too."

"The girl saw you guys," Harris said.

"Apparently so. That's why she has to go down."

"But none of them has seen us," Navarro said, waving a hand
toward Harris.

"That's why you two will be the eyes and ears on this," Dalton
said. "Until we're set up."

Harris stood, jangled the car keys from his pocket. "I'll go get us some food."

"Grab some beer," Navarro added.

"No beer," Dalton said. "I need you guys clear headed."

"A beer won't be no problem," Navarro said.

"Just food and soft drinks." Dalton looked at Harris. "Be cool. Stay under the speed limit and don't do anything stupid."

"Me?" Harris said. "I'm just a hungry tourist."

Harris left. Dalton called Frankie. He could tell Frankie was at his club—music and laughter in the background. Frankie told him to hold tight, headed into the quiet of his office.

"Tell me," Frankie said.

Dalton laid it out. Frankie said little, a bad sign. He wasn't pleased but a plan unfolded. He would call when Dennie, Bud, and Jessie arrived. He would handle Jessie. Show what happens when someone is a major fuck up. A teaching opportunity for everyone else was Frankie's take. He would also call his Tanner's Crossroads contact and get the skinny on the targets. Should have everything ready to roll in a couple of hours.

CHAPTER 57

When they reached the ER, Cain saw the medics cleaning and preparing their vehicle for the next call. Cassie stopped and asked if all went smoothly and they assured her it had. Cain and Harper entered, followed by Cassie, Hack, and Buck. A nurse stood behind the registration counter, phone to her ear. She hung up and turned toward them, and almost shrieked when she saw Buck. Her name tag revealed she was J. Campbell, RN.

"Dr. Buckner," she said. "You're back. We've been so worried."

"Me, too," Buck said. He smiled. "Sorry I missed dinner."

She rounded the nurse's station counter and hugged him. "You have a rain check for sure." She looked at the others. "He was supposed to come over for dinner but he stood us up." She raised an eyebrow, smiled. "Some kidnapping story."

Buck introduced Cain and Harper to Joanie Campbell.

"Where are the two guys that came in?" Cassie asked.

"Room one and room three. Dr. Padilla is with the injured guy."

Buck led everyone toward Trauma Room 1 and introduced Dr. Pedro Padilla. "How's he doing?" Buck asked, indicating Dennie who lay on the stretcher, his eyes now open.

"Amazingly well." He pointed to Dennie's surgical wound. "You did this?"

"On a dining room table. You should've been there. I could've used your help."

Pedro shook his head. "I'm impressed."

"Lucky," Buck said. He looked at Dennie. "And you're a very lucky guy."

"Not sure I see it that way," Dennie said. His speech was still slightly thick from the morphine and Versed Buck had given him earlier.

Buck gave a quick nod. "Actually, I think we're all lucky. You, Jessie, me. I figured Dalton would shoot us, take off, and be done with it."

"Show's what you know," Dennie said. "He's my brother. He wouldn't do that."

Buck stepped forward, gripped the stretcher's railing. "Yes, I believe he would. He murdered a family, an innocent elderly couple, and a cop. Doesn't seem to me he possesses much discrimination in who he kills."

"None of them was blood."

"Just in the way."

"Let's not forget Wilbert Shaffer," Cassie said.

Buck turned to her. "Mr. Shaffer?"

"Yeah. Didn't you know?"

"No." Buck sighed. He hesitated as if recalling something. "That's why Dalton went back inside. After we were all loaded in the SUV."

"Didn't want to leave a witness," Harper said.

Buck shook his head. "I should've guessed that."

Dennie smiled. "Well, my brother's long gone by now."

"I don't think so," Cain said.

"Who the fuck are you?" Dennie asked.

Cain walked over to the bed, looked down. "The one that's going to track down your brother and his crew."

"You'll never find them."

Cain smiled. "It won't be that difficult. Your brother isn't exactly a criminal mastermind. He's pretty sloppy."

"No, he ain't."

"You guys left enough evidence back at that cabin to hang all of you. Fingerprints, DNA, and a couple of corpses. Purely amateur."

"You could end up dead thinking that way," Dennie said.

"Maybe," Harper said. "Or maybe it'll be Dalton on the ground."

Dennie looked at her, then at Cain. "You trying to be tough guys or something?"

"If I were you, or your brother, I'd be more afraid of her," Cain nodded toward Harper. Dennie's gaze cut that way. "Or Frankie." Now Dennie's attention snapped back to Cain. "Yeah, we know all about him."

Cassie had slid to the other side of the bed. Cain gave her a nod.

"You can help your brother, and yourself. Where are they and what are they planning?"

"Don't know."

Cassie leaned her elbows on the bedrail. "We know Dalton has two other guys with him. Started with three from what Buck overheard but I had to dump one out on the side of the road."

Dennie's eyes widened a notch and concern etched his face.

"Yeah. Guy named Myrick." She smiled. "He thought he was a tough guy, too." She nudged Dennie's shoulder. "So don't screw around. Who are the guys with your brother?"

"I ain't saying shit."

Cain thumped Dennie's forehead with a finger. "Listen up. I'm sure Chief Crowe here would love to hang this entire rap on you. Make things nice and easy for her. But if your brother and his sidekicks escalate this, make a move on anyone else, it'll be much worse."

Cassie jumped in, "Right now, we have you for eight murders and conspiracy to commit such: The Finley's, Wilbert Shaffer, the couple at the cabin, and one of my officers. Maybe toss in kidnapping, though I don't think you played an active role in all of them. Getting yourself shot up and all. But you were present. That makes you at best a co-conspirator. If Dalton brings harm to anyone else, and if you impede our finding him, stopping whatever he has planned, we'll add a stack of other charges to your ledger. That'll pretty much assure you never see sunlight again."

Dennie's gaze moved around, never finding anything to land on. He mumbled, "I ain't telling you shit."

Cassie shrugged, looked at Cain. "Some folks have to stick their finger in the socket to see if it's live."

The next stop was Trauma Room 3. Jessie lay on the stretcher, wrist cuffed to the frame. Officer Rick Fowler was chatting with him.

"Anything?" Cassie asked.

Fowler shook his head. "He ain't saying nothing."

Cassie looked down at him. "That right?"

"I ain't going to talk to you either, bitch."

Cassie's eyes narrowed. "Let's add it up. You killed a family of four, a man simply working for a living, an older couple because you needed their cabin, and one of my officers. These weren't faceless victims to me. They were all nice folks. In the case of Scotty Duckworth...that was his name but I doubt you really care...he was family. So, I take all this very personally." She moved around the stretcher to the other side. Jessie's gaze followed. "But you don't have to say anything. Dennie's telling us what we need."

That got his attention.

"Yeah, he's pointing the finger for all this at you."

"Wasn't me. It was—" He caught himself. "I got nothing to say."

"Yeah, Dennie said you'd try to lay it all on his brother Dalton. But, he said it was all you."

Jessie briefly glanced toward Cain and Harper who stood just outside the door before returning his attention to Cassie. "He wouldn't say nothing like that. 'Cause it ain't true."

Cassie smiled. "I guess it's just that blood being thicker than water thing."

Jessie said nothing but Cain saw stress lines appear at the corners of his eyes and mouth. Laying it out for him the way Cassie had done was a smart move. Make him think he's the odd man out. The one with his dick in the wind. Divide and conquer.

"We'll get you over to the jail as soon as the doc clears you and we'll chat again," Cassie said. "On my turf."

Everyone gathered outside the ER entry. Cassie said that she didn't want Buck going home. That maybe he should hide out in the jail. He balked but she wouldn't back down.

"We have to assume Dalton's plan is to find you. You can ID him. We can't protect you in your apartment."

"Can I at least go by and pick some things up?"

"We'll take you," Harper said.

Cassie looked at Hack. "You and Fowler get Jessie over to the jail."

"Will do." He shuffled back inside.

Cain's cell buzzed. Mama B. He answered.

"I got some names for you," she said.

"Before you do, we found Dr. Buckner."

"And?"

"He's fine. Standing right here."

She sighed. "I was afraid it wasn't good."

"I'm putting you on speaker. Harper's here. Also Dr. Buckner and Chief Crowe." Cain punched the speaker button. "This is Mama B. A good person to know."

"Flatterer," Mama B said.

"What did you find?" Cain asked.

"The rest of Dalton's crew are stellar citizens. Robert Buddy Myrick, Chris Navarro, and Dale Harris. Myrick has three pops for assault, most recently two years ago. Navarro was named in a couple of murders but skated on each for lack of evidence. Harris is a little cleaner, at least on paper. Only has a single assault charge and it was ultimately dismissed. So these guys are careful, if nothing else."

"And connected," Harper said.

"That, too."

"We don't have to worry about Myrick," Cain said. "Chief Crowe took him off the board. Less than an hour ago."

"The world won't miss him I'm sure. So, one down and three to go." She gave a soft laugh. "I'll send the files to you."

"Can you loop in Chief Crowe?"

"Sure."

"I'll give you my email address," Cassie said.

"I have it," Mama B said.

"You do?"

"It's what I do."

"Good work," Harper said. "As usual."

"Not done yet. Just starting to dig into that attorney you asked about."

"What attorney?" Cassie asked.

"Simon Greene," Cain said.

Cassie looked confused. "What does Simon have to do with

this?"

Cain shrugged. "Maybe nothing, but he did defend Tommy Finley."

"That's what attorneys do."

"Maybe that's all it is," Harper said. "Him simply doing his job."

Cassie sighed. "First we need to find Jason and Marla."

"Marla Jackson?" Buck asked.

"She's the one that witnessed your abduction," Cassie said. "Started this whole thing rolling."

"Where? How?"

"She hooked up with her new supplier—dude named Jason Epps—in the park. Used some heroin and probably meth and saw the whole thing from there. She managed to keep it together long enough to cross the street and get back to the ER."

Disappointment fell over Buck's face. Apparently, Cassie saw it, too.

"Don't get all caught up in Marla's world," Cassie said. "She's a drug addict, maybe she always will be. Lord knows she's had multiple chances to climb out of the pit but so far nothing's worked out."

"I hate to hear that," Buck said. "She seemed so nice. Bright. I suspect she was a beauty before the monkey caught her."

"She was, and a good student." Cassie looked down, kicked at a loose pebble, sending it skittering across the pavement. "We were friends back then. Lately, more butting heads."

"Sorry," Buck said.

"Well, right now I'm concerned about her for other reasons."

"Dalton?"

"Yep."

"He did say he had some things to take care of. That's why he didn't simply leave and why he brought in more guys."

"We have to assume he'll target you. I also assume he knows about Marla and will deal with her and her new supplier Jason."

"So this isn't over?" Buck asked.

Cain smiled. "We're just getting to the fun part."

"Amen," Harper said.

CHAPTER 58

The first stop for Cain and Harper was Buck's apartment. They stood vigil while Buck gathered fresh clothing and necessities. He tossed his bag in the backseat of The Rig and climbed in.

"I can't believe I'm going to jail," he said.

Harper laughed. "Not as an inmate though. So that's good."

"I hope they have a shower. I feel like a swamp rat."

Harper twisted in the passenger seat and looked back at him. Hair matted with dirt, face drawn and pale. "You sort of look like one, too."

"It's my new image. Do you think the girls will like it?"

"No doubt. Makes you a man of mystery, or at least chaos."

"I'm beginning to feel it might be more the latter. I never figured I'd get into something as crazy as this. The truth is, my life is pretty vanilla."

"I've got to tell you," Cain said, eyeing him in the rearview mirror. "You did a hell of a job on Dennie Southwell. He looked like any other post-op patient."

"I gave it my best shot."

"By yourself?"

"I recruited Jessie and Dalton."

"They helped?"

"Well, he is Dalton's brother. But, they were both scared to death." He chuckled. "It was actually funny. Here I was the hostage, they had the guns, but I was in charge. For that hour or so it took to do the procedure, anyway. They were afraid not to do what I said."

"An interesting dynamic," Harper said.

"It was. But brief. Once Dennie was out of the woods, at least mostly, Dalton took control. Complete control." He caught Cain's eye in the mirror. "There were times I honestly thought he'd kill me."

"He would have," Cain said. "As soon as you got Dennie safely to Memphis."

"I know. He's a very dangerous person."

"We've seen worse," Cain said.

"I can't imagine."

"Afghanistan's full of them," Harper said. "Guys who'll kill entire families, sometimes entire villages, if it suits their needs."

"I've read accounts of that."

"We've seen it," Harper said. "More than a few times."

"You guys were in the military?"

"Sort of," Cain said.

"Let's say we were involved in things that aren't recorded and no one talks about," Harper added.

"That sounds sinister."

"It was."

"Are you talking about black ops stuff?"

"Dark black," Harper said.

"That's why Dalton and his crew aren't all that scary," Cain said. "Dangerous. Very dangerous. But, like I said, we've seen worse."

At the PD, Cain and Harper met JT Doyle and Liz Evans, the two officers who would hold down the fort while Cassie and Hack hit the streets. Buck headed to the shower. Cain, Harper, Hack, and Cassie settled in Cassie's office. She booted her computer and checked her emails, finding several files from Mama B.

They gathered behind her as she opened the info and images. As usual, Mama B proved to be thorough.

First was Dale Harris. A more or less normal looking guy. He wore a smirk in an old booking photo but it seemed more contrived than real. Trying to play tough for the cops. He was twenty-nine, five-ten, 160 with short, cropped, brown hair, almost sleepy eyes, and thin lips that turned down at the corners. His sheet showed the single assault arrest Mama B had alluded to. Dismissed when the victim refused to cooperate. Wonder why?

Chris Navarro, age thirty-two, six-feet, 190, and an angry face. Dark eyes, set hard, challenging. Square jaw, a fuck you attitude. This from a three-year-old mug shot. Short, spiky hair, a webbed neck, and the hint of thick, muscular shoulders. No doubt a gym rat. No doubt a handful if it came to a mano a mano match. Little doubt he committed the murders he walked on.

Lastly, a picture of Dalton Southwell. Also thirty-two, six-two, 190, lean, hard, dark hair pulled back into a ponytail—just as Marla had described. His record was a little denser. Did fifteen months for strong-armed robbery, followed by a couple on probation. That ended three years ago. Also did a month for assault, but was released when the victim decided he had made the wrong ID. Several other assault charges that never went anywhere.

"Pleasant looking guys," Cassie said.

"At least we now know who they are," Harper added.

Cassie nodded. "Now all we have to do is find them."

"Maybe they're on the road to Memphis," Hack said.

"They aren't," Cain said.

Hack hooked a thumb in his belt. "Wishful thinking."

"But we know who they're after," Harper said. "That gives us a place to start."

Cassie closed the images on her computer and stood. "Maybe we can convince Marla and Jason to join Dr. Buckner here at the jail. Sort of a sleepover."

Cain smiled. "If they agree."

"We could simply arrest them," Hack said. "I'm sure Marla's using and Jason's carrying so we'd have probable cause."

"I'd rather talk reason," Cassie said. "At least initially." She smiled. "But first, another chat with Jessie. See if he can throw some light on the subject."

CHAPTER 59

Jessie Parker. Twenty-nine and already a loser. A thug, a drug dealer, a bottom feeder. A multiple murderer. That was Cain's take. Jessie was also a dull knife. Not enough smarts to avoid getting drugged by a guy with more brains and character than Jessie was likely to see in his entire life.

The smart guy, Buck, was showering, trying to wash away the remnants of his ordeal. Jessie, the loser, sat in a hard wooden chair in the interrogation room, Cassie and Hack across from him. Cain stood next to Harper and peered through the one-way mirror/window and watched Jessie try to act tough. His words tinny as they crackled through the small wall speaker to their left.

"I don't know anything about it," Jessie said.

"Anything about what?" Cassie asked.

That gave Jessie a moment of pause. "About what we're talking about."

"What are we talking about?"

"She's good," Harper said. "Already has him sweating."

She did. Jessie's face shined, he wiggled in his chair.

"You know," Cassie said.

"I don't. Maybe you should tell me." He leaned back and folded his arms over his chest.

"Let's start with the murders of Tommy Finley and his family. You know, where Dennie Southwell got shot."

"Don't know nothing about it."

"Fortunately—actually, unfortunately for you, Dennie says otherwise."

"He wouldn't say nothing. Even if there was something to say."

"You sure?" Hack said.

"I am."

"Then we'll move on to Wilbert Shaffer," Cassie said. "The pharmacist." Jessie started to say something but she waved him away, "and the Currys. The couple whose house you took over."

"Don't know nothing about that stuff either."

Hack leaned forward, elbows on the table. "Then there was my friend Scotty Duckworth. Shot and dumped over a ledge like garbage."

Jessie simply stared.

"You must be the unluckiest son-of-a-bitch on the planet," Hack continued. "I mean, being found unconscious in the back of a vehicle carrying Dennie out of town with a guy known to be part of Dalton Southwell's crew." He scratched the back of his hand but his hard gaze never let Jessie go. "Like you are."

"Yeah," Cassie said. "He didn't make it. Myrick."

"Never heard that name before."

"Then you won't mind that I pumped a couple of rounds in his chest. He's over at the morgue."

Jessie stiffened. Some of his bravado seemed to evaporate.

Now Cassie leaned in. "What is Dalton up to? Why is he hanging around? Why not just cut and run? Why did he bring in Myrick, Harris, and Navarro?"

Jessie tried to hide it but his pupils widened, his mouth tightened.

"We know all about them. Frankie, too."

Jessie looked around the room as if seeking an escape hatch.

Hack lifted his weapon from his hip and laid it on the table, muzzle angled toward Jessie's chest. "Don't even think about it, partner. I'll shoot you dead and I'll enjoy doing it." Hack patted the weapon with one hand. "Or maybe I'll just shoot you in the leg and step on your face." He raised one foot. "I wear size eleven and a half."

"I love him," Harper said. "He would've made a good CO."

"That's a fact," Cain replied.

"I ain't got to talk to you about nothing," Jessie said.

Cassie stood, scraping her chair back. "No, you don't. You know what? That's fine with me. We'll simply hang all this on you."

Cassie and Hack left the room and joined Cain and Harper near the window. Jessie leaned on the table, his face in his hands.

"Guess we'll have to find Dalton and his guys on our own."

"Mind if we have a chat with him?" Cain asked. "Maybe explain things to him."

"What are you going to do?"

"Not waterboard him," Cain said, "if that's what you're thinking."

That drew a smile from her. She glanced through the window toward Jessie, hesitated, then nodded. "Okay. Just don't do any harm."

"Tell you what, why don't you and Hack grab some coffee? Let me and Harper handle this?"

Hack nodded. "If we aren't witnesses we won't have anything to say to the judge."

Cassie gave him a look.

"I promise," Cain said. "I won't lay a finger on him."

Cassie nodded. "Come on, Hack. We still have a long night ahead it seems and I could use some coffee."

They left.

"Glad you said you and not we," Harper said.

"Didn't want to handcuff you."

Jessie lifted his head from the table as they entered. "Who the fuck are you?"

"A couple of interested parties," Harper said.

"Yeah, I saw you two over at the hospital." His chin came up. "Not that I give a shit, but what exactly are you interested in?"

Harper stepped forward and leaned straight-armed on the back of the chair that faced Jessie. "We're curious exactly how much pain you can tolerate before you break."

"What?"

"See," Cain said, stepping up beside her, "we aren't cops. Actually we aren't anything."

"Except skilled in handling punks like you," Harper said.

"We're in a police station. You can't do that."

"Really?" Harper said. "We're in a police department? I hadn't noticed. I thought we were in some bunker in Afghanistan."

"Me, too," Cain said. "Of course, over there we sometimes dealt with guys who'd killed fewer people than old Jessie here."

Fear sweat popped out on Jessie's face. His eyes danced, as did one leg. A good sign. Fear is a funny thing. It ramps up painful sensations. Makes smaller increments more effective. Makes the person think, actually believe, that whatever is happening will get worse. It lowers defenses, creates confusion, and ultimately works well, despite what some would have you believe.

"Let's start easy," Cain said, taking a seat in the chair.

"Let's do." Harper moved around the table until she had positioned herself directly behind Jessie.

Jessie's head swiveled, not sure who to focus on.

"Look at me," Cain said. "Like Chief Crowe said, this is your situation. We have eight bodies. One a cop. Each and every one falls into your lap. Do you get where I'm headed here?"

"I don't know anything," Jessie said.

Cain smiled. "But that isn't why we're here. Harper and I. That's Chief Crowe's deal. We know Dalton's around. He's going to do something to someone. You know who. Might even know where he's holed up."

"I don't." He smirked. "Even if I did I wouldn't tell you. I ain't no rat."

"That's too bad."

Like lightning, Harper closed on him. She wadded his hair in one fist, yanked his head back, and ground a knuckle into his left eyebrow, where a nerve runs over a bone. Jessie tried to move but Cain grabbed his wrists and pinned his forearms to the table. Harper continued for a full half-minute, then released the pressure.

Jessie gasped for breath. Now his pupils were black pools. Cain could feel his pulse against the palms of his hands. About 190.

"How was round one?" Cain asked.

"Fuck you."

With Jessie's head still arched back, Harper now ground her knuckle into the nerve that ran over the angle of his mandible.

He tried to twist away, but Harper never lost her grasp just as they'd been trained as kids. Uncle Mo. Strong hands are the key to everything. Hunting, climbing, stealing, fighting, whatever. Even hostile interrogations.

Jessie's gasping took on a deep raspiness. Harper released the pressure and then his hair, Cain his wrists. Jessie took several breaths, closed his eyes. When he opened them, Cain held a knife point less than an inch from his right carotid artery.

"Want me to bleed you?" Cain said.

"You're crazy."

"I like to think of us as committed. Are you?" Cain moved the blade point to within an inch of Jessie's right eye. "Are you committed enough to protecting Dalton that you'd sacrifice an eye?" Cain smiled. "Believe me, I'm committed enough to take one."

Cain saw the fight drain from him. His shoulders sagged, his face relaxed.

"What do you want?" Jessie asked.

"I told you. Where's Dalton?"

"I don't know. I honestly don't."

"Who's with him?"

Jessie hesitated. Cain moved the knife point closer, now almost touching his cornea. Jessie froze. Afraid to move. "Okay. I'll tell you."

Cain backed away. He waved the open palm of his other hand as if to say go ahead.

Jessie glanced back toward Harper like he feared she would renew her attack. "Two other guys besides Myrick. I don't know for sure but probably the ones you mentioned. Harris and Navarro."

"What's their plan?" Harper asked from behind him.

"Find the doc—Buck—and the girl. The one that saw Dalton and me at the hospital."

"How'd you know about her?"

"All I know is that Dalton has a contact over here."

"Jason Epps?"

"Don't know for sure. He mostly talked with Tommy but I think I remember him mentioning another guy. Could be this Jason dude."

"But, you don't know Jason?" Harper asked.

He shook his head. "Never met him."

"Has Dalton contacted him?" Cain asked. "Since killing Tommy? Or before?"

"Not that I know." He hesitated.

Cain sensed there was more. "What is it?"

"Look, Dalton and Frankie have another guy over here, too. I don't know who." He looked Cain in the eye. "Dalton ain't big on giving out information he don't have to."

"This contact told him about the witness?"

"Far as I know."

"Did this guy give Dalton her name?"

"Not that he told me."

CHAPTER 60

Harper updated Hack and Cassie on Jessie's interrogation. Dalton, Harris, and Navarro were in play. Buck, Marla—though he might not know her name—and maybe Jason were potential targets.

"Dalton apparently has another contact over here," Harper said. "Any idea who?"

"What do you mean by contact?" Cassie asked.

"Someone who knew about Marla witnessing Buck's abduction." She looked at Hack. "It better not be anyone in-house."

"I can't imagine it would be," Hack said.

"If it is, I'm going to take some scalps."

It was decided that Harper would go with Cassie and try to reason with Marla, while Cain and Hack tracked down Jason and offered him the same protection. Harper climbed in Cassie's Jeep Cherokee and they headed toward Reverend John's. It was nearing midnight, the rain now little more than a drizzle.

"You think she'll be there?" Harper asked.

"With Marla you never know. More than a few times I've seen her roaming around town in the middle of the night. The park, too."

Harper sensed a deep sadness in Cassie's voice. "You two go way back, right?"

"Oh, yeah. Grammar school, and on up through high school. Marla was the golden girl. The rest of us always lived in her shadow."

"Any issues with that?"

"You mean like rivalries?"

"Yeah."

"Maybe with a couple of the girls. But the truth was that Marla was the nicest, sweetest person you could imagine. Smart, athletic, always willing to help anyone with anything. But once she got into drugs everything changed. I guess you could say we were close, then…we weren't. She became withdrawn, sometimes hostile. I didn't understand it then. I do now. She got into heroin and meth and each of those, as you know, can do a number on you. Particularly if you mix them. She got herself arrested a few times. A couple by Hack, once by me. Went to rehab two or three times but it never stuck. She always returned to the streets. Needless to say, our worlds spun in different directions."

"That's tough. To lose a friend that way."

Cassie glanced at her. Harper sensed moisture collecting in Cassie's eyes. Not true tears, but a slight glistening in the glow of the dash lights.

"The hardest part wasn't seeing the drugs take her. It was the fact that she sold herself." Cassie sighed. "For some reason that bothered me more. She sold her body on the streets for drugs."

"That happens all too often."

"I know. But when it's someone with so much going for them, an unlimited future, it seems especially sad." She shrugged. "With Marla, I took it personally, like I had failed her."

Harper touched Cassie's arm. "I doubt that."

"Well, she's dug herself into another hole. The irony is that this time, it's not really her fault."

That was true. Marla had simply been a witness to a crime. An accident of time and place and now her life could be in danger.

But did Dalton know that the witness was Marla? Or know how to find her? If Jessie could be believed, and that was a stretch, he just might not have her name. One thing was certain: based on everything they knew, what Buck had said, the fact the Dalton had called in help, there was no doubt Dalton had an agenda. A deadly one. For sure it included Buck Buckner. Maybe Jason Epps. But, Marla? Maybe, maybe not. Best to assume so.

And if he did know her name, did he learn it from Jason? Had Dalton already hooked up with Jason? Moved him into Tommy's place? Made a deal that included Marla? Harper didn't like any of those scenarios.

"Here we are." Cassie pulled to the curb in front of Reverend John's two-story, white house. He pushed open the front door and stepped onto the covered porch.

Cassie had called John before they left the PD to make sure Marla was there. She had put her phone on speaker so Harper could hear. Yes, Marla was there. Upstairs. Yes, he was sure. Did she want him to wake her? No, Cassie said she'd rather Marla not know they were coming, in case she decided to slip away. Wouldn't be the first time.

Reverend John welcomed them inside.

"Sorry to barge in at this late hour," Cassie said.

"I was still up reading."

He wore jeans, a white shirt, and a gray cardigan. Half glasses rode high on his forehead.

"What's this about?" John asked.

Cassie laid it out: Dr. Buckner had been found and was in good shape, her concern that Dalton had brought in a crew to find him, and maybe Jason and Marla.

A frown, a slight nod. "You're worried they might come here?"

"Maybe," Cassie said. "Or lie in wait for her on the streets or at the park."

John nodded. "I got me a shotgun in the closet and a handgun beside my bed." He glanced at Cassie. "And thanks to Uncle Sam, I know how to use them."

"I know you do but it's probably better if it doesn't come to that."

"What's the plan?" he asked.

"See if we can convince her to stay down at the station until we find them."

John actually laughed. "Good luck with that. She's a tad stubborn, in case you haven't noticed."

"Have I ever."

They found Marla in her room, wound up in a sheet, asleep. Cassie flicked on the bedside lamp. Marla stirred. Opened her eyes, a hand rising to block the light. She squinted.

"Cassie? What's going on?"

"We need to talk," Cassie said.

"What time is it?"

"A little past midnight."

"Well, whatever it is, I didn't do it. I've been here for hours."

Cassie smiled. "You didn't do anything wrong. In fact, you did something very good."

Marla twisted from the sheet and swung to a sitting position, bare feet on the floor. Harper noticed a few bruises on each ankle. Injection sites. Marla wore cotton, drawstring pants and a yellow tee shirt. She blinked at Cassie, then Harper.

"We found Dr. Buckner. He's okay."

"Thank God. He was so nice to me."

"But it seems the guys who took him might not be done yet," Harper said.

"What?"

"Seems they brought in reinforcements and might try to find him and kill him."

"Maybe you and Jason, too," Cassie added.

"What? Why?" Marla rubbed her eyes with the heels of each hand.

"Cleaning house," Harper said. "Taking care of witnesses. You and Buck saw them. Jason does business with them. Makes sense they'd want to cover all the bases."

Marla massaged her temples. "I don't freaking believe this."

"I want you to come down to the station with us. Stay there until this is settled."

"In jail?"

Cassie smiled. "Not exactly. Just in the department where we can protect you. Dr. Buckner is there."

"He is?"

There was the hook, Harper thought. She saw it in Marla's eyes, the way her shoulders straightened and her head came up. She had a thing for Buck. Who wouldn't? He was handsome, smart, and seemed nice. That attraction just might be the key to gaining Marla's cooperation.

"Yes," Harper said. "Look, Marla, we need to focus on finding these guys before anyone else gets hurt. If you're over at the PD, Chief Crowe won't have to put someone here to watch over you."

Marla looked around the room, considering that for a minute. "Can I change clothes? Get a few things?"

"Sure," Cassie said.

CHAPTER 61

The first order of business was retrieving Hack's and Fowler's cars from the side of Highway 43, where they had left them earlier. A quick trip up the hill from The Crossroads. Dalton's SUV had been towed and the coroner had hauled away the corpse of the late Bud Myrick. The area seemed so peaceful now. No evidence that a life and death shootout had occurred.

Cain imagined how it had gone down. Really a cop's worst nightmare. Pulling over a suspect vehicle and having the driver roll out with a gun and start shooting. Took nerves, balls, and training to survive in such situations. Cassie had done just that. Took out the bad guy and avoided being a victim herself. She was a tough cop.

After they dumped Hack's 442 back at the station, Cain piloted The Rig toward Jason's apartment. They hadn't called ahead. Didn't want Jason to have a chance to disappear into the night.

"All that stuff about you two being raised by gypsies true?" Hack asked.

"It is. The family wasn't exactly gypsies. Not real ones. Not a drop of Roma blood to be found. But we did wander around and do odd jobs, live off the land." He glanced at Hack. "And a few other things."

Hack grunted. "I can imagine."

"You probably can."

"And the military stuff? Harper ran covert operations and you did whatever you did?"

"Also true."

"That mission you mentioned…the one where you and Harper reunited. Was it successful? Did you take out the bad guy?"

"Can't say."

"Which means you did. Were there others?"

Cain gave him a glance. "Can't say that either."

Hack nodded. "Thought so."

"What about Cassie?" Cain asked. "She seems to be on the ball."

"Oh, yeah. She is."

"What she did up there along the highway was ballsy stuff."

Hack nodded. "It was." He eyed Cain. "Tell her that. She would appreciate the vote of confidence."

Cain turned onto the street where Jason's apartment was located. An eight unit, one-story complex on the right. Cain pulled to the curb, shut off the engine. They sat, looking the place over. Dark. No activity.

"You were the chief, and now she is," Cain said. "How'd that happen?"

"Her father ran the show for many years. He was born for the job, as they say. Ran a solid department until he died. That's when I took over. Cassie worked for me but I got old. Funny how that happens." He shrugged. "She was young and this job too often needs more energy." He gave Cain a look. "And Cassie, like her father, was born and bred to do this."

"She grew up in the station, right?"

"She was there almost every day. Literally from the time she could walk. By the time she was, I don't remember, sixth, seventh grade, she started working there after school each day. Filing and that sort of thing. Later she did some ride-alongs. Once she got out of high school, she became a cop. No official training but she took to it like a duck to water. It came natural to her. Then her father got killed." Hack gave a sigh. "She blames herself for that. Always has. In spite of everything I've ever said to convince her otherwise."

"What happened?"

Hack spun out the tale. The thumbnail, anyway. Cain could envision it going down. Mainly because Hack was a master storyteller.

A drizzly night. A farmhouse, rural area, acreage, long dirt road, open fields, a few clumps of trees. Not easy to approach. Three biker-types cooking meth. Chief Carl Crowe, Cassie's father, formulated the plan. Park a half-mile away, approach from two sides. Cassie and another officer would hug the tree line and flank the house. Carl and Hack from the far side, after creepy-crawling across an open field. Wet grass, cold after their clothing soaked through. They would work around to the barn, where the lab was churning out its poison. Cassie was to hold her position in case the bad guys attempted to escape that way.

When the first shots erupted, she abandoned her position, ran toward the barn, gun in hand. But, as she rounded the corner toward the rear, toward the pop-pop-pop of gunfire, she ran straight into one of the bikers. He held a shotgun, swung it her way. Carl yelled, exposed himself, attracted the guy's attention, got off a single shot that hit its mark, but not before the shotgun cut him down. Hack ended the tale with, "Ever since then she's kicked herself around for not holding her position. Not following orders."

"What she did makes sense to me," Cain said. "Go help. Not sit and hope all was going as planned."

"One thing you can say for that girl is that she ain't no coward. Believe me, I've told her so more times than I can remember."

"Thanks for telling me," Cain said.

"Just don't tell her I did. She don't care for folks nosing into her business." Hack smiled. "Don't want to face her ire."

"Got it." Cain nodded. "Let's do this."

Jason answered Hack's knock. Behind him, against the living room wall, Cain saw a desk with a computer. The screen revealing a video game.

"What do you want?"

"Mind if we come in?" Hack asked.

"I'd rather you didn't."

Cain flattened a palm against Jason's chest, pushed him back, entered. "Don't be so unfriendly."

"You can't come in here."

"Look, Jason, we aren't here for our health," Cain said. "Rather for yours."

That confused him.

Hack ran through the story. Dr. Buckner safe, Dennie in the hospital, Jessie in jail, one of Dalton's crew now the property of the coroner. The house they holed-up in found, empty, and his feeling, Cain's too, that Dalton and a couple of his guys were still around. Probably cleaning up loose ends. Which just might include Jason.

"Why would they, whoever they are, do anything to me?" Jason said. "I don't know them. They don't know me."

"Cut the bullshit," Cain said. "You know them. They know you. That puts you on the table."

"Don't know what you're talking about."

"Jason," Hack said, "we're trying to help you. Keep you safe. What we'd like is for you to come down to the station and hang out. Where we can better protect you until we get a handle on this."

Jason smirked. "Tell you what, if I need you, I'll dial nine-one-one." He walked to the door, held it open. "How about that?"

Hack sighed. "We can't make you do anything, but you just might be making a big mistake."

"Wouldn't be the first one." He smiled. "Have a nice evening."

"One more thing," Cain said. "Dalton has another contact here. Any idea who that might be?"

"No. Even if I did, I wouldn't tell you nothing about it."

As they walked back toward The Rig, Cain said, "He's not the sharpest kid on the block."

"Worse. He's an asshole." Hack stopped, looking back toward Jason's place. "But I'd hate for anything to happen to him just because he's stupid."

"Want to put someone on him? Keep an eye out? Who knows, Dalton might show up."

"That'd require manpower we simply don't have." Hack scratched an ear. "Besides, it could be days, or weeks, before Dalton makes contact with him. If he does at all." He shrugged. "Maybe they'll decide to close up shop over here and forget about Jason Epps." He glanced at Cain. "Can't say I'd mind that a whole lot."

CHAPTER 62

"Hey."

Buck had showered, slipped on jeans and a tee shirt, and now sat in the PD's break room waiting for Cassie to return. She, Officer Hackford, Cain, and Harper had left forty-five minutes earlier, saying they had a couple of things to do and would "be back shortly." He looked up at the sound of the voice. Marla stood in the doorway.

"Marla?"

She smiled. "They told me you got away from those guys."

Buck stood, unsure what to do. Embrace her? Keep his distance? Was she still a patient or a partner in all the madness? Moot point. She rounded the table and hugged him tightly.

"I was so scared for you," she said.

They broke the embrace and sat at the table, across from each other.

"Me, too. It was hairy for sure."

"What happened?"

"So much. Where to start?"

Marla smiled. "At the beginning."

He returned her smile. She looked better. Healthier than when he had seen her in the ER. She still had a bandage on her arm and it looked as though it had been recently changed. He nodded toward it.

"How's the arm?"

She held it up. "It feels better. Less pain and swelling, and yes, I'm keeping it clean and taking the antibiotics you gave me."

"Let me take a look."

He loosened the tape and unwound the gauze. It was better. The infection was clearing. She'd have a scar, of course, but it would eventually be lost among the others that lined her arm.

"Look's good," Buck said as he rewound the dressing and secured the tape. "I'll get them to bring over some supplies and change the dressing in the morning."

Marla nodded. "Now, tell me what happened."

Buck leaned his elbows on the table. "They grabbed me from the parking lot."

"I saw."

"I know. Thanks to you they knew what happened fairly quickly. Also knew what kind of vehicle to look for."

She looked down, her face revealing sadness. And more.

"What is it?" Buck asked.

"I could've missed the whole thing." A shake of her head. Her gaze lifted toward him. "I was using. Shot up about that time and was more or less out on that bench near the park's parking lot. I saw what happened, but to be honest, I wasn't sure what I saw was real. I mean, a couple of guys shoving you in the back of an SUV. How random is that?"

"But you went to the ER and told them."

"I figured they probably wouldn't believe me." She shrugged. "Most people don't, but Cassie did. She came over and when I told her she got things rolling."

"That seems to be her way," Buck said. "From what little I know of her."

"She was always the good one, even back in school. Not like me. We all knew she'd be a superstar one day and here she is, the chief of police."

"So you two go back?"

"All the way to the first grade. We were friends. Close friends. But then I got lost in drugs and everything went in the toilet." She looked down, wound her fingers together. "For me, anyway."

"Maybe all this will be a wake-up call," Buck said.

She gave a one shoulder shrug and stared at her hands, folded in her lap. "Been through that before. It didn't work."

"There's always a next time. This time."

"Wouldn't bet the ranch on it."

"It's up to you, of course. But if you want to try again, I'll help."

She raised her gaze. "I wouldn't want to disappoint you. You were good to me."

"Then don't. Disappoint me, that is." He smiled. "Or yourself."

He studied her for a beat. Her eyes were still clear and sharp despite the toll the drugs had taken on the rest of her. Her skin, and her teeth, were beginning to show the ravages of meth. Buck knew that once those signs appeared, the downhill spiral usually picked up pace. He also saw that despite all that damage, Marla's beauty still peeked through and the intelligence in her eyes hadn't yet been smothered.

"So, what happened after they took you away?" Marla asked.

"They robbed a pharmacy. Apparently killing the owner."

"Mr. Shaffer. I heard. He was a good guy."

"He seemed so. Then we headed into the hills. Dalton, that's the name of the guy with the ponytail, killed an older couple and took over their cabin. I didn't know about them or Shaffer until I got away. Anyway, Dennie, that's Dalton's brother, had been shot at the Finley house. I had to do surgery...on a dining table."

"Really?"

"Took out a kidney and patched him up."

She stared at him.

"They don't teach you that in med school."

She smiled. "Probably not."

"Definitely not. So, it seems Dalton then killed a cop and they were packing up to head out after some reinforcements arrived. I used the chance to sedate Jessie, one of Dalton's guys, and took off."

"Scary."

"It was. They turned a dog loose. A pit bull."

"What? To chase you?"

"Fortunately, I had found a shotgun and some shells in the cabin so I shot the dog and ran like hell."

Marla's eyes were wide. "This is like a movie."

"One I'd rather watch than star in."

"So, these guys, the ones that came in to help, they the ones they're worried might come after you? And me?"

"Yup. And so, here we are." Buck waved a hand. "A couple of jailbirds."

CHAPTER 63

Jason fingered a crack in the curtain and watched Hackford and Cain walk away, turning left at the parking area and disappearing from sight. He returned to his desk, stood looking at the computer screen, the video game he had been playing still paused. He exited it. No longer in the mood.

He flopped on his sofa, adjusted the throw pillow beneath his head, and stared at the ceiling. A cricket scurried from one corner, stopped, seemed to look down at him. Wobbled a few more inches, stopped again. At least the little bastard wasn't making any of those grating cricket sounds.

What the fuck was going on? Officer Hackford knocking on his door, middle of the night, making threats. He knew Hackford was a tough cop—at least that was the scuttlebutt—but Jason had never really had any trouble with him. That other dude, Cain, was still around. Hadn't he said they were looking for that missing doctor? Now that he had been found, he was still here, wandering around with the police in the middle of the night. Why?

Both of them said his life was in danger. That Dalton was going to kill him. Why would he do that? Didn't they need him now? With Tommy out, wouldn't he be their go-to guy? Or was he part of the house cleaning? That made no sense. Surely they weren't giving up on this area. Tommy had said they made good money and liked what he did for them.

Well, until Tommy tried to hook up with that other guy over in Knoxville. Jason knew that was a bad idea from the beginning and he'd told Tommy so. What was it Tommy had said? "You stick to selling and I'll handle the business."

See where that got him? Dead.

Did Dalton and the big boss in Memphis trust Jason? They didn't really know him. Would it be better to take him out and find someone else? Or better to deal with someone they already knew? On some level anyway. He was already connected to all the customers and knew the best places to do business while staying out of sight. No one else knew that. No, they wouldn't kill him. They needed him.

If that was the case, why hadn't they called him? Made contact? Set up new communication and distribution lines? Probably because their hands were full right now. Escaping from their hiding place, evading the cops, and all that. Maybe they were back in Memphis and this was all a bunch of nothing. Maybe they'd call him in a day or two and get things restarted here. Yeah, that made the most sense. Didn't it?

He stood, paced, felt his heart rate increase. Was this simply wishful thinking? Was he really in danger like that Cain dude said? Or were they simply trying to spook him?

The not knowing was maddening.

When his cell chimed and vibrated on the coffee table, he jerked that way and picked it up. Caller ID revealed a blocked number. He hesitated, unsure whether to even answer or not, but curiosity won out.

"Hello."

"Jason?"

"Who is this?"

"Your new boss."

"Dalton?"

"Don't use my name. Ever."

"Sorry."

"I have a couple of questions for you. Your answers will determine where we go from here."

Jason's senses ramped up. Was that a threat? A promise? "Okay." His voice sounded weak and strained, even to him.

"Do you want to stay in business? Take over in this area?"

That one was easy. "Yes."

"You sure?"

"Yes."

"And you'll be loyal? Do what I say?"

"Absolutely." Even as he said it, something uncomfortable niggled in his brain. A feeling that he really didn't have a choice. He was sure that he would either work for Dalton and toe the line, or he'd be dealt with just like Tommy. Was this a step up the ladder or a web he could never escape? It felt like both.

"Look, we reward loyalty and performance. We do so handsomely, if you get my drift. But, step out of line, and, well, you see what can happen."

"You don't have to worry. I'll take care of things."

And there it was. Jason had made his commitment. No reversing from here.

"Good. I'm glad to hear that. So, here's the deal. We'll be pulling out of here soon. As soon as we take care of a couple of things and deliver you some product. Sound good?"

"Sure does. I can use more. I'm running low."

"We don't want that," Dalton said. "This being a supply and demand business. So, we'll hook up in the park and make the drop."

"Sounds good. I'll be there."

"You need to bring someone with you."

"What? Who?"

"The girl," Dalton said.

"Marla? Why?"

"She's the one that saw me over by the hospital. I can't have her running around."

"Come on. She's harmless. She won't say a word. I'll talk with her."

Silence.

"You still there?" Jason asked.

"Just wondering how loyal you are. Trying to figure if you're the man we need over here."

"It's not that," Jason said. "It's just that she's…harmless."

"Not to me. It's time to fish or cut bait. The question is—are you in or out?"

"I'm in." Why not? He didn't really have a connection with Marla. No loyalty there. Besides, the money was good.

"All right," Dalton said. "We've got something to take care of and that'll give you time to get the girl. Meet us in the park. Say in an hour."

"If she'll come out this time of night."

"Convince her. That's what we hired you for."

The call disconnected.

CHAPTER 64

Cain and Hack walked along the row of cars in the parking lot until they reached The Rig. The rain had stopped though a fine mist still hung in the air. Cain had parked toward the far end, out of sight from Jason's apartment. Both men stopped near the front grill and turned back that way, Hack hooking his thumbs in his belt.

"What do you think?" Hack asked.

"I think it's likely he's in the loop," Cain said.

"Like Dalton's contacted him?"

Cain nodded. "That'd be the best bet. Or maybe Jason simply hopes he will. Thinks that's his future. So either he's been contacted and reassured, or he has a ton of blind confidence that that's what will happen."

Hack looked at him. "He certainly didn't look scared. You'd think that if he had heard nothing, particularly after the story and concerns you laid out for him, he'd have to at least consider he might be an expendable commodity. Be at a minimum nervous, maybe frantic. I didn't see that."

"Good read. So, either Jason has a pocketful of reassurance, or he's clueless but hopeful."

Hack nodded toward Jason's place. "Can't say we didn't warn him but I can't make him do nothing he don't want to."

"He thinks he's got, or will get, a better deal."

"He won't."

"Not even close."

They climbed in The Rig.

"I'll give Harper a call," Cain said. "See what they have and where they are."

Before he could do so, his cell rang. Mama B. Did she ever sleep? He answered.

"You're up late," Cain said.

"I'm always up late. Comes with being old. Us seniors sleep little and erratically."

"You aren't that old."

She laughed. "Just wait a few decades and you'll see."

"I'm here with Officer Hackford. You're on speaker."

"Nice to meet you Hackford," Mama B said.

"Mutual, I'm sure," Hack said.

"Where's Harper?" Mama B asked.

"She and Chief Crowe are rounding up Marla," Cain said. "Getting her down to the PD."

"Sounds like you're heading to the bunkers."

"More getting some potential targets out of harm's way."

"So, things are about to get hot?"

"It could," Cain said. "But, I'm sure you didn't call to wish us all sweet dreams."

"Nope. I got a friend involved on the stuff you wanted on Simon Greene."

"Simon Greene?" Hack said. "What's he got to do with this?"

"Something," Mama B said. "Just like you suspected, Bobby."

"Tell it," Cain said.

"So my guy, over at Meade, uncovered a few things of interest. Things I figured you needed to know ASAP."

Meade. Fort Meade, Maryland. The NSA. Mama B had dug deep.

She continued, "Seems back a few years ago, during the Tommy Finley trial, Greene had a flurry of calls back and forth with a burner cell phone over in Memphis."

"Any idea with who?" Cain asked.

"Not from those calls, but file this under criminals are stupid: one call came from a bar over there. Place called Turk's Lounge. The owner of record is Frank Campanella."

"You're kidding?"

"Nope and it gets better. Seems like Greene deposited around ten grand, cash, into his bank a couple of weeks after the trial."

"So Frankie hired Greene to get his boy off?" Cain asked.

"Smells that way."

"He told everyone he did that *pro bono*," Hack said.

"Maybe he didn't charge the Finley's anything," Mama B said, "but he got his blood money." She sighed. "Now it gets good. Greene received a call late yesterday afternoon from another burner. Local call. Someone in your neighborhood. The same phone called him again about two hours ago. And the cherry on top? That same phone just called Jason Epps."

"Dalton," Cain said.

"That'd be my guess. Mainly because that same number called Frank Campanella twice yesterday. Around the time of the call to Greene. All the calls originated from your location."

"Wait a minute," Hack said. "You're telling us that Simon Greene, Jason Epps, Frank Campanella, and the late Tommy Finley are all connected?"

"At least electronically," Mama B said.

"I suspect about every other way imaginable," Cain said. "Anything else?"

"Isn't that enough?" Mama B laughed.

"You're amazing as usual."

"That I am and I'm still on it."

"Okay. We're rolling," Cain said.

"Go get them, Tiger." She disconnected the call.

Cain cranked The Rig to life and spun out of the parking lot. He called Harper.

"Where are you?" he asked.

"We got Marla safely tucked away at the PD and we're patrolling downtown. Not sure what we're looking for since we don't know what vehicle Dalton has now, but who knows? We could get lucky."

"Meet us at Simon Greene's place."

"What's going on?"

"I'll explain later. We should be there in five." He disconnected the call.

"This is a strange turn," Hack said. "I mean, Simon Greene?"

"It would explain how Dalton knew there was a witness and how he knew we were on to his vehicle. Which made him call in a crew with a new car."

"So they could move around undetected and wipe the slate clean."

"Also means Dalton knows Marla's name," Cain said.

"Good thing she's over at the PD."

"Too bad Jason didn't accept your offer."

Hack shrugged. "His call. He's an adult. Well, sort of."

Cassie and Harper had beaten them to Greene's place. Cassie's Jeep was nestled to the curb out front. Cain slid The Rig in behind it. He and Hack climbed out and walked to where Cassie and Harper stood on the sidewalk beneath an elm tree.

"What's the story?" Harper asked.

Cain ran through what Mama B had said.

"Simon Greene?" Cassie said. "He's in this?"

"All we know for sure," Cain said, "is that he's had some calls from Frank Campanella and from someone nearby who uses a burner phone."

"Dalton Southwell for sure," Harper said. "Nothing else makes sense."

Cain looked across the manicured lawn toward the neat, two-story brick house. A white trimmed porch extended the width of the structure, a two-person swing hung near one end and a pair of rockers sat just to the right of the entry door.

"Campanella paid him to defend Tommy Finley?" Cassie asked.

"Looks that way."

"Son-of-a-bitch. He's strutted around for years saying he did that for free. Playing the hero."

"As far as the Finley's were concerned, he did," Cain said.

"I suppose." Cassie sighed. "So what the hell is his connection in this?"

"Let's ask him," Hack said.

Cain peered through the front windows while Hack knuckled the front door. No lights, no movement. No answer to the knock.

"If he isn't here, where could he be at this hour?" Cassie asked.

Cain looked at her.

"What?" she asked.

"We believe Dalton brought in more of his crew to clean house. That's why we have Buck and Marla undercover. Maybe Greene is on that list."

"Why? He defended a drug dealing punk. I don't see that putting a target on his back."

"But he knows Frank Campanella and apparently Dalton," Harper said. "Based on the call logs."

Cain jumped in. "The calls he's received in the last twenty-four hours, from a burner that we assume is in the hands of Dalton, means he's still in the loop. Could make him a prime candidate for Dalton's list."

"Freaking unbelievable," Cassie said.

"We better have a look-see," Hack said. "To be sure." He shrugged. "Call it a welfare check."

"You're saying break in?"

"Maybe he's a sound sleeper?" Harper said. "Maybe he's in the shower? Maybe something's happened? No matter what, we need to know and we need to know now."

Cassie nodded. "He's going to be thrilled with us invading his home at this hour."

"Use your charm," Harper said.

"I just hope he doesn't think this is a booty call." Cassie smiled. "At least he won't be mad."

Hack checked the door. Unlocked. He pushed it open. They entered.

Cassie called out. "Simon? You here?"

Silence.

Again, she yelled. Nothing.

Took five minutes to clear all the rooms, and find Simon Greene. In his home office. Slumped in the chair behind his desk. Blood smear on his chest, black hole in his forehead.

"Jesus," Cassie said.

"Dalton," Cain added.

"They set him up," Harper said. She moved around the right side of the desk. "No sign of a struggle. They executed him where he's sitting." She completed her circle of the scene. "Dalton called and arranged a meet to make sure everyone was on the same page and that everything would go on as usual. All friendly like. Greene let them in. Came in here to talk business." She shook her head. "He never had a chance."

"Which means Buck, Marla, and Jason are on the table," Cain said.

"Maybe we can now convince Jason to come into the PD," Hack said. "This just might make him see things a bit differently."

Cassie nodded toward Cain and Harper. "You guys head back to the PD. Hack and I'll swing by and lean on Jason. See if he's smart enough to read the writing on the wall."

CHAPTER 65

Buck saw the signs. The need. The monkey baring its teeth. Marla hunched over, rubbing her arms, one leg bouncing. Pupils beginning to dilate, eye movements rapid and chaotic. She avoided his gaze, preferring the tabletop, the floor, the walls—anything but him.

He sat across the PD's break room table from her. They had found some cheese and crackers and soft drinks in the fridge. Marla nibbled; Buck devoured everything. Downed two bottles of water.

"I feel like we're in jail," Marla said.

"We are."

That got a half-smile from her. "You know what I mean."

"Not really. I've never been in jail."

"That's because you do everything right. Don't you?"

"My father might not agree."

"Why?"

"Long story."

She took a gulp of Dr. Pepper. "We have time." Another half-smile.

"My father built a large medical clinic over in North Carolina. My brothers and my sister work there. A dozen other docs do, too."

"Sounds impressive."

"It is. Dad's good at what he does."

"But?" she prompted him.

"I was supposed to join the club. Finish my surgical residency and slide into a safe and warm job." He shrugged. "I chose to jump from that program and see the world."

Marla rolled her eyes. "You mean like Tanner's Crossroads?"

"Exactly."

She forked her fingers through her hair. "And here I've been trying to get out."

"Why don't you?"

"And go where? I think everywhere would be just as bad."

"Anywhere is better if you can kick your bad habits."

"Trust me, I've tried."

"Try again. And again, and again. Until it sticks."

Marla scratched the back of one hand. "Not sure it ever will."

"It will. When you're ready."

"When might that be?"

"Up to you. Most often it's when someone hits the pavement. Rock bottom."

Her head dropped. She folded her hands in her lap, stared at them. Buck waited, let her have the moment. She glanced up. "Look at me. I'm a mess. An addict. A whore. A criminal." Her eyes moistened. "Sometimes I think it'd be best if I simply ended it all."

"Then the drugs would win."

She huffed out a blast of air. "Haven't they already?"

"Not yet."

Her gaze dropped again.

"Look, Marla, the nurses over at the hospital, Cassie, too, told me about you." She looked up. "Good student. Smart. Good athlete. Homecoming queen. Prettiest girl in the school."

"Yeah, well, that was a long time ago."

"That girl is still in there. You simply have to find her. Let her live."

"She feels dead to me."

"That's the drugs talking. Look past them. See who you really are."

"What would that be? A thief? A whore?"

"A beautiful and smart woman."

She opened her palms. "I don't see anyone like that in here."

"She's there. Find her. Hold on to her."

She started to say something but her cell chimed. She looked at the screen, then answered, "Hey." She waited a beat, then said, "Hold on just a sec. Let me move where I can get a better signal."

She stood.

"Who is it?" Buck asked.

She pressed the phone against her chest. "A friend of mine. She's worried about me." She moved toward the door. "Back in a sec."

CHAPTER 66

Shame dogged Marla as she left the room. She had lied to Buck. Hadn't he been kind to her? Helped her? Even now, offered more help? In the ER he had looked her in the eye, smiled, cared for her. Treated the infection on her arm, which was now well on its way to healing. He didn't look down on her like others did. Didn't treat her like street scum, even if she felt that way about herself.

He had given her money and didn't make it feel like charity, but rather true concern. For food, sure, and she had used it for drugs. What the hell was wrong with her?

It was a question she knew the answer to. Her need for drugs was stronger than she was. That's the one thing that Buck didn't get. Not really. Sure he learned about it in med school and probably saw it many times in ERs and hospitals, but he never lived it. Never understood the grinding hunger that chewed cavernous channels inside. A monster that hid in the deep recesses, always ready to rise up and take control. Like now.

The call was from Jason. She couldn't talk to him in front of Buck so her lame excuse popped in her head and out of her mouth. A girlfriend who was worried about her. Did Buck believe her? Did he know she had no friends? None.

Definitely not Jason. He was an abusive ass. Made her do things, knowing she would in exchange for what he had. She missed Tommy. He wasn't like that. He sold her what she needed and went his own way. Even fronted her from time to time and forgave her debts when times were tough. Tommy had been good people. Not so Jason. He wanted more. Wanted her on her knees.

Yet, here she was making her way through the lobby, motioning to the cop behind the counter that she had a call and needed privacy. She stepped out the front door, looked back through the front window as if to reassure the cop that that was as far as she was going, and brought the phone to her ear.

Why was she even taking Jason's call? Because she had to. She needed a fix. With all this shit going down, she needed a safe place. A place whose door could only be opened by a spike of heroin.

She had some but it was back at Reverend John's. Well hidden behind the loose baseboard where she hid such things. She had left it behind, thinking taking it to the police station wasn't a wise move. Thinking she could ride it out for a few hours if she had to. Chalk that up as her dumbest decision of the week.

"Okay, I can talk now," Marla said.

"Where are you?"

"At the police station."

A moment of silence, then Jason asked, "Why?"

"I'm not under arrest or anything. They want me here because they say those guys that killed Tommy are after me."

"Yeah, they tried to pull that shit on me, too. I told them to fuck off."

"Are they? After me?"

"No way."

"How can you be sure?"

"Because I talked with them and met with them."

"You did?"

"Look, Marla, relax. They left. They're headed back to Memphis."

"Are you sure?"

"I waved goodbye to them."

"Oh."

"I'm the new guy here. I'm taking over for Tommy."

"Is that smart? I mean with what happened?"

"Tommy was stupid. He tried to do some crazy stuff. I'm smart. They trust me."

Marla ran that through her mind. Jason was now her only source. Maybe she could find another one. Where and who she had no idea, but there must be someone. She wasn't sure she could keep blowing Jason for her drugs.

"So why're you calling me now?"

"To see if you needed anything. They loaded me up before they left so I got plenty of everything."

"H?"

"Oh yeah. Black tar. Very pure. Got a pocketful of bags right now."

"I don't have much money. Maybe only fifteen bucks."

"Keep it. I just got a promotion and I'm feeling extra generous. I'll give you a couple on the house."

"Right. I know what that means."

"As much as I love that, and I must say as good as you are at it, those days are gone. I'm the boss now."

"You sure?"

"I am. Actually, I have a business proposition for you."

"Like what?"

"Work for me. Sell for me. You know all the folks out there that need what I have."

Marla said nothing, considering it. Moving into dealing was a big step. She wouldn't simply get a rap on the knuckles if she got caught.

As if reading her reluctance, Jason said, "You can make a lot of money and get your own stuff for free."

"Really?"

"That's how it works. You think I pay for what I use? No way. It's all in the profit."

"I see."

"Meet me. I'll explain it all and fix you up. Get you well."

"Let me think for a minute."

"Not much to think about. It's a win-win for you. Money and a free supply."

She had to admit that was the best deal anyone had offered in as long as she could remember. But, could she trust Jason? None of her past dealings with him said she could. He'd been nasty and arrogant and made her do things. But, he was the boss now. Would that really change things?

She glanced through the window. The female cop was reading something, head down. She looked beyond, toward the hallway that led to the break room. What about Buck? He had helped her, even tossed her a lifeline. Could she grasp it and this time hold on? Or would it once again slip away and plunge her even deeper into this world? Leave her with no deal with Jason and open the door for his abuse even wider?

"Where?" she asked.

"The park. The usual spot."

Another glance at the PD. Another hesitation, then, "Okay."

CHAPTER 67

The rain, at least for now, had slid to the east and the clouds had broken, allowing a half moon to silver the trees along Main Street. Cain pulled The Rig into the PD lot just left of the entrance. Through the large front window, he saw Officer Liz Evans behind the reception desk. She looked up, stood, and walked around the counter. Her hand rested on her service weapon. Cain and Harper stepped out. Liz smiled, waved, and settled back in her seat.

"What do you think his next move will be?" Harper asked.

"Something aggressive."

"You mean like storming this place?"

"It could happen."

"I'm thinking not," Harper said.

"Why?"

"He'd be at a disadvantage. Outnumbered and out gunned and on police turf. He's lost three men so far. Dennie and Jessie are out of commission, and that Myrick guy Cassie took out is permanently deleted."

"But we have several folks that can either testify against him or turn on him," Cain said. "Buck can definitely ID him and Marla maybe. Dennie and Jessie are in his world. Jessie could break. He acts tough but he's weak."

"I agree. We can always play the self-preservation card."

"Regardless, it means Dalton and crew have to get to four

people we have locked down."

"Hopefully, Jason will make it five," Harper said.

"Guess we'll see."

Headlamps washed over them. Cassie pulled her Jeep into the lot and parked. She and Hack rolled out. No Jason.

"He wasn't home," Cassie said.

"We tried calling," Hack added. "He didn't answer."

"Dalton got to him," Harper said. "Made him an offer."

"You sure about that?" Hack asked.

"Not sure of anything, but either he's incredibly stupid or he's on Dalton's team."

"Maybe both," Hack said.

Cassie propped her fists on her hips. "Hack and I talked on the way over. We think Dalton just might try to storm the PD. Try to take out all the other witnesses."

Cain glanced at Harper. "Possible, but Harper thinks otherwise."

"I'm not saying he won't," Harper said. "But he might be more patient."

"Go ahead," Cassie said.

"Here's how I see it," Harper said. "Dalton had this grand plan. Take out Tommy and his family and send a message. That went off the rails, but he adapted. He grabbed Buck and robbed a pharmacy of everything needed to patch up his brother. Bold and clever on his part. The mission morphed, he adapted. I think he was comfortable up there in the hills. Off the radar completely. Not likely to be found since we had no clue which way to look. Made finding that cabin a true needle in a haystack. But then something else happened. He crossed paths with Scotty Duckworth. That changed everything. So, he called in reinforcements and planned to send Dennie and Buck off to Memphis."

"I get all that," Cassie said. "But what do you think he'll do now?"

"Buy time. Try to eliminate witnesses one by one."

Cassie didn't seem convinced.

Harper continued, "It's actually good military planning. Guerrilla warfare. When the enemy is too big, or better equipped, make it a hit and run war of attrition. Whittle the enemy and impose psychological pressure."

"I agree with Harper," Cain said. Cassie started to respond but he raised a hand and continued. "Yes, he might go full bore and come straight at us and we should prepare for that. But, we can't keep Buck and Marla here forever. They'll leave and be vulnerable. Dennie will leave the hospital. Probably come here. He and Jessie will probably hold the line and be bonded out."

"Even though their attorney over here was eliminated?" Cassie said.

"They'll find someone. People like Frank Campanella always do."

"Someone good enough to arrange bail for two guys charged with multiple murders and a kidnapping?" Hack asked.

Cain shrugged. "Tommy Finley beat the rap."

"Thanks to Judge Hauser."

"Money talks," Harper said.

"Okay," Cassie said. "But the first order of business is to get everyone here ready to do battle. Just in case."

They walked inside.

Liz stood. "I guess Jason didn't come back with you?"

Cassie shook her head. "Wasn't home."

Buck came from the break room. "Where's Marla?"

"Isn't she with you?"

"She got a call and went out to take it."

Liz nodded. "Right out there." She looked through the front window. "Maybe ten minutes ago."

Cain hadn't seen her when they came in. An uneasy feeling rose in his gut. He pushed through the door; Harper followed. They exchanged a look. Cain circled left, Harper right. They looped the building. No Marla. When they finished the circumnavigation, Cassie, Hack, Buck, and Liz stood outside.

"She's gone," Harper said.

"Jason," Cassie said. "The call must have been him."

"She said it was a girlfriend who was worried about her," Buck said.

"She doesn't have any girlfriends," Cassie said. "Not anymore. She burned all those a long time ago."

"He offered her a fix," Hack said.

"She was getting antsy," Buck added. "All the signs were there."

"The park," Cassie said. "That's the best bet." She turned to Liz. "You and JT pull out all the weapons and lock this place down."

"You think they might try to break in here?" Liz asked.

"Could be that Jason enticed Marla away as a diversion, knowing we'd go after her. Open the door here a bit."

"Got it," Liz said. "We'll be ready."

Cassie turned to Hack. "Let's get over to the park."

"Might I suggest a strategy?" Cain said.

"Will I like it?"

"Hopefully."

"Okay," Cassie said, "suggest away."

"This smells like a set up, and not necessarily for us. Dalton got to Jason, Jason to Marla. He was instructed to lure her to the park. Like always. Middle of the night. Easy targets. Two witnesses eliminated."

"Okay." Cassie gave a half-nod. "I see that. Your plan?"

"You and Hack take the front door, so to speak. That's where Dalton will expect trouble. Head over to the ER. You'll have the park in sight and will know if anything happens."

"If they're waiting in the park, they might see us," Hack said.

"Not necessarily a bad thing," Harper said, "It might make them nervous and divide their attention."

"Or spook them," Cassie said.

"That also wouldn't be bad," Cain said. "Give us time to grab Marla and Jason and bring them in."

"We have to assume they'll be watching," Harper said. "Assume they will see you. Better if you're doing regular police work and not sneaking around. Go to the ER, go inside or maybe hang around the ambulance entrance. Casual, like cops do all the time. You'll have a visual on the park and if Dalton and his crew do see you, they'll think it's simply business as usual."

Hack chuckled. "Sort of hiding in plain sight."

"Exactly."

"Harper and I will flank the park," Cain said. "Move in through the trees from the back side. See if we can get up close and personal."

"What if they see you?" Cassie said. "Things could go badly."

Harper smiled. "This isn't our first spin around the block. We've gotten up next to people in very hostile places that had no natural cover." She shrugged. "We grew up in the forest. This won't be that difficult."

Cassie seemed to consider that. She sighed and looked at Hack. "You got a better idea?"

"Nope."

"Okay." Cassie nodded. "Let's get going."

"I'll go with you guys," Buck said.

"No," Cassie said. "You'll stay here. You're the main witness. The big prize. Dalton would want you to be there."

Buck hesitated but nodded. "I hunted a lot as a kid and know my way around a gun, so I can help here."

Cassie nodded. "Okay." Then to Liz, "Get locked and loaded. We're off."

"Just a sec," Harper said. She lifted the rear door of The Rig and zipped open a duffle. She rummaged inside, found a smaller bag, and opened it. She pulled out two earpieces. "Here." She handed one to Cassie and the other to Hack.

"What are these?" Hack asked.

"It'll keep us all in communication," Harper said. "No buttons or anything. The lines are always open. Just speak and we'll all hear."

"Clever."

"Life savers in the Mideast," Cain said.

Cain unzipped a breast pocket of his combat shirt and removed a similar earpiece. He settled it in place. Harper did the same. They tested them. All good.

Cassie and Hack climbed in her Jeep and spun from the lot.

"I'm going on foot," Cain said, "through town. See if I can pick her up before she reaches the park."

"I'll circle to the far side and come in that way."

Cain darted across Main Street, cut between two buildings and came out on Elm Street, which paralleled Main but was darker and quieter. No sign of Marla. He headed east toward the park.

CHAPTER 68

The parking deck stood at the end of Elm Street and overlooked Davis Road, the park beyond. Three stories, the top floor open, embraced by a three-foot concrete wall. Most of the park was dark but Dalton could make out some details. Open areas and clumps of trees, a pair of park benches near the entrance. The parking lot empty at this hour and beyond it, across Main Street, the lights of the hospital ER were clearly visible.

Earlier, when Dalton spiraled up to the top level, there were only three cars, clustered near the north end. Hopefully, cars that stayed overnight and not owned by someone working this late. Not a likely scenario but one that could present a problem. A random citizen could spin things sideways. He didn't have the time to worry about that right now. Better to simply deal with it if it happened. Dalton parked well away from the cars, toward the southeast corner.

Now, he, Navarro, and Harris knelt behind the wall where they had views of the park and back up Elm Street. All was quiet. They waited. Not for long.

Jason appeared and entered the park from Main, a block away. He seemed on alert, his head swiveling. He crossed the open area and planted himself beneath a broad oak tree. He lit a cigarette, leaned against the trunk.

"Now we wait for the girl," Dalton said. "Make sure they

weren't followed and then go take care of business."

Navarro pulled out his Glock, screwed the sound suppressor on the muzzle.

"You going to shoot them and leave?" Harris said. "Or take them somewhere else?" He leaned his scoped rifle against the wall.

Dalton considered both options. The chance of someone hearing their suppressed weapons was practically zero. But if one of them did run or put up a fight or scream like a scared pig, some stupid ass citizen out stumbling around might see or hear something. Then, come to investigate or call for help. Not likely at this time of night but you just never knew. He'd done bolder things. Taken out guys that were more exposed than this.

Then again, hadn't everything that could possibly go wrong happened in this shitty little town? But, herding them away to somewhere more isolated had a lot of moving parts. It also opened up the possibility they might put up a ruckus. Better to simply walk up, shoot them, load the bodies in the car and head out. They'd only have to carry them about fifty yards to reach the road a little north of the deck where the trees were thicker. Easily doable.

Either way, Jason and Marla had to disappear. With no bodies, folks might think they simply ran off. With Greene taken care of and these two, that'd be three down and the doc to go. That would be the hard part. But the cops couldn't keep him locked down in the jail forever.

He wasn't sure how Greene knew that Myrick had been killed by the chick cop, that Jessie and Buck were at the jail, and Dennie in the hospital, but he seemed certain of all that. He probably had some inside source. Dalton had actually thanked him for the info, right before he shot him in the head.

He wasn't worried about Dennie and Jessie. They'd stay strong and silent until they were bonded out, which no doubt Frankie could arrange. Maybe they'd keep Buck only a day or two before they decided that Dalton and his guys must have left town. Swinging by and torching the cabin, and all the evidence inside, would only underline that. Why burn down your hideout unless you were leaving?

Waiting around a day or two to get to Buck, the only one left standing that could connect them to the killings, would require another hole to crawl into. Maybe the motel, maybe another cabin. He'd deal with that later.

Right now, first things first.

"We'll play it by ear," Dalton said. "I'd rather take them off into the woods somewhere but we'll see how they react when we show up." He looked at Navarro. "Any hint they might do something stupid, dump them. Got it?"

Navarro nodded.

"Hopefully it won't come down to me," Harris said, nodding toward his rifle. "I don't have a suppressor for this so all hell could break out."

"That's why you jump in only if the cops show up," Dalton said. "You'll be covering our backdoor."

They settled in and waited, watching Jason light a second cigarette. The minutes seemed to drip by, then, "I got something," Harris said.

Dalton spun on his haunches, raised enough to see over the wall, and looked in the direction Harris pointed. A figure walked down the sidewalk along Elm Street toward the park. Not in a hurry, not slow. Not casual, though. Like Jason, checking the surroundings. The figure moved closer, now a half a block away. A girl with long, blonde hair.

"That's her," Harris said.

"I guess Jason did his job," Dalton said.

The girl crossed Davis Road and entered the park. She followed a straight line toward the oak tree.

"Okay," Dalton continued. "Give them a couple of minutes. Maybe let her get some drugs up inside. Make her easier to handle. Then, Navarro and I'll go in." He looked at Harris. "You all set?"

Harris nodded.

"When you see us head into the trees and toward the road, either leading them or carrying them, grab the car and we're out of here."

"Got it." Harris lifted his rifle and shoved a magazine into place.

Dalton started to move but Harris grabbed his arm. "Look over there." He pointed toward the hospital.

A cop car, a Jeep, turning into the ER parking area.

"Fuck," Navarro said.

Two cops, a woman and a heavy set guy, got out. They stood talking near the rear of the vehicle. A minute later they walked through the ER's double sliding doors and disappeared.

"What now?" Harris asked.

"Bet they're just stopping by to check on things," Dalton said. "Maybe got someone in the ER acting up, or intoxicated, or something."

"Or they're smart," Harris said. "They might know what we're up to and know Jason and the girl will be in the park."

"How could they know that?"

"Maybe Jason isn't on board? Maybe he flipped?"

Dalton considered that. "I don't think so. I suspect they think we're long gone," Dalton said.

"What about the attorney?" Navarro asked. "They ain't going to think he killed himself."

"No way they know about him yet," Dalton said. "If they did, they wouldn't be here at the ER having coffee and donuts. They'd be over at his place scratching their pointy heads."

Harris leaned his rifle against the wall and rubbed his hands together. "It's getting cold up here."

"Let's get this done," Navarro said.

Dalton looked at Harris. "If those cops head our way, take them out."

"That'll wake up the whole town for sure."

"So will getting into a shootout with them. Better they're eliminated before they know what hit them. Think you can do that from here?"

"No problem. I can shoot the eyes out of a squirrel at a hundred yards."

"These aren't squirrels."

"Much bigger targets is how I see it."

Dalton nodded. "If this goes south, get the car quick. We'll head up that way." Dalton pointed north up Davis Road. "Use the trees for cover and meet up by that cemetery we saw earlier."

"Sounds good."

Dalton tapped Navarro's shoulder. "Let's move."

CHAPTER 69

Marla didn't like any of this, nor did she trust the decision she had made. But hadn't that been her life for years now? One stupid decision after another? It started in high school. Knocking back vodka, tequila, whatever, even smoking weed. Okay, lots of other kids did that. No harm, no foul. But then that guy she met over in Knoxville and the night spent on his boat. The sex, the meth, the end of everything. Why had she let him talk her into trying that poison? Why couldn't she kick it? Return to her old self? She knew the answer. Because she was weak and made poor choices. Always had. At least after that night. She simply lacked the strength to climb from the ditch and back on the path.

As she walked toward the park, shoulders hunched, hands shoved in her jacket pockets against the cold, damp night air—at least the rain had stopped—she considered her latest choice. Work with Jason? Actually sell drugs? Enter a world where if she got caught it wouldn't be simply another trip to rehab? She'd spend decades in some cage.

Why was she turning her back on the help Buck had offered? Unlike Tommy, and Jason, and anyone else in her world for that matter, he seemed truly concerned. She believed he really wanted to help. What was she thinking?

She knew at least part of the answer. Hadn't others tossed her a lifeline? Reverend John, for sure. Cassie, too many times to remember. Hadn't she tried that path? Rehab, recovery? Hadn't she failed every time? Why would this be any different? She simply wasn't strong enough.

Had she ever been? School had been easy. Sports, too. Dating whoever she wanted, a snap. Life had been effortless for her. Never testing her abilities or her strength.

What Jason offered was an endless supply of what she needed. Maybe enough money so she could get out of Reverend John's house; for sure, off the streets. Or was it a lie? Simply another ploy to have sex with her? She didn't like Jason and she surely didn't trust him.

She was going to tell him so.

She crossed Davis Road, still wet from the rain, and entered the park. She headed toward the oak tree where she and Tommy, and now Jason, made their deals. He was leaning against the trunk, a cigarette hanging from his lips.

"Hey," she said.

"Hey yourself."

"Look, I've been thinking about what you said. Me working for you. I don't think I can do it."

"Sure you can. It's not that hard."

"Maybe I'm not sure I want to."

He dropped the half-smoked cigarette to the ground and crushed it. "That's different."

"It's just that if I get caught, it will be bad. I can't go to jail. I've been there and it scares the hell out of me."

He reached out to touch her face, but she stepped back. He dropped his hand to his side.

"Look, Marla, this is your chance to get all the fix you need. Get enough money to get an apartment. Like me. Not stay over there with that old man."

"He's nice."

"I'm sure. But doesn't he keep a close eye on things? Make all the rules?"

Marla nodded.

"With your own place it's your rules. You'd be free to do whatever you want, whenever you want."

"I don't know."

"Relax," Jason said. "It'll work out."

She looked around. "You said you had some new stuff."

"It's coming."

"What does that mean?"

"My boss. He's meeting us here. He's got it."

Her head swiveled as she inspected her surroundings. "I thought you said they were gone."

"They will be. Right after they deliver what you need."

"I don't want to meet him," Marla said. "I should go."

"Take a breath, Marla. It'll be okay."

She shook her head, stepped back. "I really should go."

Jason reached in his pocket and extracted a small plastic bag. "Aren't you forgetting something?"

God, she wanted to run. Every fiber of her being screamed that she should get as far away as she could. But the bag of white powder held her. Drew her a step closer.

"I told you I don't have much money," Marla said.

"On the house." Jason smiled. "A toast to our new partnership."

"I told you…"

"I know what you said but I also know what you need."

What was wrong with her? Why couldn't she simply turn and walk away? Tell him to fuck off and get the hell away from him?

"I don't have any of my stuff," she said.

"I noticed."

"Remember? I was at the jail when you called."

"Yeah, probably not smart to have your needles and shit over there."

"They have Doctor Buck there. To protect him. And that other guy. The one they arrested."

Jason stared at her but said nothing.

"So, are we?" Marla asked. "In danger? From those guys?"

Jason actually laughed. "Are you kidding? They're our suppliers. Our business partners. I've talked to them. Everything will go on as before. I'll be taking over for Tommy."

She huffed out a breath. "What'll keep them from doing the same thing to you?"

"Tommy was stupid. He tried to double-cross them. I'm too smart for that." He extended the bag. "You can snort it."

"I don't like doing that. It burns too much."

"Suit yourself." He gave the baggie a shake.

She took it and tugged it open. The powder inside appeared clean and pure. It almost glowed in the moonlight that filtered through the tree limbs.

"Here," Jason said. He tugged a spoon from the back pocket of his jeans. Small, not for heroin cooking but the perfect size for snorting.

She took it. She scooped up a small amount, brought it to her nose, and took a quick sniff. She recoiled, rubbed her nose with the heel of one hand. "Oh, I hate that."

"You won't in a hot minute."

That was true. The rush grabbed her, lifted her, took her over the wave and down the other side. She was sailing.

"What is this?" she asked.

Jason smiled. "A bit of meth and a touch of heroin. Your favorite combination. Right?"

"It's amazing. Wild, but…." She couldn't think anymore.

"Here they come," Jason said.

Marla turned. Through the haze in her brain, she saw two men. They seemed to materialize from the trees and float toward her.

CHAPTER 70

It was one of Cain's last missions, taking out the garbage for the military. Some small town, using the word loosely, not far from Kabul. More a collection of dingy, crumbling buildings huddled near the base of a mountain slope. The current location of a Taliban commander. One who used his network to get to the Afghani soldiers who were labeled friendlies and who worked alongside US Marines and various other military personnel. Part of the outreach program, the training program that was supposed to rebuild the Afghani military and police units.

A joke. Cain knew that much. None of them could really be trusted. The case in point being the ones that the target had recruited to kill Americans. His head count had been deep into double digits.

Cain had been deployed to the area along with three Seals, two Delta guys, and a Marine sniper, just in case.

It was a new moon and at two a.m. the sky and landscape were pitch black, the wind calm. A stealth helicopter dropped them two clicks from the village. They humped in that direction, crept their way through several dark alleys, and took up positions a block down a dusty street from the two-story house where the target was holed up. Then they turned Cain loose to complete the mission he was trained for.

Cain scurried across the street and then worked his way down a parallel alleyway. He saw no one out and about and each house stood dark and quiet. He peered around a crumbling mud wall and the target building came into view. At the end of the block, left side. Showtime. But just as he took his first step, he froze.

On the roof, directly across from the commander's hidey hole, he detected movement. A head, just above the short barrier wall that enveloped the rooftop. Then he detected the clear outline of a rifle barrel.

He squatted, tapped his earpiece, and spoke softly. "Sniper. Rooftop across from the target."

"Roger that," the reply came.

"Do you think we've been compromised?" Cain asked.

"No chatter to that effect."

Was that true? Or wishful thinking? Or simply bad intel? The CIA guys that ran his ops were good, but not infallible. Still, the mission needed to be completed.

"I'll take care of him first."

"Roger. Our guy is repositioning. He'll get a fix on him for cover."

Cain was off. He dispatched the sniper, quietly, and then the target, just as quietly. Then they were gone, back into the desert, to the helicopter, and on to the base.

That's what Cain saw now. A head and a rifle barrel. A sniper. Here in sleepy little Tanner's Crossroads.

Cain had stuck to the alleyway that ran between Main and Elm, hugging the walls, dodging the trash cans, staying away from the moonlight that had suddenly appeared. Two blocks up he slid between two buildings and peered around a wall and up Elm. Three blocks ahead, he saw Marla enter the park. Their hunch had been correct. Marla no doubt was going to hook up with Jason, making herself an open target. He saw no sign of Jason or Dalton and his crew.

Back in the alley, he made his way two blocks farther, and then slipped between two stores to Elm Street. Everything was quiet.

That's when he saw the head and the silhouette of a rifle pop up just behind the wall that surrounded the top level of the parking deck. He dropped to a squat. Were all of them up there? Or was this Dalton's cover while he entered the park? Was Dalton that smart and that cautious? Rifle cover made the most sense. For use only in an emergency to cover them if an escape became necessary. Cain didn't think Dalton would try to take out two people from a distance. Low probability of success and a lot of noise.

Only one way to find out.

He eased back into the alley and stood near three trashcans. He spoke softly.

"We have a small problem."

"Copy," Harper said.

"What?" Cassie asked.

"Looks like a shooter. On the roof of the parking deck at Elm and Davis."

"Cover," Harper said. "Clever."

"I suspect so," Cain said. "I only see one. That means that Dalton and his other guy are headed into the park."

"I'm entering the east side," Harper said. "So far nothing. I'll try to get a position where I can get eyes on the deck."

"We'll come in the front," Cassie said.

"No," Cain said. "Sit tight. He has the high ground and a clear view of the park. Let me take care of him then we can alter our plan accordingly. If we need to."

"Take care of him?" Cassie asked. "What does that mean?"

"Let's say neutralize."

"Not sure I like the sound of that any better."

"Listen Cassie, no time to argue the finer points of right and wrong here. I suspect the guy on the roof wouldn't hesitate to take any of us out. If he sees you and Hack come out of the ER and cross into the park, he'll know what's up. He'll surely have some communication line with Dalton, which means he'll not only take a few shots at you, but he'll let Dalton know what's happening. That would put Marla and Jason in danger. Time is critical, stealth even more so. We still have the element of surprise in our pocket. Sit tight and wait."

"We can go out the back way," Cassie said. "Work our way into the park from an angle where anyone on the deck won't be able to see us. That'll give you some backup."

"No," Cain said. "Not until the shooter is down and Harper and I get eyes on Marla and Jason."

"You sure?"

"He is," Harper said.

"I've got this," Cain said.

Cain returned to where he could again see the corner of the deck. No one visible. He darted across Elm and slipped between a dress shop and a gift store and into another alley. He quickly made his way to the deck. He knew the shooter's attention would be on the park so he climbed the stairs in the far corner.

The structure's open top level appeared to be about 150 feet by 50 feet. Cain saw three cars near his position and across the flat concrete a metallic gray Navigator. Near it, a single man knelt, his rifle resting on the short retaining wall. With his right eye glued to the scope, he angled the weapon toward the park.

This was the critical part. Cain had no cover, nothing to shield him from the shooter. Speed and stealth his only allies.

Cain didn't hesitate. He climbed the final three steps and walked a straight line toward the shooter. He cupped a knife in each hand, angled upward, perfect underhand throwing position.

The man never heard him coming. Cain stopped twenty feet away.

"Put the weapon down."

The man's head swiveled his way.

"Now," Cain said.

The man's calculations seemed to be that since Cain had no visible weapon, he possessed the advantage. He didn't.

He swung on his haunches, the rifle barrel rotating toward Cain. He didn't make it. Cain flicked the knife he held in his right hand. It entered the man's throat. He recoiled, gasped, dropped the weapon, and clutched at the fountain of blood that erupted from his severed carotid artery. He wavered, collapsed, his heels dug at the concrete briefly, then all movement ceased.

"Shooter neutralized," Cain said. "It's Harris. Dalton and Navarro must be in the park already."

"I'm working my way through the trees," Harper said. "Nothing yet."

"We're coming," Cassie said. "And don't say no."

"Wouldn't dream of it," Cain said. He rapidly descended the stairs. "You and Hack cover the entrance and work your way deeper. I'm heading to the north end and angling in from that side."

"Beware of crossfire," Harper said. "We're in a circle here."

"Got it," Cassie said.

CHAPTER 71

Marla's world fuzzed. The drugs wrapped her in a welcoming warmth even as her heart picked up its beat. God, she loved this feeling. Never wanted it to end.

The two men that walked toward her appeared almost ghost like. Apparitions more than flesh and blood. But as they neared, her breath caught. The tall one, the ponytail. He's the one that took Buck outside the ER. When was that? A couple of days ago? Seemed longer.

She needed to run, to hide in the trees, to get back to Reverend John's and crawl in bed, covers over her head. But, her legs failed her. She wobbled. Jason caught her.

"You okay?" the ponytailed man asked.

Now Marla saw his partner. If possible, he was even scarier. Slicked back, black hair; eyes like two pieces of coal, painfully boring into her. He wore jeans and a black tee shirt. His neck, chest, arms muscular. The oddest thought popped into her head: *Isn't he cold?*

"She's fine," Jason said. "In fact, she just got well."

"I'm Dalton," the ponytailed man said. He jerked his head to his left. "This is Chris."

Marla stared at him. She wanted to say something but could think of nothing that made any sense. Screaming for help didn't seem a wise choice.

"This is Marla," Jason said. "She's my new partner."

"That right?" Dalton said. He extended his hand. "Welcome on board."

Marla felt her hand rise and then disappear inside Dalton's firm grip. His palm was dry, unlike hers.

"You don't say much, do you?" Dalton asked.

Before Marla could reply, Jason jumped in. "Actually, she brought some useful news for you."

"That right?" He stepped closer, rested a hand on her shoulder. "Tell me."

Marla felt that if she opened her mouth she might vomit. Cold sweat lifted along her back. Thoughts swirled in her head like a flock of trapped birds. She felt dizzy.

Again, Jason saved her. "They have the doc over at the jail. One of your guys, too."

"I know."

"You do?"

Dalton nodded. "I have my sources."

"Who?"

Dalton looked at Jason. "Not your concern." He smiled. "Let's just say, advice of counsel."

"Did you bring the stuff?" Jason asked.

"Sure did. It's in the car."

"All right then." Jason rubbed his hands together. "Let's get this done."

Dalton scanned the area, glanced back toward the road as a truck rolled by headed west. "We're a little exposed here. Let's go somewhere more private where we can hammer out this new partnership and get you resupplied."

"Sounds good," Jason said.

Dalton gripped Marla's arm and tugged her toward the back of the park where the trees thickened. She tried to pull away. "I can walk," she said.

"You seem a little wobbly," Dalton said as his grip tightened. "Don't want you to fall and hurt yourself."

He literally tugged her into the trees. She glanced back. Jason followed, and behind him, the scary dude.

CHAPTER 72

Harper heard movement to her left. Footfalls and the friction of clothing against foliage. Moonlight slanted through the trees. She settled in the shadows and waited as the sounds neared. Then she saw them. Fifty feet away, now moving at an angle away from her. She cupped one hand over her mouth, and whispered, "I have eyes on them. Dalton, Navarro, Jason, and Marla. Headed north, deeper in the trees."

"We're at the main entrance," Cassie said. "We'll head that way."

"Slowly," Harper said. "Make a perimeter in case they double back."

"Got it."

Harper then heard two taps through her earpiece. Cain. Meant he was in quiet mode. He must have heard them, too. The group was likely headed his way.

Harper worked quietly through the trees, following the sounds the group made. Another fifty feet or so and the noises of movement evaporated. Then voices. Or one anyway.

"This should work." A deep voice. Probably Dalton.

Harper crept forward, staying low, until she caught sight of them again. She settled behind a hydrangea that bordered a small clearing where Dalton and Navarro faced Marla and Jason.

"So, what's the plan?" Jason asked. "How are we going to set this up?"

"Every business has to go through a little restructuring every now and again," Dalton said. "To keep it healthy and running on all cylinders."

"Makes sense," Jason said.

"Sort of like crop rotation and weeding the field. That sort of thing."

Jason laughed, rubbed his hands together. "Like me taking over for Tommy."

"Something like that," Dalton said. "Maybe more like pruning the tree."

Dalton pulled out his Glock. Navarro followed suit.

"What's this?" Jason asked.

"Business. Now get on your knees. Both of you."

"You don't have to do this," Jason said.

"Actually I do. You, and especially little Miss Sunshine here, know too much. You can identify me and Chris and I can't take that chance."

"We won't say a word. Better, we'll work with you and make you money."

"Yeah, that might be so. Right up until the cops lean on you. I don't see either of you having much backbone."

"Come on, Dalton."

"On your knees. Now."

Harper raised slightly, leveling her weapon toward the men. Take the shot or wait? Could she get both of them quickly enough? The only clear shot she had was Navarro as Dalton was partially shielded by the thicker man.

Jason dropped to his knees, Navarro moved to face him, raised his weapon. Now she saw the silencer. These guys weren't so stupid after all.

Marla began to drop but as soon as she bent and flexed her legs, she spun away, lunged forward, and disappeared into the trees.

"Fuck," Dalton said. "You hold him while I run this bitch down." He took off.

Harper stood, stepped around the shrub. "Drop the weapon."

Navarro's head swiveled her way. Surprise erupted on his face. But he recovered, kept his Glock aimed at Jason's head.

"You drop your weapon, or he goes down." He actually smiled.

Harper didn't have time to debate the issue. She fired. A single shot. It entered Navarro's throat in the soft depression between his jaw and larynx. Where it would sever his spinal cord. He never got the shot off as his brain's communication with his hand, and everything else, fractured. Navarro went limp, the gun fell. He did too.

"Navarro down," Harper said. "I have Jason. Marla is on the move to the north and west. Dalton pursuing."

"We're on it," Cassie said.

Nothing from Cain.

CHAPTER 73

Cain entered the park's north end, where the forest was thickest. He employed all his childhood hunting skills to move quickly, but quietly.

Harper's voice came through his earpiece: "I have eyes on them. Dalton, Navarro, Jason, and Marla. Headed your way."

He didn't respond but rather tapped the earpiece twice. Harper would get the message.

He worked his way to the south, alert for any sounds of movement. It didn't take long before he detected voices. Vague and distant so he couldn't make out what was being said. He dropped beneath a series of low hanging tree limbs and bear crawled to get closer.

Then a gun shot, followed by Harper: "Navarro down. I have Jason. Marla is on the move to the north and west. Dalton pursuing."

Cain already knew the latter part of her message. He could hear them coming his way. Tree limbs and shrubs rasping against clothing. Frantic footsteps. Harsh breathing. He flattened against a large tree trunk, a throwing knife in his right hand. He peeked around it. Marla came charging toward him, tried to run by the tree. He hooked her with his other arm, dragged her to the ground, and clamped his hand over her mouth.

"Don't make a sound. Don't move."

Her eyes were dinner plates but, to her credit, she nodded.

Dalton wasn't far behind. In his desperation to catch Marla, he moved rapidly and noisily toward Cain. Cain peeked around the tree as Dalton wedged his way between two shrubs.

"Stop," Cain ordered.

Dalton's feet almost came out from beneath him as he heeled the ground and slid to a halt. His head swiveled. He couldn't pick Cain out in the darkness.

"I'll kill you," Dalton said.

"No you won't."

He obviously wasn't very good at triangulating sound as the silenced shot he fired, a soft spit, was a good fifteen feet in the wrong direction. Marla flinched. Cain looked down at her, raised a hand.

"Drop the weapon," Cain said.

Another shot. This one closer. The bullet thumped a tree behind him and to the left.

"Last chance," Cain said.

Another shot. This one smacked the tree where Cain hid. Cain bent, scooped up a pinecone. He tossed it to his right. It rattled through the undergrowth. Another shot fired.

Cain slid around the tree. Dalton's attention was to his right but then his gaze whipped toward Cain. His Glock followed.

Cain's blade beat him. It entered through Dalton's right eye. He staggered and fell, the gun going off one last time, punching a hole in the forest floor.

CHAPTER 74

On the way back to Tanner's Crossroads PD, Cain made three calls, on speaker so he and Harper could each weigh in. The first was to Dr. Buckner in North Carolina. To say that he was thrilled that not only had his son been found safely, which he already knew, but that the bad guys had been neutralized and Buck was no longer in danger. He seemed unfazed by the term 'neutralized.' Cain assumed he got the real meaning and had no concerns. He did say that he hoped this might nudge Buck into considering coming back into the fold. Cain said it just might, but he didn't believe that. Buck was a free spirit.

The second was to Mama B.

"So, you neutralized the bad guys? That's excellent."

Mama B truly understood what neutralized meant.

The final call was to Reverend John to let him know that Marla was safe and that the danger had passed. He was definitely relieved, saying he could now "put his weapons back in their gun cases."

By the time they reached the PD, dawn had lightened the sky to the east. Cain and Harper climbed from The Rig. Harper stretched her back, one way and then the other.

"That was fun," she said.

"Right up your alley."

"Not yours?"

Cain smiled. "Serves me right for asking for a case."

"I meant to ask you about that."

"I'll never complain about downtime again."

Harper punched his arm. "Yeah, right."

In the PD break room, coffee was made and distributed. Cain took a sip. The warmth welcome after a night in the cold, dark woods of the city park.

"Feels good to be free of this," Buck said.

"Now you can go home and grab some much needed sleep I suspect," Cassie said.

"After I swing by the hospital and check on my patient."

"Dennie?" Hack asked. "I doubt he's still your patient, being in the ICU and all."

Buck shrugged. "I'm still the surgeon of record." He smiled. "So to speak."

"I'll give you a ride," Hack said.

"I think I'll walk. It'll be good to be outside and not running from someone."

"Tell me about it," Marla said.

"Want to tag along?" Buck asked. "I'll buy you breakfast and we can talk about our earlier chat."

"What chat?" Harper asked.

Marla smiled. "Doctor Buck here is trying to get me back in rehab."

"It'd be a smart move," Cain said.

Marla nodded toward Buck. "He seems to think so."

"But it only works if you want it to," Buck answered.

Marla forked the fingers of one hand through her hair. "After tonight it is a more attractive proposition."

"We can get it rolling right now. I can admit you for the detox stuff and then we can move on from there."

Marla hesitated as if considering it. "Tell you what. Buy me some waffles and I'll think about it."

"Fair enough."

Buck shook hands with Cain and Harper. "Needless to say, I can never do enough to repay you." He turned to Cassie and Hack. "You guys too."

"No thanks needed," Cassie said. "Just think about staying

around. We can use a good doc here."

After Buck and Marla left, Cassie turned to Cain and Harper. "It's been a pleasure working with you. I think. Not sure the coroner agrees. You guys managed to fill up the morgue."

"We had a little help," Harper said.

"Looks like we'll have a few funerals lined up," Hack said. "Not the least of which is Scotty Duckworth."

"Amen," Cassie said. She looked at Cain, then Harper. "What're your plans?"

Cain looked at Harper. Shrugged. "Sleep. We need some sleep."

"Then we might take a trip over to Memphis," Harper said. "See the Peabody ducks."

"Will I read about it in the paper?"

Cain shrugged. "I hope not."

CHAPTER 75

Two days later, Cassie sat in her office. She was cleaning up all the still neglected paperwork. Part of being the chief. Then she had a few funerals to attend. The Finleys had already been interred, but today would be the burials of Scotty Duckworth, Simon Greene, and Wilbert Shaffer.

The bad guys, Dalton, Navarro, and Myrick, had been shipped off to the coroner, as had Tim and Andrea Curry, the owners of the house Dalton had commandeered. Dennie remained in the hospital but was healing well, and Jessie was still their guest, awaiting trial. As the last men standing, it wouldn't likely go well for Dennie and Jessie.

Marla was in the hospital, fighting through detox, and Buck was back on duty. Life was slowly returning to normal. Or might be, once these funerals were behind them. It would never be completely stitched back together but at least the healing could now begin.

Hack stepped into her office. "You need to see this."

"What?"

He sat, raised the piece of paper he held. "Story on the Memphis Commercial Appeal website." He read:

Local officials have reported that the body of Frank 'Frankie the Finger' Campanella was discovered this morning in an alley behind

Turk's Lounge, an establishment Campanella owned. Police say the cause of death hasn't been released but a high-ranking official said that it was a stab wound. 'Whoever it did it was either lucky or good. The wound was in his upper abdomen and seemed to have penetrated upward into his heart.' There were no witnesses and, as of now, the police have no suspects. Campanella was reputed to have ties to organized crime, including drug dealing, prostitution, and illegal gambling. Many speculate that these connections might have played a role in his death.

Cassie shook her head. "I'd go for good over lucky."

Hack nodded. "Good bet. Wouldn't want to be on the bad side of those two."

Cassie smiled. "The good side was hard enough."

"Good folks though."

"Yeah. Good folks."

Hack stood, his knees creaking. "Hope they enjoyed the Peabody ducks."

*

ABOUT THE AUTHOR

D. P. LYLE is the Amazon #1 Bestselling; Macavity and Benjamin Franklin Award-winning; and Edgar(2), Agatha, Anthony, Shamus, Scribe, and *USA Today* Best Book(2) Award-nominated author of 22 books, both non-fiction and fiction, including the *Samantha Cody, Dub Walker, Jake Longly* and *Cain/Harper* thriller series and the *Royal Pains* media tie-in novels. His essay on Jules Verne's THE MYSTERIOUS ISLAND appears in *THRILLERS: 100 MUST READS*, his short story "Even Steven" in ITW's anthology *THRILLER 3: LOVE IS MURDER*, and his short story "Bottom Line" in *FOR THE SAKE OF THE GAME*. He served as editor for and contributed the short story "Splash" to SCWA's anthology *IT'S ALL IN THE STORY*.

He hosts the Crime Fiction Writer's Blog and the Criminal Mischief: The Art and Science of Crime Fiction podcast series. He has worked with many novelists and with the writers of popular television shows such as *Law & Order, CSI: Miami, Diagnosis Murder, Monk, Judging Amy, Peacemakers, Cold Case, House, Medium, Women's Murder Club, 1-800-Missing, The Glades,* and *Pretty Little Liars.*

Learn more at http://www.dplylemd.com.

CPSIA information can be obtained
at www.ICGtesting.com
Printed in the USA
LVHW010831121020
668565LV00013B/111